Books by Cheryl Dragon

Fantasy Castle

Kat's Karma

Lust Bites

One Weekend

Sexy Snax

Runaway Cowgirl

Anthologies

Tied to the Billionaire
Out of Bounds

Single Titles

Paid Holiday
Keeping It Interesting
A Firm Hand
Making the Pass
Devoted to Him
Best in Bed

Best in Bed

ISBN # 978-1-78686-110-8

©Copyright Cheryl Dragon 2017

Cover Art by Posh Gosh ©Copyright 2017

Interior text design by Claire Siemaszkiewicz

Totally Bound Publishing

Published in 2017 by Totally Bound Publishing, Newland House, The Point, Weaver Road, Lincoln, LN6 3QN, United Kingdom.

BEST IN BED

CHERYL DRAGON

Dedication

For all the single women out there waiting for the best!

Chapter One

Marina's Bright Idea

Close friends can be an amazing gift or a major pain in the ass. Tonight one of my friends definitely chose to be the latter. Lori, Jen and I shuffled into Jen's one-bedroom apartment done in classic styles with everything meticulously organized and accessorized straight out of Ikea.

I kicked off my uncomfortable clubbing shoes with the chunk heels that set off my black jeans and red, scoop neck fitted top. My cleavage was my best asset. Then I removed the red chandelier earrings that had been bugging me all night. "Lori, I think you are completely overreacting."

"I'm not, Marina." Lori slumped into an overstuffed chair, pulled her blonde hair into a twist off her neck and secured it with a clip. She looked flawless in a stylish but elegant print dress that showed off her slim figure. "It's my thirtieth birthday and my life is over."

Lori had a flair for the extreme and dramatic. I guess that helped make her a good lawyer. She was either going to love her birthday or hate it. Clearly, she'd chosen not to embrace her new decade.

"It'll all look better over coffee and chocolate." Jen broke up our fight, as usual, and headed for the kitchen. She was neat as a pin in a brown dress with tiny pink flowers. It wasn't too revealing at all.

Lori and I had met in college. There was no holding back when we conversed and no hard feelings for our complete honesty. Jen was a newer addition. She'd moved into the third spacious apartment on our floor of the downtown Chicago building about a year back. Our bluntness hadn't rubbed off on her yet.

We preferred to hang out in Jen's apartment because she was neat and a chef. She had pretty copper pots and pans suspended from her ceiling and ropes of garlic that scented the whole apartment. Lori and I had never complained about being guinea pigs for her latest creation. Hopefully Jen had something good tonight, because Lori was in a hellacious mood.

Normally I contributed to the party as the designated bartender. Unfortunately, hard liquor wouldn't help tonight.

"You turned thirty, not sixty." I peeled off my black leather jacket and tossed it onto Jen's couch before flopping down next to it. Out of habit, I began detangling my hair from the costume jewelry necklace I'd chosen. After grabbing a clip from my jacket pocket, I pulled my massive locks up and off my neck. No men here, so the need for beauty was over.

The scent of coffee brewing filled the loft and I hoped it would help calm Lori, the caffeine junkie. Until the coffee was ready, I could try to distract her. "Take off those super-high heels. You're bitchy because your feet hurt."

"No, I'm not." Lori took off the shoes anyway. "You don't understand. You have six months until you turn thirty. Jen has nearly a whole year. This birthday makes you think. It makes you depressed."

"No, it's just a number." Jen offered chocolate-covered scones and Lori picked at one immediately. She was naturally skinny and a true blonde. No amount of junk food put an ounce on her. If she wasn't my friend, I'd probably hate her. Of course, she envies my cleavage, so we're even.

"Try a disaster. My twenties are over. No husband, no big house in the suburbs and no kids." Lori slumped.

"No one to pick up after, less to clean and no stretch marks. It could be worse." I grabbed a scone for myself and smiled as Lori glared at me.

"I've wasted my twenties." Lori hit the coffee table with her fist.

"No you haven't," I groaned. It would be a very depressing and gray Chicago winter if Lori didn't get over this. The convenience of the three of us living on the same floor of the same building made winter socializing nicer. If Lori kept on this soapbox, however, it could make me want to tunnel my way through the snow barehanded to be anywhere else. "You've done a lot so far."

"Marina is right," Jen jumped in. "Lori, you're a top associate with a big law firm. The name is so fancy and long I can't even remember it. And your dad had no hand in getting you that job or your law degree. You'll make partner before you know it. All those hours of work got you where you are. That is *not* a wasted decade."

I added, "Most people who get married in their twenties end up divorced. You're taking your time—we all are. None of us are married. Are you saying we're all failures?"

"No, I thought I'd have at least met the right man by now. Maybe not be married, but have found him. Now all the single men have kids or ex-wives. Who wants that baggage? And you two have it easier. I've got family pressure to get married and have a bunch of kids. Both of my brothers are married and settled and all I hear from my mother is how so-and-so's daughter is engaged or got married, or is having a baby." Lori moved from the sofa to the floor and focused on lighting a lavender-scented candle on the coffee table. She stared at the flames with her blue eyes as though the fire would have the answer. I wasn't about to play into her dramatics.

"Well, you won't find a man sitting around here. None of us will. There were certainly none worthy at the bar tonight." Jen looked depressed, like Lori, as she wiped off her tawny lipstick before biting into her scone.

I'd had enough. "Fine, that's it. I'm changing the subject. Lori, what's the best sex you've ever had?" I walked to the open-concept kitchen and uncorked a bottle of wine. Coffee was not going to cut it tonight.

Lori rolled her eyes at me. "This is not the time for Truth or Dare, Marina."

"No dare. Just the truth. Face it, you've had some fun in your thirty years. So let's hear about that instead of how old and saggy you're getting. Who was the best sex you've ever had?" I headed back with the wine.

Sighing loudly at me, Lori gave in. "Nick. That mechanic I dated. I met him when the little blue Jag Mom and Dad gave me as a law school graduation present was making a weird noise. He was all greasy and gorgeous. It was just something primal. The smell of a sweaty man and oil still gets me."

"So what happened?" Jen took the glass of red wine I handed her, her attention focused on Lori.

"Everything." Lori grinned hard. "He was amazing."

"You dated?" I prompted, looking for more detail. I'd heard about Nick plenty in the heat of their romance. Now that time had passed, maybe she'd be more objective.

"Sort of. Well, yes. I could never really consider him seriously as a boyfriend. We went at it for a few months. We kept it light because I didn't know where I'd get a job once I passed the bar. He didn't want it to end. If my parents found out, though—" Lori shook her head. "He never had a chance."

"Oh, cut the cord, Lori!" I'd never understood Lori's need to please her family so much. I didn't think Lori did, either. Typical ultra-rich northsiders, which was fine, but their inbreeding tendencies shocked me. They only approved of Lori's boyfriends if they were from the same social circle and I couldn't believe those circles weren't related enough by now.

"Can you imagine me with a mechanic?" Lori asked with complete seriousness as she drained half her glass of wine in no time. She tapped her perfectly French-manicured nails against the glass uneasily. "I'm always in suits and heels. He always wore jeans and was happy with pizza and beer. It was fun for a while. We couldn't be together forever. It was a bad break-up. He was very persistent. I knew it wouldn't last."

"He was your best sex ever?" I double-checked.

"Definitely!" She smiled.

"Good. Your turn, Jen." I didn't want to dwell too long on Lori for fear that she'd get too negative about him and begin another temper tantrum about the quality of men out there.

"No, I don't want to play," Jen mumbled.

"It's not a game. This is just girl talk. Sex talk. I'll tell you mine," I assured her.

Why did Lori and I always have to prod Jen into things? She was a sensitive person, very excitable and anxious when it came to her private life. Professionally, she was successful for a new chef. Now she was ready to jump into a bigger pond. She was up for a job at a trendy new restaurant. Lori and I tended to be protective of her naiveté, but there had to be a best sex of her life.

"Yeah, I did it, so you have to, too," Lori insisted.

"Okay, Brian." Jen refused to make eye contact, and the pause following the revelation of the name went on until I was compelled to break the silence.

"Well, I'm getting off from his name alone," I deadpanned, making Lori nearly choke on her wine. "More, Jen, where did you meet him? Was it a real relationship or a one-nighter?

"Details, Jen! We deserve details."

Jen blushed redder than her hair and looked at the floor. "The culinary convention in Los Angeles last year. One-nighter, if you must know."

"And we must! As your friends, we should know all of the details," Lori added. "He was good?"

"He was great! So sweet and still good with his hands. It was wonderful, then I never saw him again." Jen shrugged and glanced at me.

"My turn." I nodded. "Lucas was in stocks. He wanted to

make a million before he turned thirty."

"You're kidding." Lori sounded terribly disappointed. "That was your best? The trader?

How dull!"

"Actually, yes, he was boring. That's sort of why I broke up with him. He was well hung, though. He had the equipment and knew how to use it. That's really all it was. Great sex, and a lot of it over a couple of months, and done. We weren't compatible. I think my personality was too much for him. Plus, he wasn't a pet person, which we vets simply can't tolerate."

"I wonder if that's the best we're going to ever get?" Lori asked. She twisted the fringe on Jen's rug uneasily with her fingers.

"Any idea what happened to your mechanic?" I asked. There was one foolproof way to get Lori out of the dumps. I couldn't outright suggest it without getting another lawyerly lecture. She'd never do it, so I had to find an indirect way.

"No." Lori sighed. "How about you and your horse-hung stockbroker?"

"Haven't talked to him since. How about you, Jen? Any idea where Chef Brian is?"

"Nope. And now we're back to being depressed." Jen frowned and took a bite of her scone.

"Not necessarily," I said. "I have an idea." I paused and admired our view from the huge windows opposite me. The Chicago skyline was a vision against the starry sky. This was either going to work great or be a bad move. I couldn't know which until we went through with it.

"This can't be good," Lori said to Jen, as though I couldn't hear her.

"It's brilliant, if I do say so myself! You're going to love it."

"Leave your high IQ out of this and let us in on your game." Lori folded her arms.

She always teased me about how I could've skipped two

grades in elementary school. She'd crammed for every test in college while I'd had a tendency not to study at all. My parents hadn't liked the idea of my skipping grades because I would've entered high school far too young. My mother had been worried I'd have trouble making friends while my father had been concerned about high school boys near his daughter. I preferred it myself. I wasn't that smart, just picked things up faster than most. Somehow my plans usually worked.

"I don't think we should let the best sex of our lives go without looking them up again, do you?" I poured more wine, knowing they'd need it for what I had planned.

"What?" Lori and Jen asked in unison.

"I think we should at least find out where they are now. Revisit them up for fun." I had no intention of giving up on my brilliant plan. Jen could use a dose of fun, too. She was far too serious.

"Are you crazy?" Lori gestured with her arms like she was arguing in court. "I'm not stalking Nick. I dumped him. I'll come off as desperate."

"No, no. It's not desperate. Do you want to look back at age fifty and wonder what could've happened if we'd done this? I don't want my life full of regrets." I tried to match Lori's lawyerly and authoritative tone. Unfortunately, I'm not that scary. A vet is supposed to put people and pets at ease.

"Checking up on our ex-boyfriends. Won't that appear really crazy?" Jen asked.

"We won't find our own guys. That could be awkward. We'll trade and check out each other's. We've never met any of these guys, so what's the harm? This way it's not as weird. We can check them out and they won't know us. Jen can research Lucas, see if he's bald, fat, or married. Run into him somewhere, strike up a conversation, whatever. We can even pretend to date these guys a time or two to get information if that's what it takes. No more than three dates so it doesn't get serious. Then we report back to each other."

"Sounding less crazy and more like a scavenger hunt," Lori admitted. "So Jen finds Lucas, then I'll take Brian and you get Nick?" Lori filled in the blanks perfectly. Like I hadn't carefully chosen my example so I'd get Nick. It couldn't have worked out better.

"Perfect! We'll meet back here tomorrow night with all the information we can dig up from the time we dated them. Full name, address, where they worked, and pictures if you've got them. Anything to help track the guy. Then we can each decide if we want to reconnect with our own ex. Deal?" I'd expected a bit of a fight. Instead, they were both smiling.

"Deal," they agreed.

"Let the games begin. The search for the best in bed!" I lifted my glass and we toasted our new diversion.

* * * *

My parents had wanted me to be a doctor, a curse of that weird brain of mine again. Then in high school, someone had told them that vet school was more challenging because of all the species of animals one had to learn and there was less malpractice insurance. I don't know whether that's true or not. Either way, I could never resist a challenge. Luckily, I've never regretted it either. Animals made much better patients and were far less trouble than a lot of their owners.

Monday was my day for surgery. A marathon of fixing animals meant hours on my feet and a stiff neck at the end of the day. Changing into my street clothes, I was looking forward to the evening.

My information on Lucas was sketchy at best. Knowing him, he hadn't gone far and was probably at the same firm building his portfolio. He could be sort of alpha at times and I hoped he wouldn't freak out Jen.

I emerged from the office the vets shared. "Anything happening?" I asked the desk clerk as I pulled my hair back in a ponytail.

"No, the puppy obedience class is about to start. You're all done." She smiled.

"Great. I'll get out of here while I can." I grabbed my bucket purse and jacket and walked to the door.

Picking up my kitten-and-puppy design umbrella to protect me from the drizzly November weather, I saw *Seth* coming in the opposite direction. Despite my intent to stay calm, my palms tingled with the urge to touch him. I took a deep breath to calm my heart, which seemed to be beating in my throat. The two men were very different. I'd definitely improved my taste over the years. Seth had a calm confidence and not the bold arrogance Lucas had flashed. As I got to the door, Seth opened it and stood back, getting wetter while I slipped by him. I tried to keep my smile to simple gratitude for a polite act that didn't happen much anymore.

I gazed down at him. I quickly pretended to be smiling at the dog, who was the patient.

I couldn't help blushing. Seth was shy, smart and totally clueless that I was attracted to him. He didn't seem to notice me, either, and gave the same polite behavior to all the staff I worked with.

"Dr. Castini." He nodded and his dog tugged at the leash, happy to see me.

"Mr. Lauden." I did my best to remain casual. I paused briefly and bent to pet the black lab puppy named Monster by Seth's nephews. I didn't want to keep him standing in the rain, so I straightened and nodded while I continued walking rather than start a conversation. He was there for the class. Monster had been on my exam table for all of his puppy shots.

It was lucky timing that he always showed up when I was working. I had no idea what his schedule was, though. I knew he was a pharmacist, lived in the city, and wasn't big on small talk. He'd gotten Monster because one of his nephews had turned out to be extremely allergic. I couldn't help but think it was sweet of him to take the dog so it could stay in the family.

I walked the few blocks to the L station and boarded the train. Unfortunately, I couldn't get my mind off the pharmacist. My secret crushes normally faded fast, but this one seemed to be dragging. Why was I always attracted to the shy, smart guys? Just like Seth. I'd never gotten anywhere with them. Those guys never made a move, at least not at me. Jen would say it was karma for how I'd treated them when I had been younger.

All through school, I'd rejected being a nerd, so not skipping those two grades had been fine with me. I hung out with the popular kids, cut class, went to parties, and had way more fun in high school than my mother ever needed to know. My grades had stayed perfect and I'd never gotten arrested, so my parents could remain blissfully ignorant of the rest.

Much as I'd tried to remind myself that this was not high school, I knew Seth would never ask me out. I had no idea why I bothered flirting with him other than the fact that he was cute with a great body and naturally polite manners. There had to be something wrong with him. When the train pulled into my stop, I put my fantasy on hold. There was one thing I had to do before heading home to trade information with the others on our search for the men from our pasts.

I entered my mom's bakery to pre-empt any nagging about never seeing my family and to get supplies. I loved it there. It looked like every Italian bakery should. Murals on the walls depicted old Italy. Thanks to my artist cousin, Anthony, the floor-to-ceiling hand-painted pictures of vineyards, fields and cottages were updated regularly.

It always made me feel at home to come to the bakery. I might not have any talents in the kitchen, yet I liked to contribute, so Jen doesn't always have to feed us and she got a taste of home baking.

My mother and her sisters had been brilliant bakers

all of their lives and when we children had gotten older, they'd opened the Three Aunts Bakery on Taylor Street. All of the daughters, including me, had worked the register during their high school and college years. Now it was my youngest cousin Penny's turn.

"Hey, Penny." I waved at my cousin and went to the kitchen. "Hi, Mom, Aunt Marie, Aunt Louisa." I dutifully gave them each a peck on the cheek and hopped up onto a vacant countertop. The old Chicago building was deep rather than wide and the oven dominated one of the walls. The island in the middle was full of delicious creations in progress. The heat was oppressively familiar. I felt at home.

"Marina, where have you been?" my mother demanded, adding spices to her dough while my aunts chimed in with similarly loving scolds.

"Work. I need a dozen Parmesan rolls, please." I picked at a new creation and got the requisite slap on the hand by one aunt while the other slipped a sample into my package of food. Whatever I requested would be tripled and just about anything could find its way in there.

"Fresh from the oven," Aunt Louisa said proudly.

"Thanks," I replied.

"How was Lori's birthday?" Mom never stopped working her dough.

"Bad. She's not happy about being thirty. I have a plan." I smiled.

"What plan? She's just going to have to get over it. I'm sixty and I don't care who knows." Mom wagged a finger at me.

"You don't care because you're the youngest," Aunt Marie cut in.

"What's the plan?" Mom ignored her sister.

"You remember when she was dating Nick?" My mother heard most things eventually. Trying to keep her out of my personal life was a fight and I picked my battles. She always got the censored version, though. When Lori and I had been in college, Mom had practically adopted Lori.

Actually, it was more Lori who'd decided my mother was what a mom should be.

"Nick? Sure. He was a nice boy. Hardworking mechanic. I took my car there after you told me about him. Lori was foolish to let him go. Nice-looking, too, and very polite." Mom added a layer of butter to the rolls as she boxed them up.

"Don't tell Lori's family that," I warned. That was very high praise from my mom and my aunts knew it.

"What? A mechanic isn't good enough for them?" Aunt Louisa asked.

"Aunt Louisa, royalty wouldn't be good enough for them. All lawyers, judges and politicians." I rolled my eyes. "They're snobs and he was good for Lori. So the plan is we're going to look up old boyfriends and put the past behind us for fun. It'll get Lori's mind off her birthday."

"Who are you looking up?" Aunt Marie asked.

"Remember Lucas?" I grimaced as they all groaned.

"That dull boy who played with stocks?" Mom held nothing back. "You don't want him. You need to find a new man." She thought Lucas had been a waste of time.

"No, I'm sure he's probably bald or married by now, so I'll be off the hook. I just had to pick one of my exes for her to find, to get Lori to do it," I explained.

"You're a good friend. We'll light a candle tonight that you find a nice boy," Aunt Marie promised and crossed herself on my behalf. Aunt Louisa nodded.

"Thanks, but I'll survive turning thirty and being single. Cross yourself for Lori." I had no fear of ending up thirty and alone. Then again, I'd never been in love. At least not the kind that took more than a few days and a new cute guy to get over. Alone was safe and easy.

"What about the tiny redhead with the freckles? Is she playing, too?" Mom asked.

"Jen?" I supplied. "Sure, she wants to find some chef she only saw a couple of times. Maybe he'll be right for her. They didn't spend enough time together to let it develop.

Whether it works or not, it's better than being depressed about our ages."

"Good! Action is always better than doing nothing. Maybe you'll find a nice man in all of this." Mom's advice was always supportive. I was lucky that she rarely criticized seriously.

"Action toward finding a good man is even better." Aunt Louisa winked.

"As long as my plan is mom and aunt approved, I can't lose." I added a loaf of her special bread to my stash. "I've got to go. We're getting started tonight, so hopefully it'll get our minds off anything negative."

"Let me know how it goes. I'm not going to tell your father about this plan of yours. I don't think he'd like it. He still thinks of you as the baby." Mom patted my cheek.

"Dads aren't supposed to approve of their daughter's love lives." I shrugged and left the kitchen. "Bye, everyone. Bye, Penny."

"Find me a man while you're at it, Marina!" Penny called as I left with a wave. Some days I think I should have gone into matchmaking. Of course, Lori was my first intentional attempt. I'd done some by accident in college and with clients at the animal hospital. Always setting up others and never finding a good one for myself. My luck had better change one of these days.

This would still be entertaining. My finding Lori's Nick would be the perfect distraction to keep her from being depressed. Hopefully this time Lori would be strong enough to keep her mechanic. We all had baggage to clean up in order to face age thirty and this might do the trick. I might have real hope for Lori and Nick if I weren't so worried she'd screw it up again.

* * * *

I arrived home to find Jen pacing in a panic with her apartment door wide open, not a good idea in the city, even with our building's reliable security. Her Wisconsin roots were showing.

"What's the matter?" I asked, setting the packages of food carefully on her island.

"The interview is tomorrow morning. I completely forgot with all of this Lori's birthday and men stuff." Jen didn't stop pacing and started biting her unpainted short nails. I glanced at my cherry-red polish and wondered how I could talk Jen into fixing up her makeup. That was a project for another day. She was stressed enough already.

"You'll be great." I popped a few rolls in the microwave to get them all gooey, hoping Jen could be tempted by my mom's latest creation.

"What if I'm not? What if I don't get it?"

"Jen, you're a great chef. You'll get the job."

"Where is this crystal ball of yours?" Jen was a worrier and never knew when to quit.

"Fine, so you don't get the job. Did you quit your old job? Are you stupid enough to walk away from a paying job because you have an interview?"

"No, of course not. But I hate that job!"

"It's better than eviction." I extended both hands and mocked a scale in distinct favor of the disliked job. "You'll live with your current job until the right one comes along. If it's not this one, then there'll be another."

"I just want tomorrow to be over with." Jen sank into the sofa as I deposited the rolls and a cup of coffee on the table in front of her. The idea of slipping a few tranquilizers into her drink crossed my mind. She'd survive.

"Tomorrow won't be the end. What are the odds they'll offer you the job tomorrow? I'm sure they have to make a decision and maybe have other candidates to evaluate. Then you have to wait."

"At least the interview will be over. You know I'm not very good with words." Jen bit into a roll and groaned. "Won't your mother give me any of her recipes?"

"So you can sell them at triple the price at some fancy

restaurant? She'd die first."

"I can't believe you never learned how to cook or bake." Jen finished the roll fast and drained the cup.

"What for? Two of my cousins work at the bakery part-time in the kitchen while they're going to college. They'll probably take it over from the aunts. Of course, my cousins will have to force them into retirement, yanking the rolling pins from them. And most of my sisters can cook. I'll never go hungry."

"What if Lucas comes back into your life? Don't you want to impress him with your culinary talents?" Jen teased.

"Not really," I admitted. "It'll be funny to see where he is. Bald, arrested for insider trading, or married with triplets. We didn't click. It's strictly entertainment value, Jen. Don't waste too much energy on this guy. He's boring."

"Maybe Lori shouldn't bother looking for my Brian." Jen walked to the kitchen to put the dishes away. "We were only together that one time."

"You liked him," I reminded her. "You lit up like New Year's Eve when you talked about him."

"He was nice, but there's no guarantee." Jen chewed her lower lip nervously.

"There are no guarantees in life, about your job or boyfriend. That's the whole point of this. We get out and do something different. If we hang around here all winter, we'll pack on ten extra pounds, which I don't need, and be depressed. Besides, Lori needs to get Nick or get him out of her system." I propped my feet up on the coffee table with my own roll and savored the smell.

"That's what this is all about, isn't it?" Jen asked.

"What all what is about?" I pretended not to follow her and took a bite.

"This whole 'best in bed' thing. You're doing this for Lori's sake."

"Well, she was the one depressed about her birthday." I waited to see if Jen would push the issue.

"Our guys are pretty random. Okay, they were good in

bed. Unlike Lori, we don't really have some huge emotional connection with them."

I grinned slyly. "You won't tell her, will you?" All I needed was for Jen to spill it. Lori was too wrapped up in the thought of Nick and turning thirty, so she'd gloss over the plot, even knowing me as well as she does.

"No, this is fun! Lori came up with his name really fast. I just hope it turns out for the best."

"Either way, she'll have some closure and can move on, with or without him. She ended things with Nick so abruptly when she took the job and put this brick wall up. She wouldn't even discuss the break-up with me. I don't think Lori and Nick ever really sorted it all out."

"And you never met him?" Jen returned to the sofa and stretched out.

"No, she was studying for the bar and I was finishing up vet school. I'd hear about him all the time, but she never brought him around. I think she thought she was supposed to be ashamed of him. Why, I don't know. I'm from the Southside, working class. Did she think I'd kick him out?"

"Her parents," Jen whispered, like they were in the room.

"Her parents have let me in their home." I shrugged. "Anyway, I've never met him. I heard plenty of stories, though."

"Like?" Jen insisted.

"You'd better not, Marina," Lori said from the doorway. "This is what happens when I leave you two alone."

"You're the late one. Jen and I got started without you. We've already covered Brian and Lucas. Right, Jen?" I defended.

"Right," Jen agreed.

"Fine, fine. I got stuck on a conference call. What smells so good?" Lori headed for the kitchen, removing her jacket on the way. She walked with confident steps, her pumps clicking on the Mexican ceramic tile.

"Mom sent rolls." I winked at Jen. "Why don't you share a Nick story and have one?" "Don't make me lose my appetite," Lori scolded me as she dove into the food.

"Come on, Lori, how can Marina find him if she doesn't know stuff?" Jen nodded.

"That isn't the kind of story I wanted to hear." I grinned.

"If all you want is a juicy story, fine." Lori settled down with coffee and pastry on the sofa next to us.

"So?" Jen pressed as she grabbed a throw pillow.

"My car was in and out of the shop for about a month and his garage happened to be on the way to my study group for the bar," Lori began.

"How soon after you met him did you two start dating?" Jen asked.

"The dating sort of happened later. Other stuff happened right away," Lori replied.

"I like a woman who knows her priorities," I teased.

"You shut up! You already know this story." Lori turned back to Jen and smiled. "Anyway, we'd been having fun for a couple of weeks and he picked me up from my study group to bring me back to the garage because my car was ready."

"I like a man who picks up and delivers." I laughed and was struck by a blue shag throw pillow, compliments of Lori, which I returned with equal force.

"We started fooling around, you know, just kissing. All the guys from the garage were gone then so it was just us. Things got a little out of control." Lori blushed.

"Go on," Jen urged.

"Well, there was this black Aston Martin there—and I just love that car!"

"A what car?" Jen asked.

"One of James Bond's cars," Lori supplied.

"Oh." Jen nodded.

"So, I started looking at it and touching it and Nick kept touching me, and before I knew it, I was naked! He'd taken my clothes off and I hadn't even noticed."

"Good with his hands," I chimed in.

"Very!" Lori agreed.

"So you guys did it in the car?" Jen asked.

"Close," I whispered.

"More like *on* it." Lori shrugged.

Jen shook her head. "On the hood of the car?"

"Wrong end," I supplied.

"Wasn't that hard on your back, lying on the trunk of a car?" Jen asked.

"I wasn't on my back." Lori's pale skin turned deep red now.

"Doggie style on the trunk of some stranger's expensive car? The two of you there naked for anyone to walk in on!" Jen's jaw dropped.

"He wasn't technically naked," Lori corrected. "He left his mechanic's cover thing on, only had time to unzip it."

"Wasn't it all dirty and rough?" Jen asked.

"Yes, just the way I like it," Lori said. "I need chocolate."

Jen bounded up and found the next best thing to sex to soothe the beast we'd created in Lori—gourmet chocolates.

"That settles it, I'm getting you a vibrator for Christmas," I said.

The laughter broke the sexual tension our fantasies had created.

"It's not the same," Lori argued.

"True. It's better than nothing. Before we have another of Lori's tales from the garage, maybe we should trade information on these guys?" I suggested.

Chapter Two

Jen on Pins and Needles

So maybe I hadn't told the exact truth. Brian was the best guy I'd felt really connected to in my life. So we hadn't technically slept together or even kissed. We'd only had a few hours of a few days to spend together at that culinary convention.

I straightened my pretty powder blue and white bedroom. When I get nervous, cleaning is the only thing that helps. I tucked the down comforter in and fluffed the pillows properly, trying not to think of Brian.

It had been one of those instant things, and we'd clicked. He was too much of a gentleman to make a move after such a short time. He didn't say that. He didn't have to. I never had the chance to give him my number. I had to catch the flight back home. He lived in Los Angeles, so it wasn't like we'd get to see much of each other.

The thought of Lori tracking him down made me cringe. She could be so dynamic and yet ruthless when she went after something. I half hoped she couldn't find him. The trail might run cold and Brian could remain a happy memory of what could have been. On the other hand, that was exactly why Marina wanted to do this—to erase Lori's regret. So why not erase my own?

As I changed into my third and final interview suit option, I crossed my fingers that Brian, if found, wouldn't reveal that things had been innocent between us. Marina and Lori would have a field day with my virginity. I couldn't help that I hadn't found the right guy yet. I didn't want to be one of those girls who regretted their first time.

Obviously, I was way behind Lori's and Marina's counts. I didn't have Lori's adventurous sexual nature or Marina's self-confidence.

Studying myself in the mirror, I saw a nearly thirty-year-old virgin who was going to blow her interview. The red suit made me look like a strawberry. I decided on the professional navy blue Lori had insisted I should wear. Lori was right, as usual. I changed and tried to get a grip on my breathing and pre-interview jitters by pacing in the kitchen. Coffee wouldn't help, so I resisted the urge to pour a cup just to keep my hands busy.

Marina entered through the unlocked door and smiled. I was glad she didn't scold me for not having every bolt fastened like she did. I'd grown up in Wisconsin, where everyone left their doors unlocked. It's habit for me. Marina had been raised in the city and locking everything was ingrained in her, just like keeping a baseball bat next to her bed or carrying pepper spray in her purse. "Ready for makeup?" she asked.

"I guess." I sat on one of the bar stools at the island, not at all ready for a makeup session.

"You look like you're going to a funeral, not an interview for a job you want." Marina set her bulging makeup bag on the breakfast bar and opened it, spreading out an assortment of powders, brushes and tubes.

"Don't make me look too made up," I begged.

"Are you saying I wear too much makeup?" Marina dabbed foundation onto a sponge and tested it on my face without the slightest hint of annoyance.

"No, it's just that I'm so pale. Your makeup blends nicely with your skin tone. I put on blush and I look like a clown." It was true. Marina had this beautiful olive complexion and I was a ghost. If I did get any sun, I just freckled, unlike Marina, who tanned even prettier than she already was. Staying out of the sun had only two advantages. Odds were, I wouldn't die of skin cancer and freckles made me seem younger. I was the only one I knew who still got carded.

"You won't be a clown. I don't know why you don't wear makeup more often. Not that you need it badly. It just evens things out. You blush too easily, then you'll be all red and blotchy. This will help." Marina smoothed the liquid over my face, careful to get every bit of skin.

"It just melts off with all the heat from the ovens." I shrugged.

"There is some really excellent matte stuff out there. It adheres to the skin. I'll find you one." Marina dusted my eyes with a neutral shadow then picked up a pencil. I pursed my lips.

Marina shook her head. "Close your eyes."

"My eyes?" I asked.

"You said you don't like mascara because the little flakes get under your contacts and irritate your eyes, so this will define your eyes and no flakes. I have to say, I think it's all in your head. The mascaras I buy are top rate."

"Like your puppies and kittens really care if your mascara is runny or flaky." I closed my eyes as directed and felt the gentle glide very close to my eyelashes. I did my best not to flinch, but luckily Marina had a practiced hand. Growing up, she had four older sisters and had learned everything from their different styles.

"My patients don't care. I do. I don't wear it for other people. I wear makeup because I like it. For a job interview, yes, it's important to show that you can dress nicely and clean up well. They won't hire someone who looks like they just rolled out of bed and showed up. That's good sense. Still, it doesn't hurt to have a makeup bag full of products that work for you in case you have a *date* or something."

"They always go after Lori." I picked up the mirror to examine the progress. Marina was gifted. My skin appeared a lot more even.

"Well, she's a skinny blonde. That's men. She can only handle one at a time, so you have to step up and take advantage of the lurkers."

"I could never ask a guy out." I hated the term 'princess' but I had nothing but older brothers and a protective dad who adored my mom. I'd had a sheltered life and dreamed of Prince Charming adoring me and pursuing me. I'd never had to be aggressive. I had brothers for that. No one bullied me because my brothers would make sure they'd pay.

"Have you ever seen me ask a guy out?" Marina posed the question as she began to work on my lips, so I slowly shook my head. I hadn't seen Marina ask a man out and that amazed me.

"You don't have to do the asking," she explained. "You just have to put yourself in their paths. Once they realize Lori isn't going to give them the time of day, their attentions will turn. You're there looking hot and friendly and available, not too slutty, and they'll be all over you."

"Why would I want a guy Lori rejected?" I asked as Marina switched from lip liner to lipstick.

"She hasn't gone through and personally rejected each of them. The skinny, pretty blonde picks the guy who most resembles Brad Pitt with the best build. There are a lot of perfectly handsome and nice guys in that wake. Even if they aren't Mr. Right, they might be Mr. Right-Now. No law against that."

"I guess. I don't like meeting people in bars, though."

"Well, Lucas' office is full of men who live their jobs like you do. Their careers are everything. Maybe you'll meet someone when you're on your mission for me. Your time would be much better spent scouting out a new guy for yourself than researching Lucas Rigby. Get a visual and a rain check and get away from him." Marina dusted loose powder over my face and blew the excess away. "There you go, perfect."

I held up the mirror and smiled. "Thanks, Marina, I'm so glad it's your late shift today at the animal hospital."

"Forget it. I love this stuff. I'll leave you the lipstick and powder in case you need to touch up. Now, no drinking, eating, sneezing, or putting your hands on your face in any way until after the interview."

"Good thing it's in half an hour." I smiled, still taken back by how sophisticated I looked. It wasn't clown makeup, but soft and subtle. "You should have gone into cosmetology and created your own makeup line."

"I don't know if I could spend my life selling things." Marina tossed the rest of her stuff back in the bag and checked her watch. "Half an hour? You better get going."

"You're right, thanks." I hopped off the stool and grabbed my purse, coat and portfolio, complete with resume and references. I dashed out ahead of Marina, knowing she'd lock the door. I wasn't going to be late when I was this well styled.

* * * *

Everything had gone perfectly so far. I hadn't stuttered or frozen up once during my interview. All that was left was a tour of the kitchen. Coty's hadn't opened yet, so everything was fairly quiet. Crews were cleaning as I entered the nearly complete kitchen behind Ralph Coty, the owner. The trendy restaurant had statues of ancient Roman gods, Indian gods and a reclining Buddha. Add a lucky white Chinese cat, very eclectic. The cozy booths and tables were all in black with bright paintings of European sites on the walls. The kitchen gleamed white and stainless steel all around me.

"The dessert preparation would all be in this area," Ralph said, ushering me to that side. Then he began speaking in French. Was this a bad dream? Had I lost my mind? I was in a panic. I didn't speak French and if that was a requirement of this job, I was out. I had the desperate need to leave before an anxiety attack kicked in. Then another man turned around and smiled at Ralph and me. "Welcome," he said with a very thick French accent.

"Jen Burke, this is my partner, Andre. He is the expert in sweets."

"Nice to meet you," I said a little too loud and slow,

but stopped myself before I said any more. I reached out to shake hands. Instead, he pulled my hand to his mouth. Maybe it was that self-defense class Lori had made me take with her, but I slapped Andre hard with my free hand.

Instantly, my face burned as the men talked in French. "I'm so sorry," I squeaked.

"No," Ralph insisted. "Andre is silly and old-fashioned. He thinks he can charm American women by kissing their hands. I told him city women don't play those games. He's lucky you did not spray him with pepper."

Pepper spray was Marina's weapon of choice on the more dangerous Chicago streets. I'd decided to get some since my best reflex toward a man I thought was being too forward was a slap out of *Moonstruck*. I played along to get myself off the hook. "You have to be careful. We city girls can take care of ourselves."

"Very sorry." Andre held up his hands and left the room muttering in French.

A tension headache built behind my eyes. I nearly rubbed my forehead to ease the pain. Luckily, I stopped in time and remembered not to touch my face or I would have smeared Marina's hard work.

Ralph laughed and put his hands on my shoulders, giving them an affectionate squeeze. "Don't worry. Andre will judge you on your work, not your socializing skills. He has only been here a few months. He didn't want to leave Paris, but I had already leased this space."

"He's a good friend." I smiled as relief replaced panic. No harm done, apparently. Two good friends going into business together. Ralph was handsome and Andre's accent was so sweet. I could get used to it here.

"Friend, yes. Well, Jen, are you interested in joining our group? You'll learn a lot of French, if nothing else, from Andre."

"Yes, I'm very interested. Are you planning on opening soon?" I wasn't sure if I'd gotten an offer or not. It sounded like I was in the running.

"About a month and a half before we open. We want to make our final decisions in the next two weeks. That gives us time to check references and see everyone."

"Of course, I look forward to hearing from you." I followed Ralph back to the entrance and we shook hands. I walked calmly down the street a block or two before I started to giggle. "That was a great first impression." I felt so stupid, yet it had turned out so great. Andre would make any blunder I made seem like nothing. And Ralph was so gorgeous! I knew crushing on the boss was a mistake, or in this case, prospective boss. I was seriously thinking about breaking that rule.

I made my way to a few shops to see the Christmas windows and found myself turned around trying to get back to the L. Damn! I wish I'd grown up here. Marina and Lori could tell where they were at all times and exactly in which direction the lake was from their position. I did my old standby and glanced up trying to find an L platform, no luck.

So now I was lost and had two options. Neither of which I liked very much. I could hail a taxi, pay it to take me to a place I knew and walk home from there. Or, I could call someone.

Money was tight and in the heart of downtown, it would take a while to get anywhere by taxi, which would be expensive. Marina was on her way to work so I couldn't call her. She really needed to work nearer the Loop. That really left only one person to call in a situation like this.

I pulled out my cell phone and selected Lori's number.

"Lori Craig," she answered.

"Hey, Lori, it's Jen." I tried to keep the fact that I was freezing out of my voice. The wind off the lake, wherever the lake was, had picked up and it was a chillier November day than I had anticipated.

"Hi, Jen. How was the big interview?" Lori asked. I was relieved she didn't seem swamped.

"Great, I just got out, actually. Want to grab some lunch?"

I asked casually.

"It's your lucky day. I had a client cancel on me. Where are you?"

"Um." I squinted at a street sign. "Randolph."

"Did you get lost again?" Lori asked, not sounding at all surprised.

I cringed at how well she knew me. "Sort of. I started looking at some Christmas windows and kept walking and got turned around."

"Give me the address of the building you're in front of and I'll be there in ten minutes," Lori said.

"You don't have to do that. Just give me directions to your building." I didn't want Lori to spend money, though it never bothered her. She splurged, went on shopping sprees, and never ran out of money.

"I was planning on having a business lunch, anyway, and now it's you. Where are you?"

I rattled off the address and hung up. How could I still get lost? I knew how. I let my mind wander and my feet kept going. The city's Christmas decorations were beautiful. I was determined not to wander again and planted my feet on the cold pavement. These pumps weren't very warm. Finally, a cab slowed and pulled to the curb. I saw Lori in the back, waving me to get in. I was rescued!

"Thanks, Lori!" I slid in next to her and rubbed my face to relieve the chill the wind had caused.

"You were just around the corner from my building." Lori shrugged then laughed. "Didn't Marina tell you *not* to touch your face?"

"What?" I asked and remembered my eyeliner. "Damn." I pulled out Marina's pocket mirror and wiped away the raccoon eyes I'd created. "At least I remembered it through the interview."

"I hope so. Where do you want to eat?" Lori asked.

"Anywhere that won't break my budget. I'm hoping this new job pays better." I applied some powder to cover up what eyeliner I couldn't wipe off. Of course, Marina would use the kind that you need industrial strength makeup remover to get off.

"No way! This is going on an expense account, so we're doing a nice lunch at least."

"I'm not business," I argued, not wanting to get Lori in trouble.

"And you're not cut out for business if you think the fat cats don't pad their expense accounts. We'll talk about my career and yours, if that'll ease your conscience."

"You pick the place, then." I wasn't going to fight Lori. She had a degree in arguing and expensive taste with or without her expense account. Her father made sure Lori never went without. Being daddy's little girl had advantages, but there were downsides, too. Part of me was glad to come from a hard-working middle-class family. I'd never have to choose between family money and the right man.

* * * *

After Lori and I had stuffed ourselves on pasta and bread, we got down to conversation — and serious ogling of the waiters. The funky Italian hole-in-the-wall had young waiters, mismatched chairs, homemade sauce and a unisex bathroom with the wine list painted on the wall. Maybe not as fancy as Lori would've liked, but we could splurge and not regret it in the morning.

"So, think you got the job?" Lori asked.

I shrugged. "After slapping Andre, I thought I was dead. Then Ralph cleared it up. They're so funny. I think I'd like it there."

"A guy tries to kiss your hand and you smack him. No wonder you don't have a boyfriend," Lori teased.

"Like you've got one," I shot back.

"Yeah, yeah. Ralph was the cute one?"

I nodded. "He's the owner and so handsome. He studied in Paris and is from Chicago originally."

"Then who exactly is Andre?"

"Ralph's partner. He has such a great accent!"

"Partner?" Lori lifted an eyebrow.

"Yes."

"What kind of partner?" Lori toyed with her water glass.

"Business." I shrugged.

"Sure. Business." She nodded.

"No." I suddenly realized she thought Ralph and Andre were gay and my fantasy went right out of the window. "No wonder Andre followed Ralph here from Paris."

"At least you two will have something in common, a lust for Ralph. Of course, Andre will actually get him."

"You don't know that for sure. Even if it's true, you don't have to rub it in."

"I'm not rubbing it in. You were on an interview and your brain was elsewhere. Moving on to heterosexual men, have you tried to find Marina's ex yet?" Lori asked.

I was glad Lori had changed the subject. "Not yet. She didn't seem to be in a hurry."

"Marina acts like that a lot. Don't let her fool you."

"You think she might want Lucas back?" I asked in shock. Marina had shown no emotion toward him at all.

"You don't know what you'll find. Maybe he was dull then. Maybe he found a sport or hobby for stress relief that'll make him more interesting. Either way, I think she should have to see him again because it was all her idea. What I really meant was that she pretends she doesn't care about being in a relationship when she really does."

"What sort of man do you think would be right for her?" I was frequently jealous of Lori and Marina's longer friendship, yet they never made me feel left out. There were times, however, when they had a whole fight and made up with a few eyes rolls, hand gestures, and subtle body language shifts.

"The right man for Marina is as hard to figure out as she is. He'd have to be smart, naturally." It constantly amazed me what odd facts Marina had in her brain. "Not a snob. I set her up with one of my cousins in college. She couldn't stand him."

"She always finds a way to avoid the really pushy guys," I added.

Lori nodded. "Absolutely. She is a guy's worst nightmare. If they're too aggressive, she'll shut them down, and if they don't make a move, she never will."

"That really surprises me. Marina is so direct and not shy at all." I'd kill to have Marina's bluntness, and the confidence to pull it off.

"She does okay in the man department. Finding the right one is the hard part." Lori seemed unconcerned. "If she met a guy who really got under her skin, I think she'd make a move eventually. Marina is picky."

"And you're not?" I teased.

"Not as picky as my parents." Lori bit her lower lip.

"True." Lori's parents and the odd relationship there forever puzzled me. Lori's dad owned the building we lived in and a lot of other property. He wanted Lori to be a princess and marry well and not lift a finger. She'd rebelled by going to law school like her father had, and she lived in the city.

Lori seemed to want to be free, then had followed her father into law and taken his money. I guess money would be a pretty good hold on someone. If my parents had a lot of money, it might have made the decision to move away harder.

"It's okay. You're right. I am picky. It's my parents' opinions I can't escape."

"Not even for Nick?" I asked, hoping to lighten the mood.

Lori's face immediately lit up and she smiled. "No, Nick was all for me. Then I grew up and got a job."

"Why here?" I asked.

"Why here, what?"

"Why get a job here near your parents in Chicago? Why not go downstate or take the bar in another state and practice there if your parents are so pushy?"

"Because I worked hard to pass the bar. I was a good

student. I write and argue great. On standardized tests, I freeze. I passed the bar and got a good offer from C.K. Dexter & Associates. They have such a great reputation and my father never worked there, so I took it. Leaving Chicago would be running away from my parents. Besides, I like living here. Where else could I have friends like you and Marina?"

"And you got to stay near Nick." I wasn't sure if that'd make her happy or not.

"Which meant I didn't have an easy excuse to break up with him. That was hard."

"And you haven't seen him since?" I asked. That was really sad.

Lori shook her head. "I avoid his garage and where he hangs out. Those places were never really my style, anyway."

I didn't believe that, though I nodded supportively. "Well, I'm sure Marina will find him and you can put him behind you for good."

"I thought I had. I believed he was just my best sex ever. Now all these feelings keep coming back." Lori rubbed her neck uncomfortably.

"Then it's good we're doing this. I hope I don't make a fool of myself over Brian or in finding Lucas for Marina. I'm not good at starting conversations with men. I'll screw it up for sure."

"Marina deserves to see him again. Just do it and get it over with. It's only one phone call to start. I'm more worried about your guy. He's long distance. How will we work that out?" Lori asked.

"I don't know. Have you talked to Brian yet?" My heart fluttered and I wondered if it was real feelings or just my normal nerves.

"No, I got his home phone number and I'll call him this afternoon. My sources say he isn't married. He has a roommate."

"Male or female?" I tried not to sound overeager.

"Male," Lori replied. "That tells us nothing. He could have a girlfriend."

"Can I listen in?" I asked.

"Not a chance!" Lori wagged her finger at me. "You'll find out the results at the weekly meeting with Marina. Brian will last until then."

"I moved to Chicago. I could handle moving to Los Angeles if Brian were the right one."

"Weather is better," Lori admitted. "Still, you can't get decent pizza to save your life."

"I could make Chicago pizza," I returned.

"I dare you to make a really good Chicago-style, deep-dish pizza for our first weekly meeting."

"You doubt me?" I crossed my arms.

"No, I want good deep-dish pizza." She smiled.

"You'll get your pizza." I nodded with confidence.

"Good, now I'd better get back to work." Lori signed for the bill and we walked to the door. "You can manage the L from here, right?"

"Yes, Mom." I spotted the platform across the street and understood why Lori had picked that restaurant for lunch.

I tried to shake the fear of what Lori might find out from Brian as a train rattled overhead. He was a very sweet guy and Lori could easily cross-examine him to the point where he'd never want to speak to me again.

I made it home and pulled out Marina's information on Lucas. Why wait? I could at least make sure he still worked at the same place and do the preliminary stuff. Going down there or speaking to him would take a little courage.

It wasn't natural for me to approach strange men, so I couldn't be as casual about it as Lori or Marina. They dealt with the public and made conversation in their jobs. I stayed in the kitchen and dealt with the same staff night in and night out.

Marina, of course, had no picture of Lucas. She had his business card. I set it on the coffee table and proceeded to pick up the suits I'd left out when dressing that morning. I put Marina's makeup on the island where she'd see it.

Housework was an excellent distraction. I was avoiding making that call and I knew it. I made my bed again and put everything in order in the bedroom before I returned to the living room and sat on the sofa. The card waited there patiently as I plumped the pillows, lit the candle and turned on some music.

I then realized I was still in my interview suit and returned to my bedroom to change. I had to be comfortable for this. Marina wasn't good at finding men so this might be her chance at true love and great sex.

Finally, in jeans and a Green Bay Packers sweatshirt — I could only wear cheese-head contraband when Marina and Lori weren't around — I settled in with my phone and the business card. A chill went through my toes, but I told myself I couldn't get up from the sofa and get socks until I made this call. *Just make sure he still works there, make contact. That's all,* I told myself.

I dialed the phone and got the right financial firm. "Lucas Rigby, please," I said.

"One moment, please," the receptionist said.

The phone rang. He still worked there. Good. *Hang up.* I could disconnect the call and that would be enough for today.

"Rigby," a strong male voice answered. Too late to hang up now without looking rude or possibly getting caught by caller ID.

"Hello," I said.

"Who's this?" Lucas asked.

Suddenly my courage took over. He had no idea who I was, so I put on my best Chicago talk and went for it. "This is Doreen McNicolas from Windy City Floral. Is this the Lucas Rigby who ordered two dozen long-stem red roses for his wife? He didn't leave a number and we can't read the address my assistant wrote down to send them to."

"Not me." Lucas hung up before I could go on. I liked my little bit of acting. It had worked and I didn't feel stupid.

Unfortunately, he hadn't told me whether he was or wasn't married, only that he hadn't ordered the non-existent flowers. Not a chatty guy.

Still, it was a victory. I had made contact and knew where he was. At least I'd have something to report at the weekly meeting. Taking today off meant I'd be working the rest of the week and wouldn't get a chance to go to his firm. That would wait for next week. Plenty of time to come up with the reason and the courage.

Now I was anxious to hear what Lori had found out about Brian, and there was nothing left to clean.

Chapter Three

Lori in Action

Enough about Nick! All the way back to the office, I had felt like a complete idiot. Much as I'd tried, I couldn't get him out of my mind. He was ancient history and not only could I not forget him, I had probably bored poor Jen about him over lunch when I knew nothing could happen. Some things can't peacefully coexist. My family and Nick were two such things. Nothing good could come from finding him again.

I plowed through the rest of my afternoon at work, trying to distract myself. The memories kept teasing me while I wrote up a brief.

Finally, I was caught up and all that was left was to call Jen's Brian. Since it was long distance, I wouldn't have the luxury of bumping into him or flirting with him to make casual conversation. I'd have to take the more direct approach.

I punched in Brian's home phone number and leaned back in my leather chair while the speakerphone rang. My view of another Chicago high-rise was uninspiring. To have a window at all was remarkable. My office was little more than a closet. Still, it was better than most associates got. I made it feel larger with mirrors and paintings that had depth. The mauve and gray walls were from the last time a company-wide redecorating effort had been conducted, the late eighties.

I guess Marina and Jen were right—I'd done pretty well for an associate without using any of my father's connections. They didn't understand that I wanted to blow my parents away with my success. Nothing I did was ever good enough. There was always a criticism behind any compliment.

For now, it was one thing at a time. That thing was to help Jen find her Brian. Hopefully he deserved her.

"Hello?" answered a male voice.

"Is this Brian?" I remembered this was a social call and put on my sweet voice as opposed to my bitchy, scare-the-hell-out-of-them lawyer voice.

"No, Brian's at work. Who's this?"

"This is Lori Craig. I was trying to look up Brian for a friend of mine. She and Brian used to date. Do you know when he'll be home?"

"Is this a joke?" the guy asked. "Am I on the radio? Brian set this up, right?"

"No, I'm looking for Brian."

"To set him up with an ex-girlfriend?" The man was laughing into the phone.

I wanted to hang up. This whole thing was crazy. He was my only contact. "That's right. Is something wrong?"

"Brian set this up for our one-year anniversary, right? This is priceless. Brian is such a practical joker. His ex-girlfriend. That's really funny!"

"Your anniversary?" I suddenly got the joke. Brian was obviously no longer into girls. "Well, happy anniversary!"

I hung up and started laughing. Jen had turned her sweet Brian firmly gay. Poor Jen! Marina and I would never let her live this down. He had clearly been confused and Jen had helped him decide. This was too much. Marina and I needed to help Jen with her gaydar.

I dreamed about how exactly I'd reveal the truth at our first weekly meeting until I was interrupted by a knock on the door. My assistant poked her head in.

"I thought you had to leave right on time today for that ultra-early holiday party?" she asked. "It's after six."

Damn! I was half an hour late already. "Thanks, Anne. I

completely forgot." I grabbed my jacket and headed for the elevators.

Ten minutes later, I pulled out of the parking garage and merged into downtown rush-hour traffic. My mother and the hostess of this party were friends from private school and were infamous for conspiring to set me up with anything male they deemed financially and socially worthy. All of their choices were dull, desperate or terrified of me. This wouldn't be a fun party.

While stopped at a red light, I imagined what it'd be like to show up with Nick. They'd all be whispering behind their drinks and looking down their noses at him. They'd ask rude questions about who his parents were and where he'd matriculated. Why did that make me grin so hard?

A honk from behind made me glance up and see the light was green. I finally looked around and noticed I was on the street where Nick's garage was. In the complete opposite end of the city from where I needed to be.

I had lost my mind.

I immediately pulled into the restaurant next door to turn around. Something stopped me. I couldn't resist inspecting the garage from the safety of my car. Nick knew what I drove, so if he saw me, I'd be caught. I couldn't help it.

Maybe he'd gotten fat and bald? I crossed my fingers and inched the car closer. I got a glimpse of him speaking to a customer and felt the urge to talk to him then strip him naked. He hadn't changed a bit, except maybe that he'd gotten handsomer. He was tall and lean like a swimmer and very good with his hands. At least he had been the last time I'd seen him. Touching him would be enough. One more kiss. Just one more time.

Instead, I hit the gas.

* * * *

Forty-five minutes later, I got off the elevator and entered one of the most expensive penthouses in Chicago with a stunning view of the lake. My parents' friends were disgustingly rich and hated to be snubbed. Every year they had their holiday party one week before Thanksgiving, so everyone would come. If they waited until the holiday season, there might be conflicts. Still, they thought of themselves as down-to-earth.

As a butler took my coat, a waiter offered me a flute of champagne, which I eagerly nabbed. The party wouldn't be all bad. They always had good food, the best alcohol, lavish decorations, and a waiter or two worth admiring.

What was wrong with me? Men were men! So why wasn't it as easy for me to fall for a rich one as it was to fall for a poor one? It couldn't be that hard.

"Lori, you're late," my mother scolded as she appeared at my shoulder.

"Sorry, got stuck at work." That excuse would go nowhere with my mother, but I enjoyed making the point that I was an adult who earned her own way. She believed that until her children were married we weren't truly adults. Unfortunately, I was the only single one left.

It was in my mother's nature to coordinate everything she could. My mother was dressed perfectly and had on just enough jewelry to signify Daddy's wealth without looking like she was showing off. I wished I had at least one sister rather than two brothers. Maybe then there would be a little less pressure on me.

"You can't spend your life as a lawyer," Mother said as though it were a law of nature.

"It was fine for Daddy."

"Of course. He made the money, and I raised the children. Motherhood is a full-time job, no matter what your generation says."

"Our nanny had nothing do with your children." I could've gone farther back.

"I beg your pardon?" I could tell Mother wanted to argue with me. However, there were too many ears to do it properly. I didn't care if she'd heard. She'd object to my tone if nothing else.

"Nothing. I don't have kids to raise or a husband to party plan for, so it doesn't matter if I work myself to death. I enjoy it."

"You're thirty years old now, Lori. Your biological clock is ticking. I don't care about medical breakthroughs. You should have children when you're young enough to enjoy them. I only hope I live to see your wedding."

"You're only fifty-five, Mother," I said a little too loudly. She pursed her lips as she looked around to see if anyone had heard her true age.

That was what she got for dumping guilt on me as soon as I was in the door. Marina thought her mother's Catholic guilt was over the top. I'd admit her family was more dramatic. My mother could serve it up cold and fast.

"I can't force you to get married or have children. Honestly, you could be a little more open-minded. There are some very nice men here." My mother smiled at an acquaintance and wandered off in the direction of the hostess.

At least this encounter with Mother had been blissfully short. Unfortunately, the evening wasn't over. I checked the room for someone I knew who wouldn't try to set me up. I was thrilled to see Diana Harris heading for me.

I was saved! A friend from high school who had chosen college and a career over society and marriage. A pediatrician, Diana took the same shit about working too much and not finding a man fast enough. There was power in numbers. She was my salvation and, with her, I wouldn't feel so alone.

"Lori, I'm so glad you came!" Diana hugged me like we were best friends. "We haven't seen each other since your parents' party last year. Are they still doing their traditional Eve of Christmas Eve party?"

I wanted to point out that they had been having that party every year since before I'd been born. For now, she was on my side, so I'd better be nice. "Of course they're having the party. How are you doing?"

"Great! And you?" Diana seemed full of energy.

"Glad to see you. My mother is on the wedding warpath and I don't have a date. I turned thirty last week." I drank the rest of my champagne in one unladylike gulp.

"What is it with that age? My mother was terrified I was going to end up thirty and alone, too."

I knew Diana was a few months older than me. I was clearly missing something. "Did you get married and not tell me?"

"Oh, I thought you knew. I got engaged." She stuck out her hand with a huge emerald-cut diamond ring.

My companion in the single, professional women's club had betrayed me. I wanted to sink through the floor. That children's song *The Farmer in the Dell* ran through my head until the last line — 'the cheese stands alone.'

When had I become the cheese?

I mustered a smile for my friend. "I didn't even know you were seeing anyone. Congratulations! How did you two meet?"

"It was the weirdest thing. I got set up on a blind date by a nurse at work for a New Year's

Eve party."

"That's pressure. A first date on New Year's Eve." Polite conversation, I could do this.

"Absolutely. I was sure it would be terrible and I'd be strangling that nurse Monday morning. I was happily surprised. Greg isn't a model, but he's cute and in great shape. He's a trainer for the Bears. We hit it off and have been together ever since. Once a month, he brings a player to the hospital to visit the kids. He's so sweet! We took a vacation to Hawaii over the summer and he proposed."

"That's great. Your parents like him?" I could only hope she'd at least have broken with tradition and gone for a man without connections.

"They adore him. His parents own a team out west but he's like us, a rebel. He won't work for the team his dad owns. He should be coming. They had a game tonight."

"He's definitely got great taste in women and jewelry!" I couldn't help being happy for Diana. Clearly, she was in love and her future husband was from a rich family, yet worked for a living. He even did charity with her patients. How had she gotten off so easily? Her man sounded perfect. There wasn't supposed to be such a thing as a good blind date, anyway.

"Thanks. I'm so amazed what happened to me in one year. Enough about me. What's new with you?" Diana tapped my arm with her left hand so the ring glimmered at me.

I plastered a smile on my face as I twirled my empty champagne flute, needing a refill. "Work is great. I won this huge case." Diana's eyes darted toward the door, and I knew I'd lost her attention.

"There's Greg." Diana waved at a tall and extremely well-muscled man. He approached for us with an equally goofy smile. Sickeningly in love, both of them! "You made it!" Diana hopped up on her toes to kiss him.

I felt like I should turn away. I decided to take the high road. "I hope this is the much-praised Greg," I joked to get them to come up for air.

"Lori's always a smart ass." Diana wrapped an arm around Greg and held tight. "Of course this is him. Greg, this is Lori, a friend from high school."

He shook my hand with a grip that felt like he used every one of those overdeveloped muscles. I had to admit that he flexed well. "A pleasure to meet you."

"You, too," he said. "Diana's told me what you two have gone through with these parties."

"We've been attending them all our lives. You'll get used to it." I didn't need *their* sympathy. Greg was the one to be judged tonight. His late arrival would be a mark against him, but his credentials were good.

"Honey, what about Andy?" Diana asked.

"He's single." Greg shrugged.

"I'm sorry?" I hoped she wasn't trying to set me up. It

was a conspiracy. My mother had corrupted Diana.

"You'll love him. Andy is Greg's younger brother and he's so cute. He crunches numbers for their father. It's a good family." Diana smiled and nodded.

"I don't know, Diana. We can't all be as lucky as you," I avoided.

"Think about it," Diana said. "We have to go say hello to my parents."

"Thanks, I will." I bit my tongue and found a waiter for another drink. My only friend in this circle, in defiance of the maternal pressure to marry well, had given in and gone to the other side. I hadn't eaten a thing since lunch and now my appetite was gone. I watched Diana and Greg get gushed over by her parents and *my* parents. They were glowing. Could the nightmare get any worse?

I needed a distraction. I went to find Aunt Gilda, the hostess. She wasn't any relation, but she'd been *Aunt* Gilda since I was little.

The manners my parents had taught me weren't a bad thing, I reminded myself. I had to pay lip service to the hostess, a frail woman whose necklace alone weighed more than she did.

"It's a lovely party this year, Aunt Gilda."

"I'm so glad you could make it, Lori. You look so pretty!" Aunt Gilda nodded in approval.

"Thank you. Is there anything I can do to help?" I asked, expecting her to politely decline.

"Would you mind chatting with Freddie for a bit? He's new to the circles and not very good at mingling, and you can talk to anyone." She'd ambushed me. No doubt my mother had had some hand in this.

"I'd be happy to," I lied. I had to admit that Aunt Gilda knew better about how to flatter people into things than my mother. How could I say no? At least chatting with Freddie meant I didn't have to chat with my mother or any more recently engaged women.

Aunt Gilda led the way to a man who stood maybe five

foot six and looked about as comfortable I did. His features were round and pudgy with a slightly offset nose. "Freddie, this is my dear friend's daughter, Lori. She's a lawyer at one of Chicago's top firms."

As Aunt Gilda left, I shook his sweaty hand and put on my fake smile. I felt like I was being punished for previously turning down the good-looking men they'd thrown at me. Freddie must be part troll. I had to start something of a conversation. "Are you new to the city?"

"I moved here for the job. You grew up here?" He downed half a glass of wine. I caught him checking out my measurements. This was going to get interesting, and not in a good way.

"All my life. We've got snow in the winter, a beach on the lake for the summer, and everything in between. How do you like it so far?" Suddenly I had a vision of Nick's image next to creepy Freddie. My fantasy life was now officially out of control. Nick towered over him by nearly a foot, never had sweaty palms, and had that sexy smile that always put me in a good mood. My body flushed and I took a deep breath.

"It is getting hot in here. We could get some fresh air?" Freddie suggested.

I nodded and we moved onto the terrace. Most of the party avoided it. The view was beautiful, despite the chilly night. The air smelled good and the quiet helped. I knew being alone with creepy Freddie wasn't a great idea. For the moment, I needed to get Nick's image out of my head.

"Would you like me to get your coat?" Freddie stood too close.

I inhaled the expensive cologne he'd apparently bathed in that morning.

"No, I'm fine, thank you. So you're in investment banking?" I had to make conversation or my imagination would wander back to Nick. I had no idea why I'd driven by his garage. Somehow, I had to forget about it. Naturally, I'd rather be having fun with Nick as opposed to making small talk with creepy Freddie. That didn't mean Nick was the right man for me, I reminded myself.

"Yes. I'm from California. I've heard a lot about Chicago winters. Are they as bad as they say?"

"They can be. Stuff brews off that lake and we can really get dumped on. It's not Christmas without snow. You'll grow to love it." I shivered and leaned on the ledge, looking at the star-filled sky.

"I'm sure I will," Freddie replied. "There are plenty of ways to keep warm."

Seconds later, his flabby arms wrapped around me as he pressed against me from behind. His hot breath on my neck made me sick. Between his body heat and cologne, I couldn't breathe and gagged.

"Get your hands off of me." I did my best to avoid his touch.

"That's not very friendly to the new guy in town." His tongue on my ear was enough. Aunt Gilda's party or not, creepy Freddie needed to be taught a lesson.

I stomped my sharp stiletto into his foot and threw an elbow into his ribs. Freddie's yelp of pain made me feel in control for the first time that day. I shoved him so hard that he fell to the ground. I stopped short of stabbing his balls with my heel — it was *so* tempting.

Instead, I left him on the ground, whimpering and cursing. Racing back into the crowded party, I found my father.

"What's wrong, princess?" He gave me a peck on the cheek. "You don't look well."

"That creep, Freddie, Aunt Gilda wanted me to talk to. I don't want to offend her by telling her that he groped me. Please tell Mother that if that's the kind of man she wants me to marry, I'll be joining a convent."

"I'll take care of Freddie, princess. And don't do anything crazy. We're not even Catholic. Your mother just wants to see you settled before I retire and we travel more. We want to know you're taken care of."

"Mom and Aunt Gilda don't have the greatest taste in

men, and I can take care of myself." I crossed my arms in a huff. "I just don't want to cause a real scene."

"Your mother found me and I'm not so terrible. Her taste can't be all bad. Don't worry, you'll find someone." Daddy tapped my chin.

I smiled. It was an automatic reaction. Much as I could openly clash with my mother, Daddy always tried to see my side, too. It was hard to argue with a man who not only called me princess, but also had treated me like one since the day I'd been born. He always took care of things calmly and handled my mother with a finesse I'd never developed.

"You've paid your dues. Go. I'll handle your mother." Daddy winked and nodded at the door.

"Thanks, Daddy." I kissed his cheek and headed for the coatroom. I was alone in the elevator in record time. My mother had a sixth sense when I was trying to get out of things. This time I'd slipped under her radar.

The quiet and solitude of the elevator made my mind whirl. If only I could have brought Nick tonight. There would have been no need for my father to handle things. Nick had simple rules and philosophies of life. When Freddie had groped me, Nick would have broken his nose and scared the shit of him. That would have been the end of it. Daddy would handle it his way, quietly and delicately.

Nick. Would any man I wanted ever measure up to him *and* meet the requirements of those rich-and-fussy women? Why couldn't I have it easy like Diana? Why was it so hard? Maybe I *should* stop by Marina's mom's bakery and find out about those convents.

No, that would be too drastic a measure. I needed to stop thinking! I needed someone who would sympathize, not tell me what I should do. I got in my car and drove carefully to the one place I knew I'd be safe. Parking the car, I took a deep breath. I then calmly walked to the door.

Leaning on the doorbell, I crossed my fingers they'd be home. Finally, the door opened, and Marina just shook her head at me. Half a second later, she registered my mood, grabbed the sleeve of my jacket and tugged me into her apartment to stop the ringing. I was in a daze.

"Want to talk about it?" she asked.

I shook my head and let my purse drop to the floor. It was only a Coach. I normally took better care of my things. Now I didn't care.

Marina nodded and grabbed my coat. Then she pointed so I'd take off my boots. Finally, she steered me toward the maroon couch. Her decorating was eclectic, to put it nicely. In her warm apartment, I felt free to be a slob and to be depressed. Jen was great. She'd try to make me feel better and would fold and straighten everything. Marina would just get me through it and not fuss too badly.

"Vodka, tequila, or rum?"

"Yes, please." I rubbed my temples, trying to do something to make myself feel better.

"That bad?" she asked.

"Don't ask. I don't want to talk about it." I knew she'd take my Nick obsession as encouragement for her little game. This was completely unrelated. Wasn't it?

"Fine. Just call me the bartender." Marina pulled out bottle after bottle and mixed up something to help me. She knew the drill. Sometimes it was six months, sometimes it was every few months. Whenever I got Nick in my head and couldn't get him out, I ended up curled on Marina's couch drunk and refusing to discuss it.

How could I admit I was hung up on the mechanic? Of all people, I couldn't tell Marina. She'd want me to go for it.

"I'll never be as brave as you," I mumbled as she gave me a drink in a plastic cup with a bendy straw to avoid last years' crimson goblet crash. I'd tried to clean it up and had ended up needing four stitches in my thumb.

"Lori, you're the bravest person I know." Marina put an extra throw pillow on the couch to catch my head when the time came.

I shook my head as I sipped. I was not brave. Marina sat in the black leather recliner with a handmade afghan.

I realized I'd barged in without even calling ahead. "Did I interrupt your evening?"

"No, I had a long day. I was just reading. Have you eaten dinner?" she asked.

"Two toast points with caviar at the Miltons' party." I shrugged and sipped harder.

"You need food." Marina started to get up.

I shook my head. "I'll eat after I'm drunk," I said around the straw.

"The way you're going through that drink and considering what I put in it, that won't be long." Marina walked to the kitchen and put something in the microwave.

A great smell wafted over the couch and hunger and alcohol fought in my stomach. Marina brought a large plate of lasagna and garlic bread on a tray and set it on the coffee table in front of me. "I said not now."

"So it gets cold." Marina shrugged. "It's there if you want." She settled into the recliner again and pulled out her needles.

It was comforting and odd that Marina, of all people, did something so old-fashioned as knit. Her grandmother had taught her and Marina claimed it helped her think and relax. It was soothing to watch, I had to give her that. I wished she had room in the apartment for a piano. That was more soothing. I hadn't stuck with the lessons because my mother wanted me to. Marina also picked stuff up quickly.

Too much alcohol. My mind had wandered.

The food called to me and I set the empty glass down. "Who made the lasagna?"

"My sister, Mary Rose. More alcohol?" she asked.

"Not yet." I picked at the garlic bread first. "My last single career friend at the party is engaged."

"See how brave you were to go?" Marina nodded.

"I didn't know until I talked to her. I know my mother knew. If I say anything, she'll claim she didn't tell me to spare my feelings. She's so evil."

"Why do you let her do that to you?"

"Like your mother never gets on your nerves?" I dug into the food.

"I've never called my mother evil."

I couldn't argue with Marina there. I'd trade for her mother in a heartbeat. Criticism in her family was masked with love and food and loud fighting rather than cool and calculating judgment. They all yelled until they got it out, then it was over.

"That wasn't all. The hostess left me talking to a creep who couldn't keep his hands to himself. I had to teach him a lesson."

"Even more bravery!" Marina smiled.

"Not really. I stomped his foot, elbowed him in the ribs, then ran to my daddy. I left him to deal with it just like a spoiled little brat." I was in the hating-myself phase. Marina hated that mood as well.

"You need another drink." Marina took my glass and headed for the kitchen.

"Marina?" I couldn't believe I was about to say this.

"Yes?" she responded when my silence dragged on.

"Have you looked into Nick yet?" I wanted her to say yes. I wanted to know if he was single or not. Mad or not. On second thought...

"No, I haven't had a chance. I want to go by the garage so he can't try to dodge me." She handed me the next drink. "So did you see him this time or just can't get him out of your head?"

"This has nothing to do with Nick. I just handled Brian today and was curious." Marina could tell when I was lying. Luckily, she wouldn't torture me about it. At least not now.

I put the straw between my lips to shut myself up and drank fast. Marina knew it was really all about Nick. My family made it so much worse.

"I'll make more." Marina raked her fingers through her wild black hair, not verbalizing her frustration at me. "I see sick days for us tomorrow."

"My liver can't take many more nights like these."

I had to put Nick behind me for good. Somehow, one way or the other.

Chapter Four

Marina's Plan—Status Check

The sunlight and sounds of a busy Chicago weekday dragged me from sleep sooner than I wanted. The wall clock read eight in the morning and I was achingly stiff. Unfortunately, I'd fallen asleep in the recliner instead of going to bed.

Lori was still asleep, curled in a red and pink blanket on my couch. I grabbed the phone and called in sick to work. Then I called Lori's office so she wouldn't stress.

It was a good thing Lori didn't do this a lot.

It had been a very long night. Lori always started as an entertaining drinker. However, if she drank enough, she became a depressed drunk who talked endlessly about her family, her future and never finding the right man.

How could I tell her she'd already found him? All that would've done was start her on a crying fit about how things with Nick would never work. Finally, she'd passed out at about four in the morning.

One more call to make before noon, I decided as I put the coffee on. I went into my bedroom for privacy. I had a good hour before Lori woke up so I'd get it all done. After a quick shower, I wrapped up in my dark purple fuzzy robe and dialed Nick's garage. I hoped I wouldn't say the wrong thing.

"Southside Mechanics," someone answered.

"Nick Jared, please." I toweled off my hair and ran a comb through it to get the knots out.

There were muffled voices then a new voice, "This is

Nick."

"Hi, Nick, this is Marina Castini. You worked on my mother's car a while back."

"I remember Mrs. Castini, nice lady. Drives a powder blue '88 Caprice. Is it giving her trouble again?"

"Actually, I keep trying to talk her into a new car, but she likes that one. Are you busy?"

"No, we're not too bad today. I can squeeze you in. What's the problem?"

"You're sure your boss won't mind?" I played along just to find out how much pull he had.

"It'll be okay. What time?"

"This isn't about the car. It's more personal," I admitted. How was I supposed to delicately change the subject to Lori when I had no idea how he'd react? I could guess Nick wouldn't be overjoyed.

"Is this a joke?" he asked.

"No, I'm calling to talk to you about a friend of mine. Lori Craig."

"What about her? I don't have any contact with her anymore." His tone was instantly cold.

"I was wondering if you ever thought about her." I wasn't getting a good feeling about this.

"Lori doesn't give a damn, so whatever you're up to forget it. Find her a prince or a millionaire or something." Disgust filled Nick's voice.

"Her mother has tried that, and it hasn't worked. I don't think that's really what she wants."

"Now I remember. Lori mentioned you. You're a meddler. Nice try." Nick slammed down the phone on the other end.

That hadn't gone well, but I had made contact. Lori was hung up on Nick, and he didn't sound indifferent to Lori. That gave me a bit of hope.

However, Nick also didn't sound at all positive toward my efforts. It was too hard to tell over the phone what his true feelings were. Maybe I was just being overly romantic. I had to believe it wasn't a hopeless case. It would, however, require some serious plotting on my part to get Nick into the game.

First, I needed some coffee.

Rummaging through my cabinets and fridge, I realized I didn't have anything good for a hangover breakfast. Not even bread for some dry toast. Time to call in the family. I hit speed dial.

"Three Aunts Bakery," Penny answered.

"Hey, Penny, it's me. I need a favor."

"Aren't you supposed to be at work?" Penny asked. I had one of those families that knew everything about everyone's life. Secrets were hard to keep.

"I'm not feeling great, and neither is Lori. Could you pack up some stuff and I'll run over and grab it?"

"No, don't come. I'll bring it over to you. It's early. Aunt Rosa can cover the counter."

"Thanks, I owe you one." I hung up the phone and tugged my purple robe tighter. I needed to put on some socks and dry my hair without letting it frizz.

Twenty minutes later, the doorbell rang and I scurried to get it before it rang again and woke Lori. I opened the door to find my cousin with a huge box of treats.

"You're a lifesaver, Penny!" I took the box and ushered her in for coffee.

"Lori looks terrible," she whispered.

"She'll sleep it off." I shrugged.

"You guys got drunk?"

"No, she got drunk and I got to listen to her go on and on. Want some coffee?"

"No. By the way, thanks for the advice. I changed my major. I'll be done in two years and recruiters are already trying to get me."

"What did you change it to?" I asked as Lori groaned from the couch.

"Nursing. Hi, Lori." Penny followed me while I got a glass of water and two aspirin for Lori and set them on the coffee table in her line of sight.

"Good choice," Lori rasped and she reached for the water.

"I agree. Penny, you're great with people, especially kids. If it doesn't feel right, you can always change it again." I suddenly felt like I was the family shrink. Hopefully, I hadn't set Penny on the wrong path. If I couldn't fix Lori's situation, how could I hope to fix Penny's?

Poor thing couldn't settle on a career that would support her or that she liked.

"The classes look interesting." Penny nodded. "Well, I better get back. Thanks again."

"Thanks for the delivery, Penny." I locked the door behind her and glanced over at Lori.

"I should be shot." Lori sipped her water and groaned, holding her head.

"No, you just need to rest." I crossed the room and sat on the coffee table. "I'll get you something bland to eat."

"Maybe later. What time is it?" A look of panic filled her eyes as she tried to focus on her watch.

"I already called your office. Don't worry, you have the whole day to recover."

"Thanks. Does Jen know?"

"No, Penny's the only one. You got drunk. It's not like you paraded naked in court or something."

"I know, but this isn't fun, post-party drunk. This is pathetic drunk."

"You're not pathetic. You had a bad night and needed to erase it for a bit. It's that time of year when our families make us crazy and we want to hide. Think of this as a warm-up for your parents' Christmas party."

"Don't remind me. That'll be here way too soon." Lori massaged her forehead.

"Think how much fun that will be. They invited me and Jen, both with guests. Not to mention *my* parents. We'll upset your mother much more than you will. My mother will bring deviled eggs or lasagna or something to clash with your menu. I'm not sure if they can make it yet. Cross your fingers they'll have other plans."

"She doesn't have to bring food. Mother is having it catered," Lori corrected automatically.

"I know, I told her. I know my mother, though. She'd feel like a terrible guest not bringing something and a bottle of wine or box of candy isn't my mother's style."

"I like your family." Lori smiled. "Even Penny's better than my cousins. She helps out, doesn't criticize and takes our advice seriously."

"She's young. She should listen to her elders. I mean, she's about to turn twenty so a woman of thirty has a lot more experience." Lori would hate that!

"You're not thirty yet. If I didn't need this coffee so much, I'd dump it over your head," she said seriously.

"Would you want to be nineteen again?" I went to the kitchen and brought the coffee pot to the couch to refill our cups.

"No, everything was up in the air then. My parents still had all the money and even controlled my dorm room situation. Things are better now."

"See, being old has its advantages."

"Older!" she insisted. "We're not old yet."

"I'm glad you're seeing the light. Now you might want to visit the inside of the shower because your makeup is smeared and your hair looks like you belong in the sixties or the B52s."

"You've seen me worse." She sat up slowly.

"True, but you'll feel better after a shower. Then maybe we can talk about this without alcohol interfering." I had followed most of her stuff last night, though odds were that she didn't remember our conversation.

"I don't know if I want to talk about it." Lori stood and took baby steps to the door, holding her head still. "If I'm not back in half an hour, call nine-one-one."

"Okay." I watched from the door to make sure she was walking into the right apartment and doing so steadily. If she made it across the hall, she'd be fine. Getting her to her apartment wouldn't help me solve the Nick situation.

Maybe if I got her really, really drunk and took her to the garage, I could solve this Nick and Lori thing for good. She'd at least admit how she felt. Though it might help if Nick were drunk, too.

* * * *

One week down, and all I'd accomplished was a hang-up from Nick. So far, this had gone very badly. At least Lori had returned to her normal routine. I'd restocked my liquor cabinet and bought extra tequila for the margaritas I was contributing to the first week check-in.

I could already smell the pizza Jen was making. I'd dressed for comfort in my loose boot-cut jeans. The cherry-red sweater was unraveling slightly on the left cuff but at least it matched my socks. I saved my sexy form-fitting jeans and cleavage-showing tops for dates, or at least leaving the building.

As I left my apartment with the tequila and margarita mix, I hoped Jen and Lori had made better progress in the past week or this would be a very fast and boring conversation. I still believed 'no regrets' was a good motto. It'd been my idea to explore it with the exes. If it backfired, I had no one to blame.

"Hey, Jen." I entered her apartment and joined her in the kitchen. True to Jen, she was in a crisp blouse, khaki pants and an apron. She already had the blender and ice set out for me. Her fancy tiered cooling trays contained two deep-dish pizzas. I saw another one in the oven as she zipped around setting out Parmesan cheese and oregano. "We each get a whole pizza?"

"Hi, Marina. No. I just had extra ingredients and wanted to use them up. If we have a lot left over, you can take it to the animal hospital with you. You said your colleagues would eat anything." Jen pulled out plates and silverware like she was having the pope for dinner.

"True, however, you might be right making extra. If

tonight depresses us, we might need them all." I poured the ice into the blender, added the rest of the ingredients, and let the blender mix us some relief.

"If that's the case, it's a good thing you got the industrial-size tequila and drink mix." She handed me a towel in case I spilled. Jen never missed a thing. "Where's Lori?"

"I haven't heard from her today. She's supposed to bring dessert." I wasn't about to forgo cheesecake because Lori got stuck at the office. I grabbed my cell phone out of my worn jeans pocket and speed-dialed her number.

"I'm coming, Marina," she answered. "I left your mom's bakery ten minutes ago."

"At least I know it'll be good cheesecake. You've got fifteen minutes, or we're cutting the pizzas without you," I informed her and hung up.

"Ten minutes," I relayed to Jen.

"Everything should be done by then." Jen took garlic bread out of the oven.

I busied myself with the blender and poured strawberry margaritas into Jen's funky cactus stem glasses as Lori entered weighed down with her briefcase, purse and two pastry boxes. Lori and her stuff were covered with a dusting of snow.

Jen ran to her aid and took the cheesecakes while Lori tried to get herself in order.

"I guess winter is officially here." I handed Lori a drink after she'd hung up her coat.

"Thank you," Lori said as her lips touched the glass. She took a long drink before elaborating. "Yeah, looks like it'll be our first good snowfall of the year. I got a strawberry cheesecake and a chocolate. I was only going to get one, then your mother insisted on both."

"Excellent!" I had a terrible weakness for cheesecake, especially my mother's strawberry one. "Was Mom still at the bakery this late?"

"She said your dad was coming to get her. I offered her a ride, but she said no. I guess her car is acting up." Lori shrugged.

"Thanks for looking out for her. She really needs a new car. Nothing fancy, she just putters around the Southside from home to the bakery and around Taylor Street. It's not like they can't afford it. She likes that boat of a car." I took a swallow of my drink and resisted the urge to call my father and lecture him about getting Mom a safer and more dependable car. Dad was proud, yet Mom had the final say on all things.

However, it could be useful. If Dad couldn't fix the car himself, I'd be the first to volunteer to take it in to Nick's garage. I couldn't count on Nick, but if the chance presented itself, I wouldn't ignore it.

"Ready for pizza?" Jen asked. "I made one pepperoni, a sausage and mushroom, and one with everything. You guys tell me if I got Chicago deep-dish right."

We dug in and settled down around the coffee table with pizza and drinks. "So, who got where with their guys?" Lori asked.

I knew Lori was curious about Nick and she seemed to have news of her own, too. I was in no rush to share until more alcohol had been consumed. Luckily, Jen chimed in first.

"Well, I called Lucas' office. I couldn't get any details about his personal life. He still works there. He was all business. Polite and not chatty."

"That sounds about right." I cut into my pepperoni wedge of pizza. I took a bite and groaned. "You got the spices right, Jen. Very good. Bland pizza isn't Chicago, no matter how deep the dish."

Jen grinned and glanced at Lori, who was stuffing her face with a slice of everything deep-dish. "Good, I'm glad you guys liked it. I'm going to visit Lucas' office and see if he has a ring on or pictures of kids in his office. If not, I'll take it from there."

"Good work." Lori nodded. "Did he sound well hung?"

"Like it had shrunk?" I tossed a pillow at Lori. She stuck

her tongue out in return.

"I don't know about that from a phone call. I was able to confirm his name, but didn't get to that personal level. I couldn't even get him to tell me if he was married or not." Jen frowned.

"Why would he?" I asked. "You didn't ask him that. Did you?"

"No, I pretended to be from a florist and the Lucas Rigby I was looking for had ordered a dozen roses for his wife and I couldn't make out the address. He wouldn't tell me anything, though." Jen shrugged.

"You lied to someone?" Lori asked.

"I'm so proud!" I clapped.

"Me, too!" Lori hugged her.

"Nothing?" I asked.

"No, he patiently waited for me to finish, told me I had the wrong man and hung up. I'll get him in person." Jen nodded. "What about Nick?"

"I called Nick's garage and I believe he *is* still single. He was busy so I'm going to have to go down there in person and talk things over. I don't want to get him in trouble at work." For all I knew, Nick could be married with kids, too. I couldn't stand it if Lori got her hopes up and they were ruined.

"Did you mention me?" Lori asked.

I felt terrible. If this didn't work, I'd never forgive myself. Regret-free was good. Opening old wounds might prove cruel. "Yes, I did."

"What did he say?" Lori put her drink down.

"Not much." That was as close to the truth as I could get. "He was at work, Lori. I'll try to get him talking in person. I didn't want to get him in trouble."

"We don't want to jeopardize his job," Jen agreed.

I was relieved Jen had backed me up. Lori was frowning, a slice of pizza inches from her mouth.

"You're right. He needs his job. Same job, same life. Probably still making the same money." Lori shook her head. "Can you imagine me with him?"

"Let me get all the facts first, then we'll worry about things. He could be married or have a bunch of kids by now. This is just to erase any doubts." I looked over at Jen to mentally nudge her to change the subject. Two nights drunk with Lori was more than my nearly thirty-year-old body wanted to endure.

"So two phone calls." Jen sipped her drink eagerly. "What about Brian?"

Lori smiled and leaned back against the couch. "I called him, naturally, because he lives in California. I didn't get to actually talk to him."

"Three for three," Jen pouted.

"No, I wouldn't say that." Lori shook her head. "I talked to his boyfriend."

"Boyfriend?" I sat up straight and leaned in. "You're kidding?"

"You mean his roommate," Jen corrected.

"No, his *boyfriend*. They were celebrating their anniversary. Sorry to bring you the bad news, Jen. You turned Brian gay." Lori suppressed her giggles.

I covered my mouth to hide my smile. "At least you know he isn't the right one for you."

Jen's forehead crinkled as she processed the information. I poured the rest of the margaritas into her glass and giggled at Lori, who smiled back.

"That explains a lot." Jen gulped from her glass now. "I'm so stupid."

"Explains what? You said Brian was your best sex ever." Lori took another piece of pizza and put one on Jen's plate, too.

"Well, he wasn't exactly my best." Jen twisted her fingers around her apron strings.

"So now you're lying to us? Why did you pick him, then? Come on, Jen, so the guy turned out to be gay, big deal. He was probably really confused when you were together." I headed to the kitchen to make more margaritas.

"No, I swear he and I never slept together." Jen's voice was getting frantic and squeaky.

"Then why would you pick him as your best sex?" Lori challenged. She pulled out the dessert and brought it to the coffee table.

"Come on, Jen. It's okay. Now you're sure the right man is still out there for you." I didn't understand why Jen was being so weird about this.

"I'm sure the right one is out there, somewhere. I only picked Brian because I don't have a best sex. Are you guys happy now?" Jen shoved another bite into her mouth.

"You've never had an orgasm?" I concluded. "Big deal. There are whole books out there on how some women have a harder time. Now I know what to get you for Christmas. A how-to book and a toy to get you there. Not all men know how to hit the mark."

"Yeah, I didn't get off my first time. It takes a little practice and some patience. Toys will help, and you'll be in the saddle in no time." Lori nodded.

"So how old were you guys when you first had sex?" Jen asked.

Lori nearly choked on her cheesecake and I poured her more liquor.

"I love Lori's first-time story," I said. It would take Jen's mind off Brian.

"No, it's not that interesting," Lori insisted.

"Come on, it'll make me feel better." Jen gave a pathetic look and Lori had to give in.

"Fine, then Marina has to tell hers, too," Lori demanded.

"Sure," I agreed. Lori knew me better than to think that would get her off the hook.

"I was sixteen," Lori began. "I broke up with this stupid guy when he cheated on me with the class slut. I even changed math classes so I wouldn't have to see him anymore. I ended up with this first-year teacher who was right out of college. He was twenty-two and all the girls drooled over him, including me."

"You slept with a teacher?" Jen's jaw dropped.

Lori shrugged. "He was really nice to me. I was doing terrible in his class because of this break-up, and he tutored me. One time he asked why I was so distracted, and I told him the whole story. The next thing you know we were naked, and I felt a lot better. No orgasm, but better."

"At school, in his classroom?" Jen asked.

"That made it even better!" Lori leaned back and licked her fork of the last bit of cheesecake.

"Did he get in trouble?" Jen asked.

"No, I didn't tell anyone. It was just a couple of times for fun. At least I knew what a real man was supposed to be like. Most teenage guys have no idea what they are doing, which would've made it much worse." Lori shook her head in disgust.

"Any teenage guy would've been done before you even got started. You were smart," I said. "I love that story."

"Your turn," Jen said eagerly.

At least this seemed to be taking her mind off Brian. "Mine was much more average and rather cliché. I was seventeen and it was the night of my senior prom. My boyfriend at the time and I had been going out for six months and my oldest sister told me to just get it over with so I'd be ready for college. She even gave me the condoms."

"I wish I had older sisters," Jen said.

"They have good points and bad points. You only had overprotective brothers, so that probably did some damage. Overall, my first time was okay. Not the best, however, it was a good first experience and I learned quickly what worked for me. Men may not ask for directions. The good ones will take them."

"I'm so behind you guys." Jen cut herself another piece of cheesecake.

Her mood was slipping again. It didn't make sense. We should have made her feel a little better. There wasn't much more we could do, other than get her that Christmas gift early.

"It's not the quantity," Lori argued. "Most guys still don't know what they're doing. You just have to find one that you can train in bed and that you can live with. That guy you marry."

I wanted to point out, in that case, Lori should've married Nick. That would be pushing it. "Lori's right, if only there was a man who did it for me in bed and who I could live with the rest of the time, I'd marry him."

"I'm so far from marriage, it's not even funny." Jen appeared to be fully backsliding into depression again.

"Come on. It can't be that bad. Brian clearly was out of this element with a woman, and so what if the others guys weren't great. They're trainable once you know what *you* like." I tried to sound realistically positive in case she thought we were just humoring her.

"It's not just the orgasm." Jen started turning red.

"Then what is it?" Lori asked.

She covered her face with her hands. "I've never had sex. I'm a virgin, okay?"

Chapter Five

Jen on a Mission

Their silence and stunned expressions said it all.

"You're kidding." Lori shook her head, bewildered.

"She's got to be kidding." Marina rubbed her forehead.

"No, I'm not kidding." I stood my ground. They really didn't believe me! I knew this wasn't going to be a fun conversation. It had never occurred to me that they wouldn't believe me. Talk about making a hard thing worse.

"Are we talking technical virginity or nothing at all?" Marina looked amused and confused as she moved to sit on the arm of Lori's chair.

"What are you talking about?" I asked. A virgin was a virgin. Right? Maybe I knew less than I thought. Or I'd lost my mind and this was all a bad dream.

"You can't have done nothing. Fooling around, hands, oral. You must have done *something*. Right?" Marina glanced at Lori, who nodded.

Sometimes I thought those two were telepathic. They knew each other too well. That expression meant something, even if it wasn't a real answer to the question. It was creepy and I felt even more isolated than normal.

"Come on, some guy had to have gotten under the underwear." Lori didn't seem to be grasping the concept of my situation either.

"No, sorry." I folded my arms tightly.

"She's stuck at second," Lori said to Marina. Lori's jaw slackened, as though it had finally hit her that I'd just revealed I had a third breast or something.

Their shock and sarcasm wasn't making me feel any better. On the other hand, I had finally managed to shock the city girls. That was a first. Maybe telling them wouldn't be so bad after all.

"Why?" Marina shoved her fingernails through her black hair and shook her head.

"You think it's going to bite you?"

Lori started to giggle and tried to stifle the noise in a pillow. "Maybe she's watched too many adult movies and thinks they're all that big."

Marina choked on her wine and slapped Lori's shoulder. "I wish. That is so completely not the case. Usually it's not big enough."

"I'm not afraid of *that*." Heat singed my face.

"Then why?" Marina asked as Lori continued to giggle. "No, Lori, stop. Honestly, why?" Marina put on her serious face.

"I wanted to wait for the perfect guy." I had no better answer. It wasn't family pressure or some religious conviction. Right now, I wanted to sink through the floor or disappear. Was it so bad?

"Jen, there is no such thing as a perfect guy. They don't exist." Marina shot a glance at Lori and finally nudged her. "Right, Lori?"

"Yeah, no such thing. No guy is perfect. Even the best require extensive training to be decent boyfriend or husband material." Lori's voice wavered. She nodded for extra emphasis.

"I know he won't be a flawlessly perfect human being. I never expected that. I just thought he'd at least be a perfect match for me. I've never had that 'couldn't control myself, had to have this guy' kind of thing happen to me." I slumped onto the couch with the realization that waiting had been a waste of time.

I curled up into the fetal position before I started crying or needed something. Those were years of my life, potential experiences I could never get back. All because I thought the right one would show up. I'd been brainwashed over the years. "I fell for the fairy tale."

"Oh, no." Marina got up and sat next to my head on the couch. She patted my hair and mumbled something to Lori. A few minutes later, Lori returned with the second cheesecake on one of my fancy china platters. The blue willow pattern I'd scrimped and saved to buy. I felt like an old lady before I'd ever been a wild girl.

"I was stupid." I dipped my finger into the piece Lori set out for me. I'd never eat like that normally. At the moment, I didn't care.

"You weren't stupid, you just never had anyone to tell you the truth about sex and men. It's never like it is in the movies. Older sisters are great for that. You only had brothers." Marina made it sound better.

"I only have brothers," Lori defended.

"You were born corrupted and boy crazy," Marina shot back. "Focus, please."

Lori looked ready with a comeback. I cut in first. "I never even had a Nick." I envied Lori so much. Even with all their issues, she'd found a guy she couldn't resist or get over. No man had ever affected me like that, and I was closing in on thirty.

"What does his name matter?" Lori acted oblivious as she feasted on cake.

"Dumbass, she means she wants to be like you and Nick," Marina corrected.

Lori paused in the middle of emptying the wine bottle into my glass and whipped the cork at Marina's thigh. Clearly, Lori didn't want to talk about *her* issues. Marina retrieved the cork and tossed it right in Lori's piece of cheesecake with a sharp nod of satisfaction. Another one of their silent fights. They were about a sex life away from being an old married couple.

"She wants heat, sparks, uncontrollable passion and all the fun and recklessness that goes with it," Marina added. "Of course you want that, Jen. We'd all love it. It's rare.

Other men aren't perfect, not total fireworks. They're fun. Don't try to achieve Lori and Nick's chemistry on your first time out. That's just setting yourself up for pain."

"Please, it's nothing special. Just animal lust. You've had something like that, Marina. Right?" Lori's question hesitated at the end.

"Not really. Lucas was the closest, sex-wise, to an animal. However, there was no passion with our clothes on. You told me once that you and Nick sizzled even when you were in your ugly gray blizzard parka and he was sick with the stomach flu. That's chemistry and emotion. It's not easy to get both in one package. I don't think you realize what you had with Nick." Marina's voice was void of any teasing or playfulness.

I only dared to move my eyes and look over at Lori. She wasn't boiling mad but her jaw was tight. That was something I'd wanted to tell Lori a million times, yet always worried she'd overreact. Lori was weird about Nick.

At least I knew Lori would take it better from Marina than from me. I could show my support. "I'd love to have what you and Nick had."

"I'd gladly trade you any day." Lori sat and lounged back in the chair as though Nick didn't matter at all. "Nick had no chance for a real relationship. It was a short-term blowout of hormones. I think you two are overestimating the emotional side of things."

"Fine, this is about Jen, anyway." Marina leaned down to look me in the eye. "So, if you really want to wait for the right guy, why are you upset?"

"Have I wasted my life? My chances?" I sniffed. Composing myself was pointless.

"Some of them, yes." Lori nodded.

"Just look at it like Lori took them for you." Marina returned.

"Like you're so innocent. You slept with more guys in college than I did." Lori scowled. "I wasn't really in love with Nick, so don't romanticize it. Marina's right, fairy tales are crap."

I nodded and slowly sat up. The emotional overload mixed with wine and tequila made my head spin for minute. "I still want the fairy tale."

"That's never going to change." Marina shook her head. "I want to be a size four. In fairy tale, I am. Here, I'm stuck at a ten and will be lucky if I ever see an eight."

Lori rolled her eyes. "You don't get a chest like that at a size four unless they're fake. And, as for you, Jen, you can either sit around not having any fun, waiting for some guy who doesn't exist to find you, or you can get out there. Why not get out and hope you bump into a guy who you can mold into the right one?"

"Mold, my ass. You can't mold anyone into anything." Marina grabbed the pitcher to make more margaritas. That poor blender was getting a workout tonight and we'd downed one bottle of wine on top of it.

"Sure you can. Just because I couldn't mold Nick into an acceptable man doesn't mean there isn't someone out there ready for me." Lori cut herself another slice of cheesecake and dove in.

"Really?" Marina asked between blender blasts. "So, in all the years we've been friends you've managed to mold me into your ideal friend?"

"Hell no, you still piss me off!" Lori took Marina's glass and finished off the last of the wine for the new batch of drinks.

"See how well that molding thing works?" Marina grinned. "A little training in bed is one thing. You can't change people. Men are 'as is' products and they don't have a warranty."

"So why bother?" I asked.

"What else is there? Unless you decide Brian has the right idea and turn gay on us, I'm afraid that's all there is." Marina returned to the couch with the pitcher and poured generously into all of the glasses.

"Maybe that's it?" Lori had that glint of teasing in her

eye. She leaned toward Marina as if to whisper yet spoke loudly. "Maybe Jen doesn't really like boys?"

"I do, too!" I insisted. Lori was worse than what I imagined an older sister would be. She loved to tease me. If I didn't argue back, she'd take it as though I agreed with her and keep going until I cracked.

"I don't know." Marina shrugged. "Never did it with a guy. Sounds pretty unsure."

"No way." I folded my arms firmly. "I may be a virgin, but I want a man."

"How should we test this, Marina?" Lori curled up in the big chair, smiling as if full of mischief.

"How should I know? I want to make sure the guy I'm after isn't gay. Who cares about women?" Marina took her glass back from Lori and poured herself more.

I shuddered at how they just shared glasses and didn't care about germs. Marina said it was just like having another sister when I'd asked her about it once. I couldn't share a glass with any of my disgusting brothers to save my life. Not with anyone, in fact. It was the same result as kissing them. That did give me an idea.

"I don't know about girls. I never thought about it," I said with a straight face.

Marina glanced at me out of the corner of her eye with a mixture of disbelief and amusement. "There are plenty of men out there who wanted you and you wouldn't let them. Try that first."

"What if Lori is right?" I stood and walked toward Lori, who appeared more confused than Marina. "What if the reason I never fell hard for a guy is because men aren't my thing? It happens."

"Sure, it happened to my cousin Anthony. We all pretty much figured it out before he was out of college." Marina sat up straighter on the couch. "Jen, don't listen to Lori. She just said it to get you worked up."

Marina wasn't sure what I was doing. She was harder to freak out. Lori's eyes were glued to me. Two could play the game and tease.

"Can you ever really be sure if you don't try it?" I casually sat on the arm of Lori's chair.

"Sure you can. Buy one copy of *Playboy* and one of *Playgirl*, study at them, and see which one turns you on. Simple." Lori shrugged.

Marina nodded. "The store clerk will look at you funny, but it would work."

I loved that neither of them knew where I was going or what to expect. It was so rare.

"That just seems so artificial. Attraction is more than just a picture. Maybe I should test it?" I began leaning way too close to Lori.

She watched me for a few seconds. When I didn't back off, she jumped out of the way and nearly tripped over the coffee table. "What the hell is wrong with you? You don't get any and one day you just snap?" Lori demanded. "People survive dry spells. Just think of it as a really long dry spell. It's just a do-it-yourself period. She really needs a shower massager for Christmas."

Marina covered her mouth to keep from spitting out her drink. She finally recovered enough to swallow. "She'll get the massager. I'm so proud." She coughed and continued to laugh.

"Proud? She's lost her mind!" Lori kept a safe distance and put Marina between us.

"Relax, Lori, Jen's finally just getting back at you," Marina explained. "You tease her enough and finally she has started to tease you back. I don't think she really wants to lose her virginity to a battery-powered device. Not that owning one would hurt."

"That's a really creepy way to get back at me, Jennifer." Lori grabbed Marina's glass from her hand and downed what was left.

"For the record, it was a joke. How is that creepy but you drinking from Marina's glass isn't? You're swapping spit," I pointed out.

"Sharing a glass isn't kissing." Lori started to laugh. "I've seen Marina naked when she needed help getting dressed for her sister's wedding. That doesn't mean I wanted to touch her. No offense."

"None taken. I wouldn't want you, either." Marina smiled. "Jen's just freaked out by germs, and while I'm glad a chef is so clean, I think we've hit on a potential problem with her sex life, should she ever get one."

"Meaning?" Lori frowned.

"Talk about germs. Sex goes way beyond spit. Maybe she's got one of those phobias about germs and bodily fluids so she just can't do it," Marina suggested.

"I'm not *that* bad!" I argued. So, I cleaned compulsively. So, I washed my hands constantly during the day, whether at work or not. It didn't mean anything. "It's the chef training, washing your hands and keeping everything clean and separated."

"How do you know?" Lori challenged. "You've never tried it. Never gotten past kissing a guy. You can't boil him before you screw him."

"Absolutely right. And with a mouth like that, Lori, I'd say you're ready to go tackle your mechanic again." Marina winked.

"That was my impersonation of you, Marina," Lori countered.

"Sure it was." Marina's sarcasm bit back.

"You go meet Nick, Marina. Spend time with him, talk to him. Then you tell me if he'd really be good for me," Lori encouraged.

"Don't worry, I intend to." Marina smiled. "After all those steamy stories, I have to see him for myself."

Lori didn't seem as smug all of a sudden. She didn't say anything.

"Brian is out. We still have Lucas and Nick to look into. Don't worry, Marina, I'm going to find out everything about Lucas this week." I changed the subject and wasn't very subtle about it.

"Find yourself a guy, Jen. Don't waste too much time on Lucas. He's not emotionally available and I really doubt that's changed." Marina waved it off.

I wasn't about to blow off my part in this. Maybe doing a good deed for Marina would get me a little good luck in the man department. "Maybe Lucas will know someone for me?" I'd have to change my thinking. It wouldn't hurt anything to hope and keep my eyes open.

"Does that mean you're ready to come over to the dark side?" Lori pressed.

"Not with the next guy I see. I definitely think I need to get some experience with men. Maybe then I'll have a little more confidence with them." At least I hoped that would be the case. I was always such a nervous wreck around the ones I was attracted to. Not with Lucas.

He wasn't for me, so I could do this right.

* * * *

I'd slept late. There was no incentive to get up early. All I had to do today was find Lucas, and I was planning to hit his building around lunch. Other than that, I had nothing to get me out of bed. So, I lounged under my thick blanket.

It had been a week since that job interview and not a word from the prospective employer. Part of me was beginning to worry. Luckily, I had a distraction. I was going to find Lucas and see if he was worth another look for Marina. After that, I needed to get a personal life of my own. There were plenty of men in Chicago. I just had to start paying attention.

An hour later, I got out of bed and showered. Since the building was professional, or so I assumed, I put on a cute sweater and wool skirt. Not quite a suit, but not my usual jeans and gym shoes. I grabbed my directions and headed out for an adventure.

I got off the L at the right stop and followed the computer printout directions to Lucas's building. The first hurdle had been a success. I hadn't gotten lost. Now I had to figure out where his office was, not to mention how to gain entry. Lori said a lot of firms had tight security.

One step at a time, I decided, as I slipped into an opening in the revolving door. Instantly, I longed for the chaos of a busy kitchen. The lobby was full of people going in every direction. I moved to a board that listed the companies in the building located near the security desk. The financial firm was on the fortieth floor.

Gathering my courage to face being completely out of my element, I turned to find the elevators. My heel caught on something. Suddenly my feet flew out from under me. I shut my eyes and cringed. The floor was hard marble and there was nothing to stop my fall.

My heart pounded faster, and the fall seemed like it was in slow motion. Then a pair of strong arms grabbed me. I gasped and clutched the stranger. I was sure it was from the panic, although those arms did feel good around me.

"Sorry, I left my gym bag right in your way," a nice male voice said.

I opened my eyes to see a man who couldn't be more than thirty-two and adorable with blue eyes, brown hair and quick reflexes.

"My fault. I'm accident prone," I said. He helped me onto my feet. His arms had felt great, though I couldn't stay there all day.

I had to find Lucas, I reminded myself. Still, I also didn't want to be rude. "Thanks," I managed as I made sure my clothing was straight, if a bit crumpled. Luckily, I had chosen one of my longer skirts.

"Any time. Do you work in the building?" he asked.

"No, I'm here to see someone." I tried to seem casual and confident.

"Man or woman?" He casually tossed the strap of his gym bag over his shoulder.

I took a good look. Very nice! He must work out very regularly for it to show so clearly under his suit and dress shirt. His body momentarily distracted me before his odd question finally sank in. "What does it matter whether it's a man or a woman?"

He shrugged. "Just a question."

"A man." I kept the answer short, not sure what to make of my evasion, then deciding it was fun.

"Lucky him. Meeting him for lunch?" He took a step closer, and I felt like we were the only two people in Chicago, even as crowds of people buzzed around us.

"No, I was dropping in to see him."

"A surprise, that's nice. Is he your boyfriend?"

"Not exactly," I stammered.

"Couldn't you wait until after lunch to see him, then?" He stepped a little closer.

"If I wanted to. Thanks for the hand. I'm going to go up now." I backed away slowly, feeling very uneasy. I wasn't scared and didn't believe myself in any danger, but he wanted something. I wasn't sure what.

Odds were he didn't work on Lucas' floor, so I could get away in the elevator if I wanted.

It wasn't as though we were alone in a dark alley.

"Wait, why not have lunch with me?" He followed me.

"Why should I?" I replied.

"I saved you a trip to the emergency room. Maybe I'm your good luck charm?" He shrugged and smiled a boyish grin that sparked something in me.

I was supposed to be trying to be more open to the opposite sex and here I was trying to run again. It was lunch in a public place. So why was I trying to avoid it? "Okay, lunch, somewhere close. I don't want to be late and miss him. This is very important."

"Very close," he agreed. His hand gently landed on my back and steered me in the direction of a restaurant on the ground floor of the same building. He must have known the staff because we got seated at a horseshoe booth in bar area right away. "This okay?"

"Fine. Is this how you normally pick up women?" I tried

to relax and be playful. I wasn't sure I could pull it off.

He smiled and shook his head. That smile was adorable!

"No, I usually race through the lobby so fast I never see anyone. Today I dropped my cell phone and put the bag down to grab it and got lucky."

He smiled as the waitress arrived and we ordered. I hoped Lucas would be as easy to talk to. From what Marina had said, I doubted it. No matter how charming this guy was, I couldn't let him completely distract me from my mission.

There was plenty of time for new guys. Lucas had a deadline attached to him. I had to report in again at the end of the week. I *had* to have something this time.

"So what do you do?" he asked.

"I'm a chef." I hesitated in asking what he did. Right now, the fantasy of a handsome stranger was more fun. If he offered up information, fine. For now, the mystery made it better.

"That's handy. I can't even boil water. I eat out all the time." He looked at me as though he was seeing right through me. It was unsettling and sexy at the same time.

"Just because you kept me from a nasty fall doesn't mean I'm your personal chef for life." I grinned.

"We'll see. So if the man upstairs isn't your boyfriend, who is he?"

I paused as the waitress brought our food. I wasn't sure how to answer anyway. It wasn't my place to spread Marina's and Lucas' business around. For all I knew, this guy could work at the same place as Lucas and he might decide it was a funny story and embarrass Lucas with it.

I remembered my self-defense course and the idea of setting clear boundaries. "That's personal." I took a bite of my cheeseburger and waited to see how he took that.

"Internet boyfriend you're meeting for the first time?" Grinning, he shoved a fry in his mouth.

"Not exactly."

"Not exactly? Am I close?" he asked as he arched an eyebrow.

"That's personal." Much as I'd have liked to go out with him, I didn't know the first thing about him and wasn't sure I wanted to learn the truth. We hadn't even exchanged names yet. Right now, he was perfect. I didn't want to ruin it.

My mystery man was maybe five foot nine inches tall, his dress shirt clearly defining his muscles. And he had the decency to care if I had anyone else. I leaned against the tall booth seat that gave us a nice measure of privacy and wondered if I'd just ruined things.

"Would you go out with me?" he finally asked.

"I don't know if that's such a good idea," I replied.

"I don't have a girlfriend, if that's what you're worried about." He passed me the ketchup when he noticed I was looking for it. I felt a little odd, like I was on display. He was such a gentleman, so I couldn't say no completely. None of the guys I'd met in the clubs had half his manners.

"What about men? Any men that'll get mad at me?" I tried not to laugh as his face dropped.

"Am I that bad at flirting?" he asked.

"No, let's just say I've had issues before and want to make sure. My radar is just off," I explained.

"I see." He nodded and leaned closer. His mouth brushed mine and I felt like I couldn't breathe. I slid my hands on his shoulders as I opened my lips. This behavior was so unlike me and felt so good!

"Convinced?" He pulled away, and I nearly followed him.

I nodded and blushed. No one had seen and I really didn't care if they had.

"So you'll go out with me?" he pressed.

I glanced at my watch, seeing it was after one already. "I need to go." I grabbed my purse and started digging for cash to cover my lunch. I hadn't planned this detour, but always kept an emergency twenty tucked away.

"They'll put it on my tab. I eat here every day." His hand rested on mine to stop me and there were those sparks I'd heard about. He'd distracted me again. "Are you okay?"

"Yeah, I just don't want to miss this guy." I felt the need to get the talk with Lucas over. What kind of friend was I? I'd come here to help Marina and had gone on a lunch date with some mystery man. He was cute, but he probably had a wife and three kids at home. I needed to find Lucas and talk with him first. "I really need to get back to what I came for. Thanks for lunch."

I dashed out of the door of the restaurant and found the elevators in the lobby. I pushed the button and tried to lose myself in the crowd. I followed the crush of people into the elevator when Mystery Man caught up with me. He squeezed his way to the back where I had tried to hide. "I'm sorry if I went too far."

"Forget it. Just quit following me, okay?" I asked.

"I'm not, I work in this building. Remember?" He shrugged.

We got a few odd looks from others in the elevator. Finally, it stopped on the fortieth floor and I made my way to the front. He was behind me. "I asked you to stop following me," I repeated.

"I work for this firm." He pointed to the etched glass door I was headed for. It was an employees-only entrance and he waved his pass card in front of the lock. It buzzed and a light turned green. He was telling the truth. He nodded for me to go in.

"What did I do?" he asked.

"Nothing, it's my fault. I came here for a specific reason and shouldn't have gotten sidetracked. At least, not until I got my business out of the way."

"It can wait," he protested.

"No, I shouldn't let myself be distracted. How do I know if he's any good or not? I don't even know what he looks like. He could have been in the restaurant or have walked out while I was coming up. I'm just not the type of person who does the fun stuff first. I have to get the necessities out of the way." I wasn't making much sense. Meeting an actual nice guy who was interested in me and to whom I was actually attracted, freaked me out.

I could have easily and completely forgotten about Lucas, and almost had. I still wanted this guy. First, I had to do the right thing, or I'd feel guilty all day, and that date wouldn't be any fun at all. Marina deserved another chance. She hadn't had the best luck lately.

"You don't know this guy or what he looks like and you're this upset about seeing him? I know everyone in the office, I've worked here for five years. I can help. At least let me prove I'm not a creep and take you to this lucky guy, whoever he is. Who are you trying to find?" He stared intently at me as other employees slipped by into the office and glanced at us strangely.

"Why do you want to help me? You don't even know me." I crossed my arms over my chest.

"Why not help? I never meet anyone who's as cute and as different as you. You've got to give me a chance. If you won't go out with me, at least let me help you for breaking up an otherwise boring day." He nodded.

He sounded sincere. Why not? It might be less awkward if I could be introduced to Lucas and say I knew someone he knew. That might make it easier. "Fine, I really need to find Lucas Rigby."

My mystery man stopped cold and stood up a little straighter. "I'm Lucas Rigby." The slight surprise in his eyes made my heart drop. I had spent my lunch fanaticizing about my best friend's ex-boyfriend. Damn it!

Chapter Six

Marina's Trip to the Garage

After we finally got my mom's old powder-blue Caprice running outside of her bakery, I climbed in. I still thought a new car was a good idea, even though she was attached to this one. The other day I'd told Nick it didn't really need work. Today, I was going to surprise him. The car had acted up off and on since that day, so I had volunteered to take it to the shop.

This was definitely my best shot at Nick. I wasn't going to pass it up. I knew any further phone calls to him would be totally useless. He was a busy guy who could avoid me if he wanted to. There was little doubt in my mind that he didn't want to talk to me.

He couldn't refuse to look over old blue, though.

I maneuvered mom's boat of a car from the bakery to Nick's garage. Pulling the car into an open bay, I was glad to turn off the engine. I'd had to get it jumped and the power had been flickering. Whenever I drove, it was usually Lori's little Jag. I'd prayed the whole way that the ancient car could make it those few blocks because this tank would be hard to get out of the road if it broke down.

I exited the car to blaring classic rock music. A handsome man, who I knew was too young to be Nick, took the keys and smiled. "Good evening," he said loudly and looked me up and down.

"Hi, I'm looking for Nick." I smiled at the helpful and cute mechanic. He was a flirt, but I had to get to Nick first. Fun could wait. I needed to settle Lori, or I might have to strangle her.

"The boss is in the office. It's straight back on your right. You're a friend?" He started writing down the plate number and car description.

"He's worked on my mother's car before," I replied. I certainly didn't want to be mistaken for his girlfriend or a random garage groupie. Lori had said that Nick was a pretty popular guy.

"I recognize it. I'm Eddie." He nodded. "I can take it from here and get started. Nick's here if you want to talk to him."

"I do, thanks." I went back to the office. It was my first time in the garage and it was everything I expected, from the dirty naked girl calendar to the grime, grit and grease everywhere. Lori, here? My mind wouldn't process that picture on any level. It was definitely a new side to her. The girl *had* to be in love.

She must've had it really bad for Nick. Worse than I thought. I knocked on the door and heard some response I couldn't make out over the blaring music in the garage.

I took whatever it was as a positive sign and opened the door slowly.

Nick was sitting at a computer and didn't even look up at first. He was cuter in the flesh than Lori's pictures. I understood why she was hung up on him. Under that dirt sat a ruggedly adorable man.

"Are you busy?" I asked.

"Always. How can I help you, miss?" He leaned back in the chair.

"I'm Rosa Castini's daughter, Marina." I shook his hand and felt the tension increase when he heard my name. Obviously I'd made an impression.

"The same Marina that called me the other day?" He pulled his hand back.

"That would be me," I confirmed. "I know that probably wasn't the best start. I've been Lori's best friend for years. This isn't some joke or attempt at messing up anyone's life. I just want to talk to you about Lori in person. And since my mom's car needed to come in, I thought it would be a good time."

"I don't think there is anything to talk about. Lori made her choice and she's happy." He shrugged. "I don't want to be sucked back in, only to get kicked out when she's done with her second roll in the dirt."

"If you think she's happy without you than there's a lot to talk about." I closed the door then sat.

If he intended to dismiss me, I wouldn't make it easy. Mom said he was a gentleman, so I hoped it would last. He was clearly hurt and, in men, hurt turned instantly to anger. They could never be wrong. Instead, they became defensive.

"This is old news, ancient history. I'm sorry she turned thirty. I'm not a consolation prize." He crumpled a piece of paper and shot it into the garbage can.

He remembered her birthday? I hadn't said a word about that on the phone to him. "This isn't about settling, for either of you. I don't think she's ever gotten over you and the fact that you remember her birthday and age so readily makes me believe the same about you."

"Because I remember her birthday, I'm pining away for her? Sure, that's an engagement ring right there. Look, your mom's a nice lady, and I'll take good care of her car, but if you think I'm taking care of anything else, you're crazy."

"It's not the first time I've been told that. Lori has called me nuts several times, in fact. You two actually have a lot in common."

"Hardly. You must be insane if you think that. I don't need a princess or her lunatic best friend in my life. I have my shit together."

"Doesn't stop me. I know when I'm right." I crossed my legs with confidence. I wouldn't be bullied or ushered into leaving. His sarcasm was thick with a hint of something deeper. Otherwise, why hadn't he prodded me to leave yet?

He stood, and I wondered if I was about to be escorted out. Instead, he paced behind his desk. "Let me tell you what I know. I know Lori is great. I also know Lori *was* crazy about me. I really know Lori won't disappoint her family for me. And I knew all of this years ago. There's your free history lesson, now let's move on."

"Time changes things," I argued. "Both of you have changed and yet you're still hung up on each other. Another thing you two have in common." I put on my best soothing tone that worked on frightened animals that ended up on my table. Out of their element and under stress, any animal could turn on any human — even their masters.

Nick reminded me of a wild cat backed into a corner. My tone could help. I'd bet he'd still fight me.

"I remember you. She talked about her friend in vet school, Marina." He shook his head.

"That's me. I've graduated since then. So what?" I wondered if I'd given Lori some bad advice when we were younger that was about to come back and haunt me. Lori had ranted so much about him, I'm sure I'd told her to both dump him *and* marry him at various times.

He went from dismissive of me to intensely curious in a flash. "So, you've been friends with her a long time. I never met you when we were dating. She didn't let me near her real life. I'll bet you've met her family. Haven't you?"

"I was busy in vet school. It was nothing personal with me not meeting you back then. I spent more time on the phone with Lori rather than getting to see her in person. Our schedules both sucked. As far as her family, sure, I've met them."

He stepped around his desk and leaned down face-to-face with me. "Do you really think they'd let someone like me in their family tree? Pollute the gene pool? I'm not stupid. If she won't fight, there isn't a chance."

I saw the pain in his eyes, and the frustration that ran deep. He'd been rejected and was as proud as Lori was. Her parents wouldn't like him whether they met him or not. I wasn't going to lie to him about it.

That, however, wasn't the point. "Lori's parents don't get

a vote. It's not their call. Maybe Lori wasn't strong enough to stand up to them back then. Things change. Only Lori's opinion matters here. It's her decision."

"You're absolutely right and she made it already. She's not here. She had her chance. I've never gotten a call or Christmas card since she dumped me. I could've dropped dead and she wouldn't have cared. If she wants to talk to me, she knows where to find me. She won't. She's got a lot of pride to go with that pretty pedigree, if you hadn't already noticed." He left.

I took a deep breath and felt like a failure. All of that passion and feeling still churning and yet neither of them was willing to stick a toe in the water. Idiots! Wasn't it eating him up inside?

At least I'd broken past that macho shell and seen he had feelings. Too bad I didn't have a secret video camera. Lori would never believe me if I told her. She'd chosen to be in denial of it all. I had discovered he was the boss. That was something. Not that I'd tell Lori that.

I walked out and saw my first mechanic, Eddie, approaching. "Good news," he said.

I smiled. "I could use some."

"It looks like it's the alternator, not the engine or anything real serious. I'll get to it first thing tomorrow. With winter setting in, there is a lot more work to do. Don't worry, Nick said to take care of your mom's car."

"Thanks. Just give me a call when it's ready," I said.

"Sure, you'll want the battery changed, too. The alternator ran it down to nothing. We can recharge it. Honestly, if it was my mom, I'd go get a new battery."

"That explains why jumping it only worked for so long. Fine, it's my mother's car so I want it safe. Let me know." I smiled a better smile now that my mind wasn't on Nick and Lori. There weren't real sparks with this guy. He was potential information and nice to look at.

"Not a problem. She always brings us cookies and stuff. Nice lady." He nodded in the direction of the office. "You find the boss okay?"

"I found him. I couldn't get him to listen to me. First things first, I found him." I folded my arms and tapped my toe in childish frustration.

"It's about Lori, right?" he asked.

I looked up in surprise. "Is he talking trash about my friend? I never got the impression he was that bad." My blood began to boil. Maybe Nick wasn't so good after all.

"No, no trash. Everything I've heard about her is very respectful. There is a lot of stuff left over. He's whipped over her. His sister told me it was a few years ago and he never got over her. You're her friend?"

"Yes. We shouldn't talk here," I whispered. I didn't want to get him in trouble and Nick seemed the private and touchy type. "Would you give me a call later and we can discuss this?"

"Anything to help the boss quit being a moody ass. Everyone who worked here back then said he was a great guy and fun to work with."

"I'd appreciate the help. My cell number is on here, too." I handed him my business card and headed out to the L, feeling a little better. I needed all the help I could get with Nick.

In the end, it would come down to Lori or Nick making a move. I could get as much information as possible to try and convince them they belonged together. If that meant I had to go around them and to others, then that was what I'd do. Nick was a match for Lori, just as stubborn. He was her secret type of man, attractive without being really polished.

* * * *

Two days later, I was at work and thankfully, for once, Nick and Lori were not the first thing on my mind. I had my hands full with a litter of kittens someone had left on our doorstep. They were in good condition for being only a few weeks old. The shelter was full, so we'd keep them. I didn't mind a bit. They'd cheer the place up for the holidays.

"Who just leaves adorable little kittens?" asked the secretary, who was hand-feeding one during a lull in the office traffic.

"Just be glad they brought them here and didn't leave them in a dumpster," I advised. I'd seen my share of surrendered or abused animals. This litter was lucky. They were barely chilled when we'd found them and whoever had left them had done it not long before we'd opened. Every member of the five-kitten family was a decent weight and healthy.

"They're so cute." She cuddled her orange tabby that was half asleep.

"Yeah, too bad I can't take them home." The only drawback to an apartment was living with no pets in our building. I had plenty to play with at work.

The bell rang on the front door and the secretary started to balance getting up with not disturbing her creature. "I got it," I said. I had been weighing in the all-black runt who didn't like to be put down and let her cling to my collar. The animal seemed content, though its little needle-like claws needed to be trimmed.

I pushed through the swinging door to see my favorite patient and owner, and neither looked very happy. "Mr. Lauden?" I got his attention. Seth approached me in a rush.

"Dr. Castini, I'm glad you're here. Monster got into something." He handed me the whining puppy as though it were a ticking bomb.

I felt the kitten dig deeper into my neck as the dog whined. I scooped the kitten and put her safely in a basket on the counter.

"Let's take a look." I stayed calm and focused on the animal, even as I noticed Seth's casual attire. Jeans and a sweater weren't his usual. Maybe it was his day off. "Did you see what happened?" I moved us to an exam room and rested Monster on the table.

"No, he just started whining. We were in the park. He was running around then stopped and started whimpering like he'd hurt himself. He walks fine and I don't see anything like a scratch or a splinter." Seth stood close behind me. His concern, as well as his body heat, was palpable.

I ran my hands over the puppy's coat. No reaction. His legs, torso and face all seemed fine. Carefully, I lifted his lip and was greeted with a low growl. "That's it. Here's the problem."

"What is?" Seth asked.

"He bit something. Puppies love to eat things." I changed where I was touching on the dog's snout and the growling went away. Slowly I pressured the puppy to open up.

Monster flinched, and Seth flinched behind me. Nervous owners were always more work than the patient. Luckily, it just meant they cared.

Monster shook his head and spat out a tooth.

"He's teething." Seth picked it up.

"Sure, maybe it wasn't coming out and was hurting him. He might have bitten down on something else at the time it came loose and hurt his gum." I examined the dog's mouth. "Nothing major. A scrape. Looks like he bit into his own tooth not realizing what it was. It'll heal fast. I'll give him some antibiotics, just in case."

Seth took a deep breath and exhaled, petting the dog. "That's a relief."

"Hold his head. I don't want him to jump," I instructed. Seth held the puppy as I stuck the needle in. Monster growled again, louder this time. "All done." I scratched Monster's head.

"Who is that?" Seth asked and pointed at the basket. He got very close and used a single finger to pet the little black kitten.

"We got a litter of strays in this morning. She was getting weighed when you came in. She decided she liked my collar better than sharing space with her brothers and sisters. Want to hold her?" I offered.

"Think Monster will mind?" he asked.

"As long they meet young, dogs and cats can get along.

She has a lot more to fear from him than the other way. He could swallow her whole." He picked up the kitten. Clearly he had an affection for pets, even if his nephews had been the ones to introduce Monster to him unwillingly.

"She's so small. Can they be adopted at this age?" he asked.

"No, too young. It'll be a few weeks before we can do that. She can't eat cat food yet. Until then, they'll have to be hand-fed since no one knows where the mom is." I gave Monster a little attention so he didn't feel left out. "Looking to adopt one?"

Seth paused. "I don't know. Monster is a handful. I don't know if I could handle another pet."

"Well, there is plenty of time to change your mind. They'll be here for a few weeks at least. Then, we'll find them homes." I thought he looked cute with the black little ball of fur purring in his hand. The kitten was content to stretch and rub against Seth's fingers.

Now I was jealous of a cat! The kitten had certainly gotten farther than I had in the months I'd known Seth. If only I could purr, maybe he'd want to pet me.

I stopped myself. I had to get over this crush. It was stupid and not going anywhere.

This one was so different and odd. I couldn't get a handle on it. Why could I flirt well with every other man on the planet, but with this one I just got too mixed up inside? It wasn't like me.

I blamed work. I focused on the animals more than men. Right now nothing was stopping me from turning on the charm. I wasn't about to ask him out, but I could at least let him know I was interested. I told myself to say something before he packed up to leave.

Just then a lab tech came in. "Everything okay?" she asked.

"Sure," I replied. I had to think of something. "Would you watch Monster for a minute? I'm going to show Mr. Lauden the rest of the new litter."

Not that he'd asked or anything, though he smiled and followed me to the back. The rest of the kittens were in their cage, huddled up in a group nap.

I took the little black one from Seth's hands, ignoring the sparks from his skin as best I could. It wasn't easy. He hadn't shown the slightest bit of interest in me beyond being his vet and I didn't chase men. If they weren't interested, I wasn't going to throw myself at them. I'd seen my older sister, Nina, make a fool of herself over a guy, and I vowed never to act like that.

"Here you go. Back with the family." I gently placed the black one at the top of the heap and she snuggled in. To be spoiled house cats, that was what I hoped for all of them. Not a bad life.

Seth was inspecting the different patterns. "Two orange, two black with spots, and one all black? Odd mixture for siblings."

"These aren't purebreds like Monster. Very questionable parentage. Probably have different fathers, too." I shrugged and wondered why I was suddenly discussing feline mating habits with a man I had a crush on.

"Different fathers?" He folded his arms, looking interested.

"It's just the law of nature. Goes back to the days when cats lived in groups, like lions. If there is a chance the kittens are the offspring of that male, they won't hurt them. So females generally don't discriminate as much. Protects them from a fight and their kittens from harm if the males knew there was a chance the cubs were theirs. It's all survival instinct."

"And leads to pretty cats." Seth smiled. "Which is your favorite?"

I shrugged. "I'm partial to the all-black one. She's the runt. Black cats are supposed to be unlucky. I'm usually the opposite of normal people, anyway, so she'd probably be lucky for me."

"So instead of seven, your lucky number is thirteen?" He laughed.

"Something like that." I nodded. "Of course, that kitten wouldn't work for you."

"Why not?" He sounded a little defensive.

"Monster is all black. If the kitten fell asleep on Monster, or the other way around, you'd never find the other one. Besides, people would think you're weird. A black lab puppy is cute, but a black cat, too? You'll be the weird guy at the end of the block," I teased.

"And you're sure I'm not already?" he teased back. "There's a lot you don't know about me."

Success? Was this actually a conversation with the silent Seth? One with humor, teasing, and not pet related. Just then my cell phone buzzed on my hip. "Sorry," I mouthed as I answered the phone. "Marina here."

Nick's voice on the other line changed my whole mode. "Hi," I said. Did I dare hope he'd gotten over his ego and mental trip and would talk to me?

"Don't go talking to my sister," he warned.

It took me a minute to process that statement. I recovered quickly. "Nick, I don't know your sister," I replied honestly.

"Sure, you don't. Lori and she were close. I'll bet Lori told you that. Guess who called the day after you left my garage?"

"I'm not responsible for your sister calling you," I said firmly.

"No? You didn't get her to nag me about Lori? She tried to guilt me, and fight me, and called me a coward," he shouted.

"No," I said flatly. "I've never spoken to your sister. I have no idea who she is. I'm sure she'll tell you that herself if you just ask."

"Of course she'll stick to your lie. She wants me with Lori. They both wanted sisters and never had them. I'm calling to tell you it won't work."

"How did you get this number?" I asked. Better to change the subject since we were going in circles.

"Eddie left a copy of your business card in your file for

contact information on your mother's car," he snapped. "I'm telling you to leave my family alone."

"I didn't do it, Nick. I don't know your family and don't want to. And if you act this childishly over a silly phone call I didn't make in the first place, I'm not entirely sure you're good enough for Lori." I hung up the phone and realized Seth was still next to me. "Sorry, my friend's ex-boyfriend. He's a little off."

"Sure, I understand." The spark was gone. That playful feel had disappeared.

All I could do was go back to professional mode. "I'd give Monster soft food for a few days to let the scratch heal, then back to his dry stuff. And only soft treats, no bones or anything hard until then."

"Sounds good."

I led the way back to the exam room, but Monster was not missing us at all. He was the center of attention. Seth led the puppy out to the front office.

I stayed in the back and went into the office. I didn't need any of my co-workers thinking I had a crush on him. The litter of kittens had been a safe way of being alone with him. He'd shown interest. The hospital always preferred to place kittens with clients we knew and had other pets with the right disposition. Monster would be perfect for a feline companion, someone to play with while Seth was at work.

Seth might already have a girlfriend for all I knew. It definitely wasn't me. I'd almost gotten a little luck there. Like always, fate intervened. Either that, or fate had kept me from pushing too much and making a fool of myself. Maybe it was better this way.

Add to that the 'good' news that Nick now thought I was contacting his sister. What would account for that? What would make his sister bring that up now, of all times? I hadn't gone that far yet.

My cell vibrated again. "Marina," I answered. I was ready to go home and go to bed. Forget dinner, exercise, or anything else. Just start a new day.

"Marina, it's Eddie. I'm sorry Nick went ballistic on you."

"How did you know?" I asked.

"I used to date his sister. I called to find out what I could for you and she's on your side. She thinks Lori is good for Nick. I guess she called Nick to try and shake him. He stormed in here today and wanted to know how to get in touch with you. It was that or he was going to go through your mother. He was that pissed off."

"It's fine, Eddie, thanks for trying. Are you busy tonight?" I asked. I couldn't believe I was doing this. I told myself it was for Lori. I knew that mechanic had been flirting with me, so why not give it a try?

"Tonight?"

"Yeah, if you talked to his sister, maybe you can tell me what she knows and what you know. I need to be informed if I'm going to keep playing this insane game." I rubbed my forehead, not really wanting to go out. This was for Lori's own good and putting it off wouldn't make it any easier. Maybe if I did have a little fun of my own I'd be more clearheaded. Five months without a man wasn't good for my health.

One more Nick ambush and I might tell him where to go for good. I'd snapped at him and hopefully that would throw him off my ass for a while.

"I can't tonight. How about Friday? Lunch? I'm off at eleven so I can meet you wherever."

I mentally flipped through my schedule. I had the day off so we could talk as long as needed. "Fine." I rattled off a place near enough to be convenient and far enough away from the garage to not be a likely drop-in place for Nick. Eddie agreed, and that was one less thing to worry about. I'd get some more information, at least.

The good news was Nick's sister was on the right side, even if she'd set off the panic button in Nick a little prematurely. Maybe, once Nick settled down, he'd see his sister's point. The odds of her reasoning with him were better than mine. I still wasn't confident.

Too bad I was having lunch with Eddie and not Seth. Eddie was business, not play. I'd flirt to get what I wanted out of him and forget it.

Seth was a completely different situation.

Chapter Seven

Lori in Denial

I was growing more and more obsessed with the whole Nick situation and had almost called Marina to cancel. Not that she would have. Not Marina. I didn't really want her to, anyway.

I couldn't think about what Marina might have found out about Nick. Which naturally meant I couldn't stop thinking about him. I avoided my own apartment and the memories there.

Still, I'd left work that Saturday and was back at my apartment before Marina returned home from work. It was her scheduled Saturday — damn her. She'd avoided every subtle attempt I'd made to get information. If I'd been any more direct, she'd expect it was eating at me to know Nick's reaction. Of course, she already knew. I didn't want to act as though I was desperate. Then I'd have less wiggle room if I couldn't bring myself to see him again.

If Marina knew just how much I wanted to know, she'd start in about what I had with Nick and what was I waiting for. I hated it when she was right and the doubt nagged at me continuously.

Every time I got close to calling him or going to see him, too many times to count in the last week, that sense of panic returned with a vengeance. He hated me and I knew it. I couldn't stand the idea that he hated me. Neither of us were easygoing or forgiving types.

I wandered around my apartment for a bit. It was sparsely decorated, to say the least. I had expensive things and believed less was more. Unlike Marina's clutter of family photos and knickknacks, I kept it simple. I envied the fact that she had so many happy family memories while I preferred to forget mine.

I changed into a more casual outfit of sweats with the Northwestern emblem on them and matching socks. Then I circled my living room, avoiding what I wanted to do. The memories called to me. I had to resist. There was no use in torturing myself with them.

Eventually, I'd give in.

I checked my mail, the answering machine, personal emails and even tossed out some of the gross stuff in my refrigerator. It wasn't distracting me.

Finally, I headed to my antique roll-top desk and unlocked the bottom drawer. I reached in and removed the mementos. I sat on the floor cross-legged and carefully put the contents of the drawer in my lap.

One picture of Nick and me, framed. His sister had taken it the day after I'd passed the bar and we'd been out celebrating. She'd given it to me, even after I'd broken up with Nick, only days after that celebration. She was the sister I wanted, but I'd felt too guilty to even call and thank her when the card with the picture had arrived in my mail.

Next was a stainless-steel chain with a medical alert medallion hanging from it. Nick was allergic to various things and I'd ordered it for him.

We'd been out to dinner one night and his throat had started to close up after he'd eaten something that contained shellfish. It had been a scary night in the ER. Getting him the necklace had been the best solution I'd been able to come up with. That way I wouldn't worry every time he ate without me.

He'd worn it for a few months and one night it had disappeared. Six months later, after we'd broken up, I'd found it behind my headboard. He'd gotten a replacement right away because I'd nagged him. Keeping the first one had been an odd impulse. I'd just wanted it.

I clutched the cheap metal until I felt the heat of his chest in it. I could still see it on him. I was losing my mind. This cheap piece of metal meant more to me than my entire jewelry collection. The rest of my jewelry was real, expensive and some was antique. This was worth nothing.

But, I couldn't get rid of it. I flipped through the other pictures of me and Nick on the shore of Lake Michigan, in his garage, and one picture I'd snapped of him naked. No one had ever seen that one.

The rest was a less interesting mix of movie stubs, concert tickets and other treasures from our various outings. The silly teddy bear he'd won for me at Navy Pier was always on my bed. I'd forgotten how many lies I'd told people about its origin to cover it up being from Nick.

Suddenly I piled it all in the drawer, slammed it shut and locked it. I couldn't take it anymore. Fighting back tears and frustration, I refused to allow myself to dig deep into my closet and pull out the sweatshirt he'd loaned me one night when I'd been cold. He'd never get it. It was my bottom. If I pulled it out, I'd truly have hit bottom.

I collected myself and decided to head over to Jen's rather than be alone with my thoughts. If I didn't change my direction now, I'd never go over there. I'd spend a depressed night alone. Drinking with friends was better than getting drunk alone.

I'd grabbed an array of cookies, cakes and brownies at the coffee shop and bakery on the ground floor of my office building on my way home. It wasn't as good as Jen's or Marina's mom's, but it would do. As usual, I'd overbought, because only a bad hostess ran out of food.

I balanced the huge tray and managed to make my way from my apartment to Jen's door and nudged it open. The girl would never learn to lock her door.

"The refreshments are here," I announced.

Jen took them from me and settled them on the island. "You know some of us don't have an overactive metabolism like you do," she reminded.

"Then you need to find a good man to burn off the calories with," I teased. It was a relief to have conversation. My own thoughts had been torturing me all day. Work hadn't cured it, and a trip down memory lane had only fueled it. Now, my friends could help distract me.

"Marina called. Work ran late. She's finally on her way." Jen removed the lid from the tray of goodies and began sampling. "Not bad."

"It better be good for what I paid for it. I requested extra caramel turtle brownies."

"They're delicious." Jen covered her full mouth when she spoke.

I smelled coffee and joined Jen in the kitchen, pouring myself a huge mug. I took a regular fudge brownie. I didn't deserve the caramel turtle one. I had failed to keep Nick off my mind.

Jen noticed my pastry choice. "You love the caramel turtle ones. What's wrong?"

"Nothing is wrong. I just haven't been to the gym in a week."

"Like you'll gain an ounce." Jen dug in the fridge and opened a bottle of wine for later.

"I go to the gym to keep toned, too, and your metabolism is supposed to fall off after thirty." I left Nick, my true excuse, out of it. Food wouldn't tempt me. I needed my mind on other things as quickly as possible.

"Then I have one more year to abuse my metabolism." Jen grinned triumphantly and took another caramel turtle brownie to taunt me.

"Evil." I gave in and took one for myself. "Any news on the job?"

"No, I'm not sure if I should call or what." Jen frowned and took a huge bite.

"Give it another week then follow-up. Hiring always takes longer than they say it will. Don't count yourself out yet." I took another sip of coffee and it soothed my nerves. "Any progress with Lucas?"

"I think we should wait for Marina for that conversation, don't you?"

Jen didn't seem upset, only a tad uneasy.

I shrugged and backed off. Lucas wasn't a real prize except for his earning potential.

Marina didn't look at men monetarily anyway, so to her, he'd be a waste.

"Has Marina said anything to you about Nick?" I did my best to sound casual.

Jen shook her head. "No, not a word. I'm sure she's started, though. Marina wouldn't let us down. It was her idea. Hopefully their schedules worked out."

"I'm not worried about her *not* doing it. I'm more worried about her *over*doing it."

"You don't want her to *not* explore the option?" Jen looked very concerned.

"Of course not," I backpedaled. "She just tends to go a little overboard at times. That temper and she always has to be right."

"Good thing I didn't tie him up and drag him back here to be our personal sex slave." Marina sounded proud of herself as she sneaked up behind me and broke off a piece of my brownie. "I thought about it, then figured the virgin might get too excited. You don't really like to share, anyway."

"You're so twisted," I snapped. I didn't share well as it was, but that was mean.

Jen turned red and said nothing.

"No, I'm funny and you're damned touchy today." Marina poured herself some coffee and grabbed her own giant cookie full of chocolate and macadamia nuts. "What crawled up your ass and died?"

"Nothing, I'm not touchy. I don't care if you have him chained up naked in your apartment right now smeared with chocolate sauce." My God, what a lie!

I waited for lightning to strike me dead where I sat. Marina knew it wasn't true, either. The very idea of Nick touching another woman, especially a friend of mine, made me understand crimes of passion.

Marina sat in the chair across from me and rolled her eyes. "I don't need your rejects, thank you."

She didn't believe my act and she shouldn't. I noticed that Jen turned away and dug through the fridge rather than comment. Odd for her, even if Jen didn't always get our humor. I knew Marina would never touch Nick, even though he was exceptionally sexy. He wasn't her type.

"You could do worse than Nick," I pointed out.

"Please, I've heard too many stories. I'd start laughing imagining *you* with Nick." Marina grinned. "If I actually saw him naked, I'd die of hysterics. That's your boy toy. And if you never see him again, I still couldn't. As far as I'm concerned, he's a eunuch."

"Hardly, but if that works for you." I started to giggle too when something crashed in the fridge. "Everything okay in there, Jen?"

"Fine, no problem." Jen closed the fridge and joined us — blushing.

Marina looked at her then at me with a frown. I shrugged and she nodded. We both knew something was off with Jen, just not what. It was an efficient method of communication.

I smiled and took another bite of my brownie. I'd never find another friend like Marina. Or another man like Nick, I realized. That didn't mean, however, that he was the right one for me. People got obsessed with the wrong people all the time.

Hopefully, Marina would have some news that would ease my mind. I had no idea what would do that, but I could hope. I'd run through tons of scenarios in my head and I couldn't have covered them all.

"So, what did we find this week?" I asked. My part of the deal was done. I had nothing and was eager to hear both of their results.

To not appear too eager for Nick's news, I looked at Jen first.

She set her coffee down and nodded. "Well, I went to

Lucas' office and made contact. He was very nice and polite, but I didn't get far. No wedding ring. He didn't get bald or fat, and he's cute."

Marina nodded. "Not very interesting, right? Dull as a day at the DMV."

Jen blushed. "We didn't discuss current events or have any real conversation, so I can't honestly judge. He was on his way to the gym. I'm going to run into him again this week and try to get more information. I didn't find out if he has a girlfriend or not. He's not married."

"No big loss, either way." Marina kicked off her gym shoes and propped her socked feet on the coffee table as she tossed another piece of cookie into her mouth.

I could tell Marina would've preferred to hear Lucas was married or fat. No such luck. Jen seemed to think he wasn't so bad. I'd heard enough details about him over time to know better. Marina found his financial obsession dull.

Lucas could be polite and charming, a good first impression that he couldn't keep up. Except in bed, which of course, was why Marina had continued seeing him for a while, even when she'd known there was no future.

"Maybe he'll be worth another look. You think?" I asked so Jen wouldn't feel her efforts had been in vain. For Jen, approaching a strange man and having a real conversation with him was a big step. This wasn't small talk.

Jen nodded. "I think I should find out more, at least. He may have a girlfriend. I'll investigate." Jen gave Marina a half-hopeful smile.

"Don't take it personally if it doesn't work out, Jen. These are all long shots. We're just making sure we did the right thing." I thought I sounded pretty convincing.

"What did you find?" Jen asked Marina.

"I went to the garage and met Nick, who was not overly eager to talk. I started things off. He isn't married and, from the sound of things, doesn't have a girlfriend, and his appearance has *not* gone downhill."

I knew that much. I was still embarrassed that I'd driven

by his garage on a whim. At least I knew the physical attraction was still there.

"Are you going to talk to him again?" Jen asked Marina. I was glad. It got me off the hook.

"I'm going to give him a few days and try again. He's got my mom's car for repairs, so he'll have to see me again when I pick it up, if nothing else."

"You used your mom's car to get to him?" Jen was stunned.

"Good idea," I admitted. "We didn't end on the best of terms. He could've thrown you out and that would have been it." I'd sort of expected that reaction anyway, even though his boss probably wouldn't have approved of him doing that to a paying customer. Nick wasn't the type to act like that anyway, not with a strange woman.

"He wasn't like that. The car needed work anyway. It was a safe opening in any case. He had overreacted. I think I'll have a better talk with him now that the ice is broken." Marina freed her hair from its ponytail and sunk lower in the chair as she rubbed her eyes. "I'm beat."

"I have wine breathing on the counter," Jen offered in a tempting voice.

"You're the best." Marina smiled.

Jen brought the wine and I sat trying desperately to think of a new topic of conversation.

I didn't want the focus to stay on Nick and me.

"So, Lori. Excited about Nick?" Jen asked.

I took the wine she offered and decided I needed it more than I wanted to toss it at her. "There isn't that much to be excited about. We're not compatible and, anyway, he's not interested. He didn't do back flips and welcome Marina."

"Are you interested?" Marina asked.

"If I couldn't make it work before, there is no reason to think it'll work this time. We're checking to make sure we don't leave any regrets in our twenties, not to repeat the mistakes of our past." I drained half of my goblet of wine.

"Some mistakes could be fun to repeat." Marina grinned.

"Maybe you and Nick could just hook up again for some horizontal fun and see what happens."

"I don't think that's a good idea." I had to think of a cute comeback or Marina wouldn't let up. "Then what would I do with my new vibrator Santa is going to bring me for Christmas?"

Marina and Jen both laughed.

"It's going to be good, but I don't think it's a permanent replacement for the real thing. Otherwise, men would be considered obsolete by now." Marina stretched and yawned. "I'll make sure Santa gets you rechargeable batteries and a deluxe model vibrator."

I tried to retaliate, but we were all laughing too hard. Jen poured more wine.

"Come on, I want to hear about new men. Let's leave history alone for tonight." I looked at Marina. "Any movement with the slug?"

"Seth is not a slug," she defended. "He's just shy and smart."

"And so slow he can't figure out you want to rip his clothes off and screw his brains out."

I nodded. "I don't think he's good enough for you."

"That is slow," Jen agreed. "You're not very subtle, Marina. It's not your style."

"I don't throw myself at my customers, Jen," Marina defended. "I'm not about to start that. Seth seems nice, not the type to troll for random sex in bars or out to pick up women everywhere and anywhere."

"And the nickname 'slug' lives on. I know you like smart men, but really, you can do better." I smiled as Marina glared at me. It was always fun to turn the tables on my friend.

* * * *

I spent all of the next day, Sunday, in bed. I had my laptop up and running and was looking up case research, or so

I told myself. I didn't want to face anyone that day and allowed myself to hide.

Monday came and I had to go to work. I made it through another day at the office. Thankfully, nothing special was on my schedule. At six o'clock, I couldn't find any other reason to stay at work. My bed sounded like a good place to be depressed. I packed up and ventured out for the day.

I sped through downtown, at least as fast as the traffic would allow. My mind was lost in the commercial-free satellite music system I'd had installed. I knew my way home with my eyes closed.

Unfortunately, my subconscious betrayed me yet again. I arrived at Nick's garage stunned and ready to turn around and go home. I couldn't leave.

I told myself I'd just see him once and leave. I didn't see his car parked anywhere. Maybe I'd missed him. He might have left for the day already.

Why had I even come? Did I actually think I'd get up the guts to go in? I wouldn't. I doubted I'd ever cross that line. So why did I torture myself? I noticed Marina's mom's powder-blue Caprice safely in one of the bays.

I needed details. I knew Marina hadn't told me everything. Asking her would only encourage her to think I wanted Nick back and she'd work harder. Why was I torturing myself? I couldn't figure it out. From one extreme to the other. I needed a drink. Or maybe a shrink.

What I really needed was objective advice, which I couldn't get from Marina now. I had a better idea. I drove a few blocks south and east and arrived at the Three Aunts Bakery. I paused, finally forcing myself to get out of the car. I needed real, honest, cut-to-the-chase advice. Not friend advice. I needed mom advice.

I entered as Penny was packing up.

"Hi," she said.

"Hi, is Mrs. Castini here?" I asked.

"Sure, Aunt Rosa's in back. I have to go. I have a big test tomorrow. Lock the door behind me, would you?"

"No problem. Good luck." I bolted the door behind Penny and walked slowly to the kitchen.

I saw Mrs. Castini and one of her sisters fussing in the kitchen.

"Hello, Lori," Mrs. Castini said. She didn't sound at all surprised to see me and waved me in. "Don't lurk in doorways, dear."

I entered, careful not to disturb any of the trays or canisters of ingredients. "I hope I'm not interrupting anything."

"Nothing. You remember my sister, Louisa?" Mrs. Castini waved her hand in the direction of her sister.

"It's nice to see you again." I nodded.

The older woman smiled. "You, too, dear, is my daughter gone?"

"Penny? Yes, she said she had a test to study for," I supplied.

Marina's Aunt Louisa headed for the door, wiping her floured hands on her apron. "I'll tidy up out front. We're done baking for the day."

"How are you doing?" Mrs. Castini pulled a tray of buns out of the huge oven. "Last one."

"They look delicious." I inhaled. They smelled just as good.

"Sit here. You need some food." She dished out two steamy rolls from the previous batch and poured me a glass of milk.

"I'll never eat two full rolls," I protested.

"You'll try." She patted my arm. "You're a rail."

I knew I would. Replacing happiness or men with food wasn't the answer, at least not for long. "Thank you. How are you doing?"

"Good. My car is trouble. Other than that, life is going well. How are you?" she asked.

Mrs. Castini sat at the counter across from me and waited. I didn't feel pressure or expectation. I wanted to spill my guts.

"I'm not sure," I said honestly. "Not feeling like myself

lately."

"Work?" she asked.

"No, that's fine."

"Marina?"

"No, she's great."

"Your family?"

"No, not exactly."

"Men?" I could guess that Mrs. Castini had left that for last, strategically. Marina had probably filled her in. Mrs. C was a mother to the core. I knew better than to even try to lie to her.

"One man," I admitted.

"My mechanic?" she asked.

I blushed. "Marina told you?"

"She told me about the looking up of your ex-boyfriends. Is Nick a problem?"

"I haven't talked him in three years. It's just weird." I bit into the roll finally.

"What's weird?" she asked.

"I can't get him out of my head. I believed I was over him. I just can't stop thinking about him." I felt like a whiney teenage girl talking about some random high school boyfriend. My mom never had these sorts of talks with me. Maybe I needed this?

"He's a nice boy," she said.

"I know that. It just can't work. We're too different." I heard the words and they didn't sound as convincing as they felt. Marina's mother wasn't my mother. Family pressure could be extreme. The rules were different in what they considered good men. Hopefully, Mrs. Castini could help me.

"Sometimes differences make people work harder at things and that can make the relationship stronger. You don't want to fight for him?"

"I don't know. Our differences didn't make us stronger. They only made us fight." I couldn't look her in the eye. Marina's family had blue-collar roots, too. I didn't want to offend her. I didn't care if Nick wanted to spend his life under a greasy car. There would be consequences and I didn't want to disappoint my family.

"What was the fighting about?" she asked.

"My family, mostly. His family was pretty nice to me."

"Was your family mean to him?"

"They never met him. I never brought him around." I shrugged.

"Why not?"

That was the question I didn't want to answer, but knew I had to. It was where I got stuck every time I thought about the situation. "My family would never approve of a mechanic. At the least, they want me to marry another lawyer or a doctor. My mother has a pre-approved list of men for me. Nick is definitely not on it."

"What if you don't love a man who does that sort of work or is on your mother's list?" She started to pick at the roll I wasn't eating. Such a mom thing to do—I loved it. I *did* need this, even if she didn't have the answers. Just being here helped me feel less jittery.

"My mother is so odd. She wants me to follow in her footsteps, make a good social match, quit practicing law and raise kids."

"What do you want?"

"I want to keep practicing and find the right man and have kids." I needed my financial independence.

"It's your life. She can't make you quit."

"No, and I won't quit my job. She's almost accepted that fact. If I brought Nick home..." I shook my head. "I don't want to lose my family, either."

"Do you really believe your family would throw you out of their lives?" She seemed unconvinced.

"I don't think they'd do *that*. It would be too easy for them and not enough punishment for me. They'd invite us, include us, and I'd never hear the end of it. Everyone would judge him, look down their noses at him, and make us feel uncomfortable. And the comments behind his back would be harsh to say the least."

"That's when you leave until they respect you. If he's worth it, you take the stand."

Not what I'd expected from Marina's mother. "Walk away from my family?"

"Not forever. There are times when you must take a stand for what you want. I have five daughters. I've had many boys come through my door and I didn't approve of all of them."

"You're different." I smiled at her.

"You're not like any of my daughters, either. Doesn't make us wrong. Why did you come here today, Lori?" she asked.

I thought about that for a minute. "Right now I need advice. What do I do?"

"First, you have to figure out if you really want Nick or if you just want to rebel. You might want to rebel and you're hung up on the drama. Even if your family doesn't know about it, it's still rebellion. Again. Using him for that isn't right."

I processed the words and stored them. "What if I'm not rebelling? What if he's the one?"

"Then you hold on to him and let your family do what they're going to do. You never know, they might not act the way you expect. Once your decision is made, you don't go back on it. The hard part is listening to your heart. Your brain tries to get in the way too much. You and Marina have that much in common."

I nodded slowly and felt better. There was no answer in the advice, far from it. I had more thinking to do. It was comforting. "Thanks," I said.

"Are you going to talk to Nick?" she asked.

I got up and paused. "Not yet. I have a lot of thinking to do first."

"Good, you were listening. I'm proud of you." She smiled and walked with me out to the front of the shop. "Come back any time."

"Thanks, I will." I hugged her before she let me out. I wandered back to my car in a daze and drove home with my brain whirling.

I'd spent so much time thinking about what would happen *if* I tried to see him, what he'd do or say, or what I'd do rather than what my family would say if they ever met him. I'd never for one second considered whether I'd been using Nick to break loose from my parents or whether it was deeper. Before I got myself worked up about anything else, I had to figure that out.

Chapter Eight

Jen at It Again

Four days had passed since I'd met Lucas. I'd tried my best, only I couldn't stop thinking about him. Once I'd found out who he was that day, I'd pretended to be late for work and left. He'd given me his cell number before I'd gotten away. I felt bad blowing him off but didn't know what else to do.

I didn't know if I wanted to call or what to say if I did. I stared at the phone. Circled it, picked it up, even dialed Lucas' number then hung up. This was the sort of thing I needed a second opinion on. I'd considered asking Lori, but she and Marina were too close. Lori wouldn't keep that type of secret from her.

If only Marina's ex weren't Lucas, I wouldn't have a problem, I'd have a date. A real date with a nice guy. He had a job and went to the gym. I'd seen his place of work and the stinky gym bag for myself. I'd been lied to often enough by men. Lucas wasn't like that.

It was my day off. Instead of the twenty errands I had to run, I was frozen thinking about my best friend's ex. I needed to do my laundry. I was down to my granny underwear, as Marina would call them. I also needed to finish the deal I'd struck. I had to talk to Lucas about Marina and keep my end of things.

I didn't know if I could do this. I needed more information. If I were near him, I'd have a hard time staying focused.

I didn't want to do it over the phone – I wanted to see him again!

Back in my bedroom, I checked my appearance. I'd left my hair down and my blouse slightly open. This time my skirt was a little shorter and my heels a little higher.

I checked my makeup. Marina had come through with the essentials and I'd put them on without looking scary. I dabbed on perfume and turned off my brain. I grabbed my purse and coat. No turning back now.

I ran to catch the L and squeezed into the compartment. I had to see Lucas, to explain things. At least that was what I was telling myself. Most importantly, I had to explain why I couldn't date him. He'd asked me out and I'd avoided answering.

What had I been thinking? Until the weekly meeting, I'd let myself actually dream about Lucas. Not just dating him, but X-rated dreams. Lori and Marina would've been very proud of me. Objectifying and lusting after a man I barely knew. He wasn't just good on paper, he had a great body and I wanted him. How sick was I?

On the bright side, I finally got it! I finally felt that lust and passion for a real guy who was available. I couldn't share it with my friends. I couldn't tell them I wanted my best friend's ex-boyfriend. Marina would blow it off and let me have him. That was her nature.

Lori would kill me.

As I got off the train, I realized what a terrible friend I was. I had to do better this time. Tell the truth and not get swept in by his charm. The guilt was eating at me and I had to settle it somehow.

I entered the building as the lunch rush was letting out. I didn't want to make a scene in his office or get him in trouble at work. I stood on a convenient bench and hoped I wouldn't miss him in the sea of people.

Finally, I spotted him and moved toward him, calling his name. It was noisy, but I was louder. I didn't want to miss him. I got close and grabbed his arm. He turned and removed his tiny headphones with a grin.

"Hi," I said. Not a brilliant opening line. I wasn't flirting,

I reminded myself. Not this time. This time I was in control.

"Hey, what are you doing here?" he asked.

We moved to the side to avoid getting run over or the finger from people trying to make the most of their lunch hour. "I was in the neighborhood," I lied.

"I'm glad. I was hoping you'd call. I really want to get your number." He pulled out his cell phone and I could tell he was ready to program it in.

"I have to talk to you about something – the thing." I suddenly sounded like I was missing some brain cells. What was wrong with me?

"Want to go to lunch?" he asked. Lucas wasn't an easy man to say no to. And Marina and Lori believed there were no truly nice guys left in the world.

"Didn't you have plans?" I looked around self-consciously. As though Marina was going to appear and object. Lori was who I had to fear if I blew it.

"Nothing that can't wait until after work." He took that as a yes and steered me toward that same little restaurant we'd gone to before. I couldn't say no. It might be easier to talk over food. Too early for a drink, yet I wanted one.

"Did you get the job?" he asked.

My mind had been so focused on the feel of his hand on my back that I barely heard the question. Oh, that was right, I'd told him about my interview. "I haven't heard yet. I'm going to call because they may be behind. Opening a restaurant is more work than running one."

We ordered and I tried to think of something else to talk about. I didn't want this to be over so soon. Why ruin the meal? Why not make it last?

"Are you worried about the job?" he asked.

"No, I was just thinking." I realized I'd been quiet too long.

"About me?" He grinned.

"You're sure you don't have a girlfriend?" My cheeks tingled in embarrassment.

"No, I'm trying to ask this cute girl out. She keeps changing the subject and won't give me her number. She just appears and disappears from my life like a ghost. Maybe she's not real." He leaned in.

I knew I should have backed away. We were in public. I'd never made out with a man in public. This wouldn't be a quick kiss, I hoped. Lucas wasn't just any man. He was Marina's ex. He'd slept with Marina. But he felt, tasted and smelled too good.

His mouth was warm and soft, not too pushy, definitely confident. Marina was right about one thing—he knew what he was doing with his hands. I could only imagine how good he'd be in bed. I already had.

The plates landed on the table and I pulled away. I was making out with a man I barely knew in a public place. The odds of getting caught by Marina or Lori were slim since they were both at work. I felt the same terror of being caught by the waitress.

"Sorry." The waitress grinned at Lucas and winked approvingly at me.

"Will you go out with me?" he asked.

I took a French fry and chewed slowly. Instead of pushing, he handed me the ketchup. He'd remembered I like ketchup. I melted like a sap and looked into those soft blue eyes. He was too good to be true. Of course, there was one glitch—Marina.

"Okay," I said.

"Okay? Was that a yes? You'll go out with me?"

"Yes, first we need to have that discussion." I put the condition out there now that he'd forced me to talk. The option of avoiding the topic was tempting. I couldn't do that to Marina, though.

"I'm ready when you are." He took a big bite of his burger and washed it down with root beer. Root beer. For some reason I found that cute. I hadn't had root beer since I was little, and I'd loved it. And it was cute on him. He wasn't ordering a beer or something macho. What a romantic fool I was.

"I want you to meet a friend of mine first, Marina." I waited for a reaction. His face remained blank as he chewed.

"Who?" he asked.

"Marina." If he didn't remember Marina, I'd just lost all respect for him. If he was the type of man who forgot women as soon as he was done with them, I'd change my mind quickly. There had to be more than one Marina in all of Chicagoland. Plus, it had been a few years.

"Oh." He nodded. "You want a friend to meet me in case I'm an ax murderer?"

"No, you went out with her a few years ago, Marina Castini. She's also one of my best friends." I didn't know what else to say.

"And my ex. Is that why you came to find me?" he asked slowly.

I nodded. "It's a long story. I need to make sure you're not still interested in her."

"She sent you to find that out?" He appeared confused. "Why wouldn't she contact me directly? Not that I'm sorry. I got to meet you this way."

"That's not really the whole story. It's a thing for our other friend, Lori. To get Lori to agree, we all had to pick exes to find. Marina picked you. I wasn't supposed to pick you up."

"If I remember our first meeting, I picked you up — literally." He smiled again.

"That wasn't supposed to happen, either. I'm here to find out if you're worth a second look by her, not for me to be attracted to you."

"And if I'm not interested in her?" He shrugged. "Then what?"

"I never thought of that. I mean Marina is gorgeous, smart and confident. I wish I were half as confident as she seems. You know how she is."

"Don't put yourself down or I might not take you to dinner." He had his hand on the back of my neck, massaging softly. "You're unique."

"You barely know me. I know you two didn't have a ton in common. Neither do we. Don't you think you deserve to see her to be sure? You and Marina had something. There isn't anything really between us, yet. Won't you at least meet her for lunch and see?" The guilt was killing me. I wanted them to smooth things over so I could be sure whether I could date him with a clear conscience or not.

Lucas rested his head back against the large booth. "Will you be there?" he asked.

"If you want me to." I didn't think that would be comfortable, but if it got him there…

"That's the only way I'll go. Then we'll have dinner that night."

"You seem awfully sure you won't want Marina back." I didn't trust that. Marina was a strong personality and gorgeous.

"I'll keep an open mind." He put his hand on his heart then stole one of my fries.

I hadn't even touched my lunch, I realized. With things finally settled, I was starved. "I'll talk to Marina and let you know when."

"Make sure to use my cell. My business line gets jammed and I don't want to miss it," he added.

"No problem." He was very particular about that cell phone. I started to wonder if he was holding something back. Marina did say he lived his job and it was high pressure. Maybe everyone got him on his cell.

Then I remembered the first time I'd called him at the office and it had gone through the receptionist. Maybe personal calls at his firm were monitored and it would get him in trouble.

It wasn't like he owned the company.

Either way, I had a date with him, and Marina, and hopefully it would all be out in the open and I might be able to date Lucas after all. First, I had to make sure that Marina got her chance. She'd had him first. This should be strange *and* uncomfortable. Once I saw them together, maybe it would hit me.

* * * *

After lunch, I'd wandered the streets, keeping an L track in sight so I wouldn't get lost. I'd been trying to figure out how I was going to bring this up to Marina. Eventually, I got cold and went home.

I did the laundry and cleaned the apartment. I still didn't know what to say to get Marina to come to lunch. When the clock read six p.m., I knew she'd be home. If I didn't do it fast, I'd never do it. Then this mess would just continue. I had to get them together so they could be sure they weren't right for each other. I needed a clean conscience.

Ignoring how obviously selfish I was being, I grabbed a chilled bottle of red wine and padded in my sweats and fluffy orange Garfield socks from my open door over to Marina's. I knocked, knowing it would be locked.

She opened the door and I waved.

"Are you busy?" I could tell she'd just gotten home.

"No, come on in." Marina left the door open and headed back to the kitchen as though nothing was out of the ordinary. To her, nothing was. She didn't know what I'd done. What I was about to drop on her. Should I tell her how I felt or just wait and I see how the lunch went? That was my sticking point. I feared it would just spill out of me once I started talking.

"How was your day off?" she asked.

"Good. No news on the job yet." I knew if I told her I was interested, she'd probably tell me to take him and refuse to go to lunch. She hadn't really been that interested in Lucas to begin with. That was the easy way out.

"My sister sent over some dinner. Like I'm going to waste away. Are you hungry? There's enough for four people." Marina opened the microwave to check on it then closed it, adding time.

"Sure. I've got wine." I was barely listening.

"Great, open it while I go change."

She headed to the bedroom and I began the routine task of uncorking wine as my brain spun wildly.

My other option was a lot harder, though much more honest. At least I was getting Marina and Lucas together for their true reactions. If Marina had taught me one thing since we'd begun this little game, it was what people said wasn't always what they felt.

Of course I knew that, and it applied even to my very best friends. Lori had lied to Marina and me when she'd said she was over Nick. It was clear as anything that she wasn't. She was being stubborn.

It was settled. I definitely wouldn't tell Marina I wanted her ex. This way would give Marina a real chance to see him again, I told myself.

Deep down, I knew it was because I didn't want to see the reaction. What if she'd harbored a secret desire to be back with him and just couldn't admit it even to herself, like Lori? Maybe Marina was just better at hiding things and there was an outside chance for her and Lucas.

"Forget where I keep the glasses?" Marina was next to me, taking two glasses down from the cabinet above my head. I had just been standing there, wine cork in one hand and the corkscrew in the other.

I shook myself awake. "Sorry, I was daydreaming." I took the glasses from her and began to pour.

"Must be a good dream." Marina shrugged.

"Yeah, that I got the job at the restaurant." I'd been a tad too enthused.

"You're a terrible liar, Jen." Marina checked the food again and removed it from the microwave steaming. "What's going on?"

"Nothing."

"Nothing? You never hang out here. You hate my mess," Marina pointed out.

She spoke the truth. Her couch had a sweatshirt over the arm. There was yarn in the recliner and magazines and newspapers all over her coffee table. "I just wanted to talk about

Lori and figured she'd never look for us here together. How are things going with Nick?" Marina nodded and seemed to accept that excuse. "Nothing new really. I'm more and more convinced Nick is perfect for Lori. He seems all calm at first and turns out he's every bit the pain in the ass drama queen she is. What a mess." She dished out food onto funky dishes her cousin had had hand-painted for her and gave me a plate full of pasta and bread.

"There is such a thing as too many carbs, Marina." I couldn't have eaten all of that if I'd tried.

"No wonder you're almost as skinny as Lori. Your mother never fed you." She rolled her eyes and sat cross-legged on the couch.

"I ate a big lunch, too." That was the truth. I'd eaten a burger and fries with Lucas and rarely ate two big meals a day.

"You'll take the rest home. I certainly don't need it." Marina took a swallow of wine. "Anyway, Nick's pissed off at me because he thinks I called his sister to try to get him to talk to Lori."

"Did you?" I asked.

"No, I didn't even know he had a sister. Lori might've mentioned it. I forgot to play that angle. I'm not stalking the bastard. I only wanted to talk to him. Lori had gone on about his great family when they were together, but mostly about him. Never got that specific. This guy at the garage, Eddie, sort of cute and a massive flirt, is going to help me with some info on Nick."

"That's good. What about the sister?" I frowned. Trying to keep up with Marina's super-fast mind and mouth was a challenge. The thought of what it must be like when she and all her sisters got together boggled my mind.

"Wait, it gets better. Then I find out Eddie used to date Nick's sister, and he called her to get info on Lori. That's how she found out I was trying to get them back together.

Then she called Nick and now Nick thinks I called her to get her on my side. If I wanted a soap opera, I would have watched one. I did *not* want to get involved in one. Why did I do this?" Marina groaned.

"Do what?" I mostly followed her spiel and wasn't sure what to make of it. She frequently answered her own questions within seconds.

"This, this whole stupid game that made you feel bad about being a virgin and me having to find out about Lucas. Lori is a mess. She can pretend all she likes, but this is making her crazy. If she won't face it, then what's the point?" Marina put her plate to the side and shook her head. "Maybe it was a big mistake."

"No, I don't think so." I frowned again.

"Because your part is over and done. What about Lori? Did I just extend her misery of turning thirty?" Marina raked her fingers through her hair, massaging her scalp.

"Better she finds out now if Nick is the right one or not than regret it at fifty. Isn't that what you said? No regrets. I don't have any. Clearly, Brian wasn't the right one for me. At least now I don't have to wonder or hide my lack of experience anymore. I feel like I can get out there now, and you guys are behind me."

Marina frowned and examined her nails. She analyzed her decision, second-guessing herself. "Lori is different."

"She's an adult. She can take it. You're not afraid to see Lucas again, right?" Maybe if I steered her in another direction she wouldn't derail this. Lori and Nick seemed like a fit. Lori was just stubborn.

"Afraid? Hell, no. I don't care. Why should I have to? Have you seen him again?" Marina reached for her plate and looked calmer.

"Yeah, today, in fact. He wants the three of us to have lunch."

Marina glanced at me in disbelief with her mouth still full. "You're kidding," she managed without hardly opening her mouth at all.

"No, he doesn't have a girlfriend or a wife. He isn't fat or bald. He did say there was a woman he's interested in. He'd like the three of us to have lunch and catch up with you. Would you mind?"

Marina licked her lips and I could tell she was pondering her answer. "Jen, I don't know. That's old stuff to dig up again. I understand that's the point. I really thought he'd be married with kids by now. That's what he wanted. A wife, two kids, a house in the suburbs with a dog and a white picket fence, where he could show off his wealth in fancy cars and lawn ornaments. We only had a spark in the bedroom."

"That doesn't mean you can't have lunch to be sure. Please, it'll make me feel like I did my best and fulfilled my part. If there's no spark, you never have to see each other again." She was going to chicken out. "I'm not saying you two should get back together. It might smooth things over."

No, she had to go. She had to! I had to be sure he was clear and free for me. At least I believed she didn't really want him now. My spirits were up. I might be able to date Lucas.

Pouring herself more wine, Marina shrugged. "Okay, as long as he's buying."

"Obviously. Don't worry, I didn't tell him you wanted to get back together or anything. I made it sound like a coincidence and old friends catching up. He didn't ask too many questions." Relief washed over me. I could have a clear conscious and a gorgeous guy who was actually nice, with a little luck.

"That sounds like Lucas. Not the chattiest guy in the world. Probably just wants to brag about his portfolio. Show off what I passed up. If it'll make you feel better for me to see Lucas, then you'll put my little trip down insanity lane to rest, I'll go."

"Excellent! Where?" I wanted her to pick the place so she didn't freak out.

"How about that new Mexican place we keep meaning to

try? Looks good." She seemed to perk up at the mention of good food that Lucas would pay for.

"Great. How's Monday?" I asked.

"Make it Tuesday. He should wait to see us." She winked and took her dish to the sink. "Was he civil to you, at least? He can be thoughtless."

"More than civil. He was very nice. You don't get far without people skills, Marina. He had to learn them sometime." Time changed people's perception of things, too. Marina had dumped him for a reason. Now she only really remembered the bad stuff, except for the sex. The Lucas I knew wasn't rude or showy with his money.

"Good, because if he was mean to you, I'd have to give him a lecture. He hated my lectures." She stood at the sink, paused in her dish rinsing and beamed in remembrance. The man who'd be right for Marina would be a very patient and yet very tenacious person. Lucas was persistent. He lacked that measure of patience, which I found intriguing. I had no patience on the job or man front.

"No, no lecture necessary, I promise you. Just think of it as a last meal with him. Then we can focus on fixing Lori and Nick."

"I'm half-tempted to give up. Neither will budge." She shrugged.

"Can you blame him? She dumped him for being poor and not good enough for the family. Not for being a jerk, or cheating on her, or because they weren't getting along, or because there were no sparks. Would you want snobby in-laws?"

"I get the picture," Marina interrupted. "I understand why he's mad. I should've known this would deadlock. He has every right to hold his ground. She's the one who needs to go and talk to him. The effort needs to come from her."

"That's not likely." I shook my head.

"Maybe, maybe not." Marina searched the ceiling for an answer. She had something cooking in that brain of hers and I wasn't sure I wanted to know what it was.

"Do you think he'll talk to her if she does make an effort?" I asked.

"Yes, I do." Marina sounded confident. "He took out his anger on me because I was there. They need to have a blow-out fight. Get everything off their chests, then they can move forward."

"Are you thinking of locking them in the garage alone together one night? That would be great. We could watch through a security camera and everything." I was intrigued. Marina's mind was far more devious than mine and I'd come up with that much myself.

"Oh, my God, we've created a voyeuristic monster." Marina laughed. "No, that won't be necessary. It'll be fine. I've already pushed too much. If Lori can't go after him herself, she doesn't really want him or doesn't deserve him. I just need to talk to her. Let her know he'll listen once the venting is over. And the sister thing will help. I need to tell her everything once I've talked to Eddie, then leave her alone." Marina nodded sharply.

"Since when are you anti-meddling?" I feared my friend had lost her mind.

"I'm not. There is good meddling and bad meddling. Good gets her to do it, bad is me forcing her to do it. If Lori can't face her family and stand up to them, she shouldn't string Nick along. It won't work."

"Do you think she can?"

"Lori is thirty years old. She's a self-sufficient adult who argues for a living. She can do this. The old excuses she has used before don't matter. If she doesn't do it now, she'll regret it.

And not just Nick. She'll be under her parents' thumbs forever. Cross your fingers she wants him bad enough." Marina dug through the fridge for some ice-cream cones and tossed me one.

"I don't need this." I had imagined getting naked with Lucas and feeling sexy. Ice cream landing on my hips didn't help the picture.

"Sure you do. We both struck out. Lori's the only one left with a chance at a man." Marina flopped down on the couch and handed me the ice cream.

"We don't regret it," I added. I unwrapped the ice cream cone so she wouldn't suspect.

Extra work out tomorrow, no question.

"Very true." Marina nodded as the phone rang. She grabbed it and glanced at the ID first. "Lori. I was wondering where she was. Since this Nick thing started, she's been very bad at being alone with her thoughts." Marina grinned and answered.

Chapter Nine

Marina's Plan Looks Iffy

I was intentionally early for my lunch with Eddie. I wasn't looking forward to it. The information for Lori wouldn't help if she refused to try at all. That was my biggest fear now and a real possibility.

It wasn't a date or anything, but Eddie was cute, so I went halfway and wore my funky black boots under boot-cut jeans and finished it with a dark blue sweater that showed off my assets without the plunging neckline. I needed to feel like a woman who was desired for a change. However, I didn't get the feeling Eddie needed a big flashing green light.

Before lunch, I had to get a little advice, so I went down to Mom's bakery. Penny was swamped at the register. I nodded at her and slipped into the back.

"Hi." I was met with a full kitchen, including Mom, aunts and two cousins. They all greeted me as they kept on with their work, except for Mom. She could tell this wasn't a normal drop in just to say hi.

"What's wrong?" She nodded for me to follow her into the supply room.

"Lori. I'm beginning to think I didn't do such a good thing." No reason to waste time on the formalities. Mom was busy. I was due at this lunch. I needed a reality check on what I was doing to my friend.

"Why?" Mom organized things as we chatted. Her hands rarely stopped moving.

"Nick isn't very receptive and Lori doesn't seem to want

to make the first move, either." I pulled my compact out of my purse and dabbed powder on my forever oily T-zone. "She's so damn stubborn."

"Should she talk to him?" Mom asked.

"Nick's theory is that she broke off the relationship so she should make the effort to come back. I don't disagree. However, she's stubborn." I snapped the compact closed and tossed it back in my bucket purse.

"Give her a little time," Mom said.

"That's the thing, if she won't go and talk to him after all this time, will she ever? Did I just drag up ancient history and torture my friends for what I thought was a good idea?"

"You had good intentions, dear. But things don't always turn out the way you want."

"So why do I hear that old cliché of 'the road to Hell being paved with good intentions' running through my head?" It had been an impulse to combat Lori's depression and I'd thought it would all just click.

"Don't worry, you did the right thing." Mom nodded with her back to me as she straightened spices. "Lori will understand that in time."

"How do you know that?" I asked. Mom never said those fake mom sayings just to pacify us. That was what made her advice so useful.

Mom turned and smiled knowingly. "Lori stopped by to see me."

"You're kidding?" My jaw dropped. Lori had sought out maternal advice.

"She just needed to talk to someone older. Her mother sounds very unreceptive to all of this." Mom shook her head disapprovingly.

"I doubt Lori's mom even knows about this or that Nick existed. I don't get that relationship. Her whole family is a bunch of snobs."

"At least she's talking to someone. I'm not sure if I helped, but she seemed to feel better." Mom turned to me and frowned.

"I'm sure you did. She's been quieter lately. Thinking is my guess." I wasn't about to ask for details of their conversation. Mom never shared private stuff from talking with my sisters. I knew she'd give Lori the same privacy and respect.

"She should give it some thought before she acts. Unfortunately, she can think all she wants, but that won't get her Nick back. Sooner or later, she'll have to go after him. Assuming that's what she wants. He has to be worth it in her mind," Mom said.

"Oh, I'm sure that's what she wants. Otherwise, she wouldn't care about my talking to him. Lori certainly wouldn't have come to see you if she wasn't confused, at least. She's been acting so weird lately." I'd known Lori long enough to see even a minor mood change. This wasn't very subtle.

I didn't want it to be permanent depression or for her to start smoking again. Nothing was worse than her on nicotine withdrawal, except possibly Nick withdrawal. At least the cigarettes were out of her system. There was no such thing as a Nick patch.

"Love makes people act weird. You've done the best you can. It's up to her now."

"Almost." I nodded. "I have one more thing to do. I'm meeting with a friend of Nick's and we'll see what he can tell me. Maybe I'll get something that'll help Lori decide. Nick's already tied in knots about it. Maybe all I need is one more piece to push her over the edge."

"In the end it's up to her," Mom warned.

I nodded. I knew she was right. "Whether they end up together or not, I really want her to at least talk to Nick. She needs to put this behind her. He's either the one or he's not. He can't be the one that got away forever. I can't still be hearing about this guy when I'm eighty. And she'll never stop. I can just see Lori and me puttering around a nursing home. Having to listen to her stories of Nick would make me want to call Dr. Kavorchian. She's my best friend, but the drama will kill *me*."

"I think she'll talk to him, eventually. She has to get brave enough first. That or she'll hit rock bottom being without him. Either way, feelings don't just disappear. Let her think it through and she'll come to you about it. How is Jen doing with this?"

I took a deep breath. "Pretty good, surprisingly enough. Her ex-boyfriend turned out to be a gay guy and she's really a virgin. She bounced back."

"I could've told you the virgin part." Mom smiled. "She's clearly shy."

"Those mom powers get scarier every day." I shook my head at her. "Anyway, she's found Lucas and doesn't find him as annoying or boring as I did. I'm having lunch with them next week."

"You don't want him back." It wasn't a question, just a fact.

"No. Jen wants the lunch so she feels like she held up her part of it."

"Sounds fair, since that's what you want Lori to do," Mom agreed.

"That's mainly why I'm going along with it. I need to show Lori it won't kill her to see an ex again." I folded my arms tightly.

"When are you going to start finding new men then, and stop pulling out the exes?" Mom asked.

"Is this a thinly veiled 'when are you getting married' talk?" I asked.

"You know I'm in no rush. Still, you haven't had a serious boyfriend in a while, either. The family is beginning to talk about you turning into an old maid. You're too smart and attractive for that."

"Mom, in order to be an old maid, I'd still have to be a maid. Born again virginity is crap, mine was gone a long time ago."

"You know what I mean. No one wants to see you old and alone." She waved off the sex talk. No better way to halt a conversation with a good Catholic mother than to throw your sex life at her.

"When I find the right one, I'll let you know." I was a bit shocked at Mom's questions. She hadn't been one to push marriage. I was closing in on thirty, however. My sisters had all been married by my age.

Even worse, my mother had given birth to all five of us by then. At the rate I was going, I'd never have any kids. That thought made me want to hide under the covers for a split second. Then a saner me took over. I wasn't ready for kids. Not yet.

"Don't wait until I'm dead. I'd like to see the wedding." Mom smiled.

I glanced at my watch. I had some time left. I wanted to get out before the conversation really got out of hand. "I'm going to be late for lunch."

"Is he cute?" Mom asked.

"He's not good potential. Just good information on Nick." I knew Eddie wasn't husband or even boyfriend material, even though he was attractive.

"Oh, well. Good luck."

"Bye." I made my way out of the bakery and felt weird. My mom had actually brought up my getting married. The creepy chill of Catholic guilt ran down me. I tried to shake it off and went to the restaurant. Eddie might not be marriage material, but he was good enough for now.

* * * *

I beat Eddie to the restaurant and got a table before the lunch crowd took them all. It was a little Greek restaurant in the neighborhood where I grew up. Hardly pricey, but this wasn't a date.

I ordered a Diet Coke and flipped through my appointment book. That damn lunch with Lucas. I had no desire to see Lucas, but at least I could point out to Lori that I was willing to put him behind me face-to-face. Jen didn't count since she'd never actually had a real relationship and her guy was long distance on top of it. Lori had no such excuse. If I could swing it to work to my advantage, maybe it would be worth putting up with him for one lunch.

"Sorry I'm late." He sat across from me in his work shirt and jeans.

Eddie was cute. I had to admit there was some attraction.

"No problem. Get stuck at work?" I asked.

"Yep. I have the rest of the day off, though. All yours." He grinned.

"Let's order, then get down to the Nick information." I smiled and scanned through the menu quickly. He wasn't the best conversationalist in the world. He was a means to an end. And not terrible to look at.

We placed our order and I waited for him to begin. After a few minutes, I finally had to ask. "Did you learn anything new about Lori and Nick?"

He downed his second cup of coffee. "Right. Nick's sister is totally behind this and called him again to give him hell. Once she opened the can of worms, she figured why not keep the pressure on?"

"And?" I pushed.

"Nick's sticking to his position. Lori has to come to him."

"You men and your egos. He'll be miserable, of course he'll keep his pride." I jabbed the straw back into the pop glass. "Will he listen if she does come?"

"Yeah, I think he wants to see her. Hear what she has to say," he suggested.

"I don't want her to go to Nick just to have him humiliate her and send her away. If he's just in it to make her miserable, he can forget it. I won't see my best friend hurt by this."

"Nick's not like that. He isn't out for revenge. If Lori isn't willing to come to him, I don't think he'll believe she really wants him. Nick has as much to lose himself. She could make him look like a fool if he goes to her," Eddie said.

"I understand that. She's very hot-tempered." Our salads arrived and we busied ourselves with eating for a bit. "Is there anything else?"

"From what his sister says, he hasn't had a serious girlfriend since Lori. That's years. That's a long time." Eddie frowned.

"Lori hasn't had a *real* boyfriend either, not since Nick. Lots of first dates, though no one really made it to boyfriend status." I kept coming back to the conclusion that I was right. Lori had gone to my mom for advice, and Nick was talking about her, if only to his sister. This might turn out okay.

"Nick gets set up a lot, but they never last. One-nighters here and there." Eddie shook his head. "If he were happy, I'd say why the hell not."

Our food arrived so I didn't have to respond to that. One-nighters had their uses.

I did a quick calculation and it had been nearly five months since I'd had any fun. Eddie was suddenly looking better and better as a short-term solution.

"Has he been acting up lately, too?" I asked. "I hope he isn't taking it out on his staff."

"Nick's as grouchy as ever. He's going to start losing employees if he doesn't change. Not that he's rude to the customers. He was always moody. Since you called, he's been a total ass."

"Lori's been pretty incessantly bitchy herself, when she's not being quiet and moody. They deserve each other. At least then they'll be annoying each other and not the rest of the free world. What did we do to deserve this?" I asked. "I say we lock them in a room and leave them alone for a week."

"They're lucky to have friends like us," he said. "I bet we'd find them having a sex marathon if we did lock them up. To be this nuts over each other after three years."

"Lori owes me big time if this works out." I picked at my club sandwich.

"How long have you been friends?" he asked.

"Over ten years." I shrugged. "She'll pay me back one of

these years. That's the good thing. I can pull her into this and if it works, great. If it doesn't, we'll still be friends. She'll never let me forget it. We've got that sort of friendship. We couldn't cut each other out of our lives if we tried."

"That bugged Nick." Eddie stuffed another fry in his mouth and didn't continue the thought.

"It bothered Nick that Lori has a friend she's stuck by and been loyal to for ten years?" That made no sense. Did he think I'd sabotaged him and Lori? I had nothing against him. I was on his side. She should never have broken up with him. She didn't listen to me.

"No, it bothered him that Lori never introduced you to him. I guess she talked about you a lot. He never met you or any of her family or other friends. He felt like a secret and that she was ashamed of him."

"He mentioned that. Her family is a different story. I was finishing vet school and she was studying to pass the bar. That was the busiest time in both of our lives. Our friendship lasted. We barely saw each other at all for six months. It wasn't personal. Our schedules conflicted all the time. Now that he *has* met me, I don't think he likes me very much."

"He doesn't know you well enough to like you. I think he respects you, though." Eddie drained another cup of coffee. "That's better with Nick."

"Why would he respect me? He barely met me and we argued most of the time." I hadn't gotten that vibe from Nick at all. I'd detected mostly hostility from him. "Nick probably wishes I'd never shown up. I know Lori hurt him, but I didn't think it would still be so raw. And yet he's so stubborn he won't make any effort."

"You came and confronted him. Nick likes direct people. He respects the employee who tells him the truth rather than the guy who tries to get away with shit or kiss his ass. Nick never misses a thing. Probably a big part of why he's pissed at Lori."

"I can't blame him. Lori's my best friend and I love her.

She's so fucking stubborn sometimes it has made her do stupid things. A great guy like Nick and all that amazing sex and she isn't sure what to do." I rolled my eyes and wanted to shake Lori, not that it would help.

"He never said anything to me or anyone I know about their sex life. I've seen Lori's picture so I'll bet it's amazing," Eddie said.

"He has a picture of her still?" My ears perked up. That was promising.

"Yeah, in his desk drawer. I'm sure he has more at home. He was out sick one day and we were looking for an invoice and I found the picture in his desk. A picture of both of them together at some party or in a bar. I'm pretty sure he isn't over her."

Now I knew for certain. A man refuses to brag about the sex to his buddies and coworkers and he held onto her picture. He was in love.

"I'll bet Lori has stuff like that and she's hiding it somewhere from me." It was classic Lori. I'd seen a picture, sure, but she was the type to keep tokens and I'd never seen any of them. Those keepsakes had to be very special to not share with her best friend.

"Sorry I couldn't find out more. Nick's been very touchy and his sister is trying on her end. She didn't give up too many details. I'm her ex." Eddie paid the check and we walked out of the restaurant. "Do you have a car?"

I shook my head. Still, Lori would keep things and I contemplated potential hiding places. That was exactly the sort of sentimental thing she'd try to hide. She didn't like to let on she had an emotional side, even to her friends at times. I saw Eddie still looking at me and remembered his question. "I took the L," I said.

"I can give you a ride." He nodded to a Harley-Davidson motorcycle.

"Okay, thanks." I knew Eddie wasn't my type instantly. My college boyfriend had had a motorcycle and that had been a disaster. 'Never date a guy with a motorcycle' had become a rule. It blew out my hair, gave me wind-burned cheeks, and the bike's vibrations had done more for me than the guy ever had. Of course, he'd thought he rocked the whole world with his small dick. Even so, motorcycles still turned me on.

I got on behind Eddie and held on. His body was nice and he still smelled like grease. The roar of the machine vibrating between my legs didn't help much. I gripped him and my purse tightly as the wind whipped through my hair. You had to be crazy to drive a motorcycle in the dead of winter. The danger only helped turn me on more. Fortunately, there was no ice or snow on the ground.

Chicago streets were dangerous enough in a car and motorcycles made you feel that much more exposed. We flew through the streets and I was free. It had been far too long since I'd had sex. This hadn't been how I'd planned it. Eddie wasn't the man I'd been after. But for now, I was attracted.

As he parked in front of my building, I told myself not to invite him up. I'd just pull out my box of toys and have fun alone. Unfortunately, I'd been doing that too much lately and I knew I'd crack.

"Thanks for the ride and lunch." *Don't let him get off the bike*. If he didn't, maybe he wouldn't want to come up and I'd misread the signs.

"Sure, hope I helped." He got off the bike and moved a piece of my hair that must have been blown into an odd direction.

"You did, thanks. I think Lori and Nick have a chance if they'll be civil." I gave in to my hormones. "Do you want to come up for a drink or something?"

"Sure." He followed me and I was very glad Lori and Jen would be at work until Eddie was safely out of our building. A girl needed more than a vibrator. I'd be much happier if it were Seth behind me.

We made it inside my apartment, hopefully without any of my neighbors seeing him. I locked the door behind us and he had me pinned to the door the second I turned around.

He was a pretty good kisser but lacked any subtlety or polish. I reminded myself this wasn't about romance, only taking my sex life off life support. I quieted my brain and let my body take over.

I unbuttoned his dirty work shirt and tugged it away as I pushed him into the room. The shirt landed on the back of my couch. I walked him toward the bedroom as I kicked off my black boots and he removed my sweater.

It took my body a few minutes to remember what it was doing. He undid my bra and massaged my breasts with his rough hands. Men were fascinated by large breasts. Were they real or fake? Some men were actually disappointed that they were real and didn't look like porno tits that stood up at any angle. Mine were hereditary.

Eddie seemed indifferent to their being natural, still enjoying them. It was always a challenge to get men to pay attention to the more sensitive areas of my body.

I shimmied out of my jeans and he got the idea. He removed the bikini scrap of cotton then roamed his hands over me and pushed me onto my bed. When he dropped his jeans and boxers, I could tell he liked what he saw of me.

Since he was already hard, I got to judge what I was in for. Not bad, not great length, maybe eight inches and it didn't look like it was going to get any bigger. It was enough to do the job.

He leaned down over me, kissing me for a moment, then he kissed down my neck to my tits and stayed there. Too long, keep going, my brain screamed, and finally, he tongued down my stomach to the spot that desperately needed the most attention.

His tongue on my pussy was so much better than a vibrator. It was different at least. That feel of flesh was so intoxicating. Or maybe it had just been so long. I spread my legs wider as I grew wetter.

Eddie would make the right girl a great sex toy if they

could stand his lack of a personality. I rocked my hips. I needed to be fucked, not just licked. When I reached for the drawer of my nightstand, he caught on.

I watched him put the condom on. For a real boyfriend, it might be fun to tease him and do it myself. For a one-nighter, in an afternoon even, he could do it himself. At least he didn't try to get out of the condom thing. That would put a halt to all of the fun.

Ready for the main event, I pulled him onto the bed and had him lying flat on his back in no time. I didn't want to risk him being a bad thruster. That was the easiest way to never hit orgasm. I'd do it myself and we'd both be happy. I straddled him and he didn't object.

I eased onto him and it felt good. I pressed down, ground to the base of him until there was no more. This wasn't going to take long for him. Quickly, I picked up the pace, fucking him hard. It had been too long and I didn't need anything soft or gentle.

My body took over, finding the right angle to hit those perfect spots. Eddie groaned and talked dirty, encouraging my efforts. I wasn't listening. Finally, my orgasm approached and I snapped my hips down faster as I cursed. A few more strokes and he shouted and jerked into me as he slapped my ass.

Men, what was it about slapping or spanking that turned them on? At least he hadn't done it all through the sex. That would've ruined it completely. I rolled off of him and enjoyed the sensation of my lingering orgasm. Not the best by any measure, still not the worst. Not bad at all. Mission accomplished.

Chapter Ten

Lori in a Fury!

I'd spent all morning blowing off the brief I should've been reviewing and making a list instead. Originally, it contained Nick's pros and cons. Lots of pros and very few cons, except that he probably hated me right now. He was polite, strong, good-looking, great in bed and understood me. That last part was what hurt. He'd understood me and that was how I knew he hated me. I understood him, too.

Then I made a list of everyone I cared about and what their opinions would be on the Nick situation, if they knew. That was a little harder. Of my friends, only Marina had met him, and not under the best of circumstances. Fighting aside, Marina seemed to feel Nick was worth pursuing on my behalf. That told me something positive.

My family was a huge con. Lumping them as one felt like cheating, so I tortured myself further. I listed family members one by one and what they'd have to say. Only one distant cousin might like it and she was fifteen with a bolt through her lower lip.

Dumb. I knew it was a dumb thing to do. What I wanted was supposed to matter. Hard as I tried, I couldn't discount everyone else's feelings. Marina would say it was because I was the baby. I couldn't stand to hurt people.

There was some truth to that theory. All my life my brothers had fought off bullies for me, scared off the big dog down the hall from our childhood apartment, and told me which teachers were easy and which were hard. That made it easy to please everyone. I'd never had to go it alone. As the only girl, I didn't have to compete for attention like my brothers had. I was the only *princess*. And if I stuck with the family line, I'd never have to work for attention.

I'd never disappointed them before. Not in anything big, anyway.

That was the hardest realization. I'd never once in my life done something against them or without first calculating the family's reaction to it. I avoided making waves. Unless I counted the time when I'd been five at that pool party and had taken off my bathing suit top.

I didn't see the problem. The boys didn't have to wear a top. I was excused because of age, though my mother never let me forget it.

The first time I'd taken my top off for a guy, I'd felt my mother lecturing me. I still felt her lecturing me, and I didn't get any breaks anymore. I had to live up to my mother's high standards or face the reaction.

Law school had been a surprise to them. In the end, they'd thought it was cute. I had gone to the same law school my brothers had. My mother had justified it to herself. Something to keep me busy until I found the right husband, then something to make me look like an impressive wife. That was it. I wasn't a rebel. I was well-rounded.

Nick was a different story.

I reviewed my notes, pages upon legal pages of notes. I'd listed everyone I knew. Why did I care what my ugly cousin Marjory would think? She only got a date when one of the old family biddies set her up with their friends' sons or grandsons. I ripped out all the pages and fed them to the shredder next to my desk.

Then, I took out a big red Sharpie and made a list of questions or points to discuss that did matter. To me at least. Nick wasn't perfect. It wasn't that easy. It had been a while since I'd been around him, so I had to think this through. I knew I'd forget logic as soon as I got near him.

I needed to talk to Marina and find out all the details. I'd followed her mother's advice and had given it a lot of thought. Now I had to find out what Nick was thinking. Or at least what Marina thought he was thinking.

I ripped out that page and grabbed my purse, briefcase and coat. I walked out of my office leaving the lights, my computer and everything else on. I went straight to the receptionist's desk in a hurry, no doubt looking like a crazy person. Didn't matter. I suddenly had to know everything. No more sticking my head in the sand or covering my ears. The whole awful truth was all that would pacify me now.

"I'm taking the rest of the day off. Rearrange whatever, tell them I'm sick. See you tomorrow." I didn't wait for the reaction. I went right for the elevators and hit the button for the parking garage.

I called the animal hospital and they told me she wasn't there. So I drove straight home and practically sprinted up the stairs when the elevator in our building took too long. Patience was not a virtue I'd ever pretended to have.

I rang Marina's doorbell repeatedly then pounded on the door like the emergency it was. *Please let her be home.* She had to be home.

I heard her moving around inside and thanked whatever WASP religion my mother would have called us. Or maybe I'd find out from Marina's mom the right saint for the hopeless cause I was and get a statue of them. I'd need more luck if I talked to Nick. *If.*

The door to her apartment opened a crack, stopped by the chain. "It's not a good time, Lori. I'll call you later," she said.

Was she kidding?

I needed to talk.

I was ready.

What kind of friend had she turned into? "Marina, let me in. I want to talk about Nick. Come on." I pushed on the door and peeked in. I could tell she wasn't fully dressed. Just a T-shirt that came down to her upper thighs.

A man, score! She needed to get some. I hoped it was that Seth guy she was always talking about. I was about to ask and promise to come back for the details. Then I saw the couch behind her and I stopped cold. There it was.

She didn't. Not Marina. She wouldn't!

"You bitch!" I yelled. I started pounding on the door like a woman in a Lifetime movie. Nick's garage uniform shirt was on her couch. I'd recognize it anywhere. "How could you?"

"What?" Marina shouted back. "Lori, stop screaming. I'll let you in."

Marina closed the door and undid the chain. The door then opened wide and I lunged for her. I half fell into the room, I was so furious and confused. Marina closed the door before all the neighbors stormed in. I recovered and went after her again.

"What the hell is wrong with you?" she demanded.

She caught my wrists every time, deflecting me as I did my best to swing at or choke her. Damn her for having four sisters. She could do this better than I could. I'd never fought another girl before. No man had ever been worth fighting over before. I'd scratch the eyes out of any woman who took Nick away.

Even Marina.

"You slept with Nick!" I started crying on top of the screaming and crumpled up that list I'd finally made and tossed it at his shirt.

"Oh, my God. You're an idiot!" Marina yanked me by the arm to her bedroom.

"I don't want to see that," I protested. "I don't want to see him in your bed."

She was stronger and pulled me past her rumpled bed to the bathroom where the shower was running. Marina opened the door and tugged the curtain back. I cringed for half a second. A man I'd never seen before was rinsing off and looked confused at first.

"Room for two more." He winked.

"Dream on," Marina replied. "Get dressed and get out. Lori and I have important things to discuss. I just had to prove to her you weren't Nick."

"That's Lori." Marina's random man seemed totally oblivious to his nakedness and intrigued by me. He must work with Nick. Duh! How stupid was I? They all wore the same shirt. I'd just lost it over nothing.

"She's not here to see you," Marina told him and closed the curtain. She pulled me out of the bathroom and shook her head at me, cursing under her breath. "You really think I'd sleep with Nick? I'm that hard up that I'd ruin our friendship over some sex?"

I sat on her bed and half-laughed and half-cried. This was what being hysterical felt like. I'd never in my life fainted, but if Nick had been in Marina's shower, I knew I would've passed out cold.

"I don't know. I saw the shirt. I knew that shirt. It was all a blur after that. I went crazy. I'm sorry I tried to kill you." Those were words I never expected to say to my best friend.

"Forget it. If you'd tried, I'd have kicked your ass. It never occurred to me you'd show up in the middle of a workday. You should know better than to think I'd do that to you. We share a lot of things, Lori. However, men aren't *ever* going to be one of them. I promise you that." Marina tugged on her jeans then handed me a tissue. "Here, your mascara looks awful."

I fixed my face as Marina's random boy-toy left, still suggesting a threesome. Marina tossed him out and locked the door.

"So, why are you here in the middle of the afternoon? What's the emergency? Is something wrong?" She slicked her hair back into a ponytail. Now that the drama was over, the concern set in.

After being alone with him, I felt off. I'd gone ballistic over nothing and accused my best friend of something that rationally and deep down I knew she'd never do to me. "I need a drink first."

Marina returned with a drink in under a minute.

With a generous glass of raspberry vodka on ice in hand,

I finally sat on Marina's couch and actually started to calm down.

Marina was puttering and I just wanted everything to stop. I wanted to have the answers. Marina came in from the kitchen.

"I'm sorry." I took a long drink and exhaled. Then I looked at Marina and started to giggle.

Marina had opted for red wine and put down a plate of her mom's holiday fudge. She started laughing, too, as she flopped back into her recliner.

"He's not bad. What happened to Seth?" I asked. "What were you thinking?"

"I was thinking I hadn't had sex in five months. He had the right equipment and wasn't a total asshole." She shrugged. "What were you doing running out on work in the middle of the day to come pound on my door with yellow legal paper? What's wrong? That's not normal, even for you."

That reminded me. "Where did I put that paper?" I dug through the cushions and found it under a pillow.

"What is it?" Marina stretched and ignored the fudge as I dove in, getting chocolate smears on my notes. She'd had sex. She didn't need chocolate. I sure as hell did. Lots and lots of chocolate.

"I made a list of Nick's pros and cons." I licked my fingers.

"Great. That'll really help." Marina rolled her eyes at me.

"Wait, then I wrote up a list of how everyone I know and love would react if I brought Nick to my parent's Eve of Christmas Eve party."

"Again, no surprises." Marina propped her toes on her coffee and table and wiggled them.

Don't get me wrong, I was glad she'd had sex, but now I felt deprived. I wanted Nick. Her toes were a glittery red that I liked. A sexy color — maybe Nick would like it, too.

"I know. I know that was a stupid thing to do. That's why those lists went in my shredder. This is a list of things I want to know from him. I want to talk about the list and what I liked about him." I unfolded the crumpled list and stared at it. First, I wanted her opinion, without my influence. "What did he say?"

"What about your list?" Marina asked.

"That's the big thing. What did he say about me? I know what I want to hear. I want the truth. I've lived on fantasy long enough."

Marina took a drink of her wine. "He said he was hurt. He felt like he wasn't good enough for you or the family. Apparently, it really bothered him that he never met me while you two were dating."

"Why you?" I asked.

"Not just me. Did you introduce him to anyone in your life?" she asked.

"Were you going to introduce me to What's His Name in the shower?" I shot back defensively.

"That's different. That's recreational sex. You and Nick went out. Eddie said he saw the picture in Nick's desk. You two at a party or something. You guys had an actual relationship. And you never let him meet your family or any of your friends."

I opened my mouth then closed it again. There was nothing to say. I'd never thought about it like that. I'd loved having Nick all to myself.

"I don't blame him for feeling second-class. He should be pissed at you. He never met any of your friends? Not even a friend from law school?" Marina asked.

I shook my head. "I guess I talked about you a lot. I wanted you to meet him. With him, it was too good to be real and I didn't want to screw it up. What about you? Did you like him?"

"When we weren't arguing, he seemed nice. Lori, when you're the topic of conversation, he gets worked up. He's a very direct guy. There's a lot of emotion right beneath the surface. Mom says he's a nice guy who's fair and respectful."

"High praise." I knew Marina's mom was a hard lady for young men to impress. She had five daughters and any man brought around had to be up to her standards. Luckily, her standards weren't the same as my mother's. Her standards made sense and were good to rely on.

"Very," Marina agreed. "He's hurt. You're the one who broke it off. He isn't about to come to you. You'll have to go after him. That wasn't negotiable."

"I deserve that." I stared at the list. "Do you think he wants me to?"

Marina nodded. "Men don't usually argue so fiercely about women they don't care about. I can tell you that as an absolute truth from dealing with my four brothers-in-law. They may tease their wives, but if anyone else bothers their women or even says a word against them, they get very defensive and aggressive—like Nick."

I smiled. I tried to stop and couldn't. "Think I can do it?"

Marina looked back at me. "I think you'd be a dumb bitch not to try. And if you don't, I don't want to hear the name Nick out of your mouth *ever* again. It would be more than I can take."

"Sorry," I said. "I know I've made too big of a deal about this since I broke up with him." I'd never realized how much I talked about him.

"That's not what I meant." Marina got up and moved to sit next to me. "You can talk all you want to me, Jen, or a shrink, if it helps. It won't solve anything. It sure as hell won't change anything."

"I know, I know." I had no other response.

"You need to have it out with him. He's either worth it or he's not. You have to decide, then win him back." Marina shrugged.

"My family." I shook my head. My courage was slipping just as it began to feel real.

"Get over it. Your family will either accept it or they won't, and you guys can come to my house for Christmas next year. Mom loves extra people. She gets sick of it being just her own daughters." Marina grabbed a box of tissues out of a bookcase for my inevitable waterworks.

"What if he doesn't want me?" I took a tissue in case and rested my head on the back of the couch.

"Lori, you can argue your way in or out of almost anything. I've seen you do it. Talk yourself into it and go do it. I have complete confidence in your ability to argue rings around Nick. And if you have to, seduce him. Men listen better when they're naked." Marina grinned.

"I can do that." I nodded and pointed to her toes. "Can I borrow that nail polish color?"

Marina got off the couch and brought back the bottle of nail polish. "Keep it. It's you."

I turned the bottle over and read the title of the slightly slutty color. "*I'm Not Really a Waitress.*" I began to giggle. "That's me. Ready for seduction. I just don't want to chicken out."

Marina shook her head. "Why don't you sleep on it? Clear your head. Do your nails. And when the doubt comes back, just think about what your mother would tell you to do. Then do the exact opposite and don't look back."

Marina knew me too well. "Thanks, I'm going to go try and take a nap." I downed the rest of my drink and hugged Marina tightly.

I walked carefully to the door.

"You forgot your Nick yellow page." Marina brought it to me.

"Rip it up. I need to do this on my own." I nodded. "I hope the next time I find you half-naked with a man, it's Seth in your shower."

"Me, too." Marina tore up the pages and locked the door behind me.

I held onto my new nail polish and picked up my briefcase and purse that I'd left strewn in the entryway, a tribute to my rush to save Nick from Marina. I felt like an idiot as I fished my keys out of my purse, went into my apartment and flipped the lock.

I tossed my purse and briefcase into a corner without another thought. My proper heels followed them. I carefully set down the bottle of polish then stripped off my blazer, blouse, and skirt.

I padded to my bedroom in nothing except a bra and pantyhose. I didn't see the point of underwear under pantyhose and Nick had found that so sexy. Rummaging in the back of my closet, I knew exactly where his sweatshirt was. I pulled it over my head and hugged it around me.

Digging through my linen closet, I found an old bottle of nail polish remover and a bag of cotton balls. I had a standing appointment in the salon to get my nails done in a neutral mauve. Not this time.

I wasn't very good at doing my own nails, but I was going to do them myself in trashy red. I was going to be so sexy he'd have to forgive me. At least he'd hear me out.

I set my supplies on the coffee table. In the kitchen, I poured myself a glass of water and grabbed a pint of chocolate ice cream from the freezer. I set those on the coffee table, too.

Finally, I went to my desk drawer and unlocked it. I spread all of the keepsakes on the coffee table. The pictures made me smile as I sat and began to remove the most boring and appropriate color from my nails.

The phone rang and I didn't move a muscle. The machine picked up. Who else? My mother's voice was like fingernails on a chalkboard. "Hi, Lori. It's your mother. I tried your office and they said you went home sick. Let your father or I know if you need anything. Gilda called and has a young man she'd like you to meet. I'll set up a dinner for this weekend. Call me when you get this."

I glared at the phone and didn't move. "No, I'm not going," I said. And I meant it. "I'm getting the man I want."

Before this weekend, I'd have Nick back and, even if I failed, I wasn't going to let my mother play social director of my life any more. Telling her 'no' never helped. If I simply refused to show up, she'd be mortified. A couple of incidents like that and she'd stop trying.

Why hadn't I done this before? She'd leave outraged messages on my machine or at work, sure. Who said I had to listen or return them? Marina was right, do the opposite and it would feel great! It felt like I was already back with Nick.

My nails were now clean and I ran to the bathroom to wash my hands. I glanced into the mirror and saw the dull and proper Lori. I pulled my hair out of the neat clip and let it flow messily over my shoulders.

Nick liked it better and so did I. Why had I changed it? I couldn't remember now. It didn't matter anymore. Now it would all be different. The way it should be.

I went back and looked at that picture of Nick and me again. Nick and I were happy and I liked myself better back then. I missed that. I removed my pantyhose and sat back down to put that funky red on my nails, and not just my toes, like Marina. I was going for it all.

Suddenly I wasn't so scared. Instead, I felt free. I couldn't wait to see my mother's face when I brought Nick to their holiday party.

First, however, I had to get Nick to come with me. To take me back. I blew on my nails and noticed Nick's medic-alert necklace among the stuff on the coffee table. I hadn't put on any jewelry today. I slipped it over my head, careful of my nails. I wasn't going to take it off until I had Nick back and he could take it off me, naked.

And I'd get what I wanted. It had taken me a few years to realize the truth. He'd forgive me. He had to! Marina had forgiven me for trying to kill her, so how could Nick not for breaking up with him?

I got up and went to the large mirror hanging on my living room wall. I admired his stainless steel, cheap necklace on me. It meant more than all the expensive jewelry my parents had given me.

Nick would forgive me and fall for me all over again. I'd take Friday off and go see him. This was a once-in-a-lifetime thing. I wouldn't get a second shot so I had to do it right. I'd make a hair appointment, get everything waxed and build up my courage.

Chapter Eleven

Jen's Night Out Clubbing

I'd blown it. Totally ruined everything. That realization just kept looping in my brain as I sat on my couch. My life was taking a nosedive and I couldn't seem to fix it. Everything I did was wrong.

In minor things, it had been a bad day at work. Thoughts of Lucas had made me careless. I'd caused a grease fire that had nearly singed my hair. That had trigged an all-day fight with a coworker. I had good reasons to hate that job. Unfortunately, still no news on the new job and I was resisting the urge to call. I didn't want to look desperate, and it was too soon.

That was bad enough. Then there was last night.

I'd gone on a date with Lucas. A real date, at night, to a fancy restaurant that I'd chosen and we'd had wine. I felt terrible.

It had been great in the moment. He had showed up at my door with flowers in hand and dressed in a cute suit. It had been a complete surprise.

I couldn't say no. I didn't want to. We hadn't had *the* lunch with Marina yet. If that was over and she'd expressed no interest, then maybe my conscience wouldn't be torturing me. That voice in the back of my head kept telling me that I was a horrible person and a failure at friendship.

What if Marina never forgave me? I couldn't help it. I couldn't stop it. I'd tried. This lust thing had sounded fun, a force I couldn't control yet. Would I ever be able to?

Of course, last night during the date, my enthusiasm had

drowned out the nagging voice of reason and caution. I'd even invited him into my apartment. I finally understood what all the fuss was about sex. I couldn't help it. We hadn't done everything, but I now got why I wanted it so badly. The chemistry was intense with the right guy.

It was attraction. It was lust. I couldn't blame the wine or anything else, either. I'd invited him in and curled up on this very couch with him. He'd smelled so good and I hadn't been thinking.

Not that I'd actually slept with him on the first official date. Though that depended on your definition of sex. I didn't let it go past that. Still, it was a first for me. Great, wonderful, guilt-inducing.

I was miserable. I'd betrayed my friend. I was half-tempted to cancel the lunch and tell Marina what I'd done. If she wasn't going to care if I dated him in the end, would she care when it had started? Why possibly make her mad or embarrass myself?

What I needed to do was stop thinking about it. I couldn't change history. I couldn't confess to Marina now. Why hurt her if she wasn't really interested? I had to get my mind off Lucas and the whole thing. Maybe Lori could help. I willed my depressed body off the couch and out into the hall, where I knocked on Lori's door.

"Hey you." She opened the door and nodded for me to come in.

"Hi." I didn't even try to sound happy.

"What's wrong?" she asked.

"Just stuff. Life." I shrugged. I couldn't divulge the details to her. Telling Lori was the same as telling Marina and it worked the other way, too. They didn't keep secrets well. I could use the job thing, I decided. "I haven't heard about the job yet."

"That sucks." She nodded again.

"I need to distract myself. Get my mind off it. Any ideas?" I flopped onto her couch and curled up with a paisley throw pillow.

She glanced at the clock then back at me. "You need to get out."

"Out?" I wasn't sure if I wanted that.

Lori held up a finger and picked up the phone. "Marina, get over here. We need your expertise." She didn't even say goodbye.

"All of us?" I asked.

"Of course." Lori looked at me like I was crazy.

Marina walked in seconds later. "What's the problem? My only expertise is animals."

"And alcohol. Jen's depressed about her job and life in general. Are you up for a night of partying?" Lori kicked off her work heels.

"I have the late shift tomorrow, so sure. Where do you want to go?" Marina asked,

"I was thinking The Rattler. Don't you know the owner?" Lori winked.

"I know Louie from high school. I haven't seen him since the reunion almost two years ago." Marina didn't seem too thrilled with the idea.

"You can get us in. You said he was flirting with you at the reunion." Lori clearly wanted this. She had a plan for fun.

"Yeah, fine. Go get dressed. We'll leave in half an hour." Marina turned before she left. "Lori, you're driving."

"No problem." Lori smiled and ushered me off her couch to go make myself presentable.

I shuffled along the hallway. Getting drunk in one of our apartments would've been enough. Now I had to get dressed, pay for drinks, and worry about men hitting on me or *not* hitting on me.

However, dancing did sound good. The music might bring back some energy and help me forget the guilt. It would be too loud to think in that club.

Feeling a bit better, I dug into my closet and found a cute dress. It wasn't quite sexy, but it did show what little cleavage I had to its best advantage. I felt a bit better just changing out of frumpy sweats and into something that made me feel like a woman.

I did an up-twist with my hair, enough makeup to make me not seem scary, and shoes that were nice enough not to be vetoed by Marina or Lori, yet they wouldn't kill my feet if I danced all night in them.

I stepped into the hallway and found Marina. Her outfit screamed sexy in a low-key way. Black skirt and blouse with a black scarf that had just a hint of a red pattern for spice. She could pull it off. In all black, I would seem like I should be at a funeral.

Lori was always the last to join us. Marina saying thirty minutes meant she expected to have to drag Lori out by her hair at forty minutes.

"Is The Rattler fun?" I asked.

"It's okay. Always crowded, plenty of people. Loud, trendy and all that stuff."

"Hot guys, then?" I wanted to sound like I was looking. I'd said enough nice things about Lucas, not that she cared. I hoped she didn't.

"Hot enough to get Lori's attention. But they're not in her class." Marina looked over her shoulder as Lori's door opened. "Just what she likes."

"Quick. Aren't you proud?" Lori did a model's twirl for us. The cream halter top dress with flowing skirt hugged her.

"Thoroughly, let's go." Marina clearly lacked enthusiasm about tonight.

"Don't drag us down, Marina. You'll have Louie all to yourself and maybe Seth'll be there," Lori teased.

"I don't think he's the type." Marina led the way into the elevator.

"See, a stuffy slug." Lori nudged me.

"He's not stuffy or a slug. Seth just doesn't strike me as the type who would go to a crowded bar, though, he might have friends who drag him out." Marina turned to me. "Have you called about that job?"

"They said two weeks. That's almost up. I'll call Monday. I'm just nervous."

She nodded as we exited the elevator and piled into Lori's little Jag. Driving with Lori the Adventurer was never dull and often more exciting than the club. She cut people off, sped and gave the finger like the Chicago native she was.

Even in thick traffic, we were valet-parked outside The Rattler in fifteen minutes, door-to-door. I willed myself not to feel carsick. I was determined to have a good time, even if it killed me.

The line to get in was fairly long, considering the cold weather. Marina spoke to the doorman and we were ushered in around the ropes. I heard the doorman tell Marina he'd let the owner know she was there.

We walked in and Lori snagged us a table near the bar right away. "Perfect spot to get drinks and look at guys, who will hopefully buy us more drinks." Lori grinned.

I'd learned from Lori that barhopping and location had a strategy. She was in stealth mode. No doubt hoping to forget about her man problem. Not a word of Nick had been spoken.

"What do we want? I'll get the first round." Marina fished her credit card out of her purse.

"No, no," a male voice behind her said. "You don't pay for a thing."

"Hi, Louie." Marina smiled, and he kissed her on the cheek. Although clearly not overjoyed, she faked it well enough. "These are my friends Lori and Jen."

He shook hands with us, flirting and smiling. "Our club always has more room for gorgeous women. I hope you don't mind if I steal Marina for a bit."

"I'm here to spend time with them, Louie," Marina protested.

"Just a bit. My sister is here and I know she'll want to say hello." He pushed Marina a little away from us and leaned over. "You two order anything you want on the house. I told

Mickey. He's the bartender over there, so no worries. See you later."

"Thanks." Lori flashed a killer smile.

"That's weird," I shouted in Lori's ear.

She nodded. "Marina won't be gone that long, don't worry. Just reunion time."

"Did they date?" I asked.

"No, I think he'd like to." Lori grinned at the attractive waiter who approached and took our drink orders. He insisted on throwing in the appetizer sampler. Who were we to argue with a guy who looked that good in tight jeans?

"Why is she so hung up on Seth when she has a man right here who has a business and money?" I asked. "Not that Seth sounds bad. He can't be that great if he isn't interested in her."

"Taste and attraction are very peculiar things. Why did I go after Nick instead of one of those snobs my mother keeps throwing at me?"

I nodded. The drinks arrived and kept me from opening my big mouth and asking what she was waiting for. Marina and Lori were after different things in men. Attraction was a funny thing—I had no room to talk. I tried to think of something polite to say. Before I could, Lori's eyes bugged out of her head.

"What?" I turned.

"Don't turn around." She kicked me under the table.

"What is it then?" I asked.

"Nick," she mouthed.

"Where?" I didn't care what she said, I turned around. I craned my neck to see if I could spot him.

I'd only seen pictures and they were only a few years old, but I managed to pick him out of the crowd. A bit underdressed to be clubbing, but good potential. He was tall so I had a nice view of his face and solid shoulders. Nick looked better in real life.

"I told you not to look," Lori whined. Whining Lori was not a good sign and she didn't even have a full drink in her.

Whoops, as I glanced back at the table, I knew I'd thought too soon. She'd already downed the first drink and had signaled the bartender to send over another. Great, drunk Lori was a handful.

"He doesn't know who I am," I reminded her.

"That's right. He doesn't," Lori said.

"No, whatever it is. The answer is no." I sipped my drink and kept shaking my head whenever her gaze shifted back from Nick to me.

"Come on." Lori stomped her heel on the chair.

"No," I repeated.

"You don't even know what I want."

"I can guess enough bad things to say no to whatever it is." I shook my head to reinforce it.

"Marina would do it for me," she pouted.

"Then get Marina to do it." I'd already been party to enough trickery and deception of my own.

"I can't. She's already talked to Nick. He knows her." Lori's eyes never left him now.

"If he sees you with me, then you can't send me, either." I smiled.

"So don't go and talk to him." She swatted at me. "You don't have to talk to him. Just mingle near him and see if he's with anyone."

"Why do I feel like I'm in high school?" I rolled my eyes at her.

"Because the relationships between men and women never truly mature past that stage. Does he like me? All that crap. Look at Marina. She won't ask a guy out. Her rule, I understand it, because one of her sisters made a total fool of herself over a guy. I think you can casually ask a guy out without losing your allure."

The waiter brought her one additional drink. She downed it in record time and requested to go from mixed drinks to vodka on the rocks. "Go mingle near him." She literally bounced in her chair with insistence.

"Wait, it looks like he's with someone." I watched as a tall woman with large assets whispered something in Nick's ear. "I think we can see better from here. He hasn't spotted you yet."

"That's because that silicone tower is all over him. I'll bet nothing in her is real. How dare he?" She grabbed her other drink and tipped it back.

"He's single. You haven't staked a claim. Did you brand his butt with 'Property of Lori' before you dumped him?" I shot back.

"No, but that's a great idea!" Then her eyes got bigger. "Yes, the cavalry has arrived!"

"Who? Silicone City's boyfriend show up?" I turned.

"No, Nick's sister. She was always on my side." Lori sat up high to watch. "See, she's getting him to leave. Damn. He's leaving."

"If you want to talk to him, I'm sure I could catch him," I offered.

"You wouldn't spy for me, but you'll sprint through a crowded bar?" She scoffed.

"Yes, because spying in a bar is pointless. Getting him to come back and talk to you is productive. Not to mention you've had too many drinks to be running anywhere in those shoes." I shrugged and pointed to her super-high heels.

She dropped her chin in her hand. "He's gone. Good thing we're not paying for drinks. I'm going to need more."

"You've got a ton of money. I don't want to hear you complain." I finished off my first drink and the waiter brought me another. Apparently, Lori's reputation had rubbed off on me. In this instance, I was glad.

"I know. It's better when men pay for it. And if that man wants to get in your friend's pants rather than yours, that's the best free drink there is. No pressure." She nodded.

"Speaking of Marina, I think we should go and find her. She's been gone too long. Probably in desperate need of rescuing." I glanced at my watch. It'd been nearly half an hour and that was too long for my comfort.

Lori blinked at her watch. "Okay. She'll be glad we saved her and we have to make sure they didn't sell her to the gypsies."

Lori laughed at her own statement and got up from the table, carefully. "The gypsies," she repeated.

"I don't get it," I confessed.

"It's an old saying. Never mind." Lori grabbed her drink and I remembered to take mine as we headed off in the direction Marina and Louie had disappeared.

After asking the bartender, and Lori nearly grabbing his ass, we wandered toward some private rooms in the back, where we spotted Marina half-involved in a conversation with three guys, one of whom was Louie, and two other women. I waved to her and she perked up.

"Excuse me." I could read her lips. Louie followed her out, of course.

"Why is she drunk? She was supposed to be the driver." Marina asked me after assessing Lori's condition in half a second. Marina shook her head and sighed heavily.

"Nick's here!" Lori lifted her glass quickly. If it hadn't been empty, she'd have showered us all with raspberry vodka on the rocks.

"He's here?" Marina asked.

"He was. He and his sister left a few minutes ago," I filled in then nodded toward Lori. "I could really use your help."

Marina nodded. "I've got to get back to my friends, Louie. Nice seeing everyone." She waved at the room then grabbed Lori's arm.

"Wait," Louie insisted. "I know you need watch your friend, just give me your number. I'll invite you to the next private party."

Marina smiled and pulled a business card from her purse. "Thanks, Louie." Before he could press for her home number, she turned and steered Lori toward the table. "How many vodkas has she had?"

"Three. She started with vodka and cranberry juice. Then she saw Nick and switched to straights."

Marina nodded. "She drinks that when she wants to get drunk."

"Nick looked *so* good, Mar." Lori didn't fight too much as Marina shifted her into the chair.

"I'm glad. Why didn't you talk to him?" Marina asked.

The waiter appeared and Lori was totally distracted. He'd brought her another drink. "No, that's for me." Marina's reflexes had Lori's eyes spinning. "A coffee for her, please."

"I don't want coffee," Lori whispered.

"You're not passing out on me. You get coffee." Marina nodded to the waiter with a stare that let him know she meant business.

"You're mean." Lori pouted.

"Why didn't you go and talk to Nick?" Marina asked.

"What for? So he can yell at me and walk away? Humiliate me in public? No, thank you." Lori shook her head hard and rubbed her forehead. "I'm drunk."

"No shit." Marina sipped the vodka brought for Lori. "That man is going to make you an alcoholic."

"Same difference." Lori shrugged.

"What does that mean?" Marina asked. "Different from what?"

"When I was dating him, he made me a nymphomaniac and when I'm not dating him, I'm an alcoholic. So I went from being an 'aniac to an 'olic. It's okay." Lori smiled and giggled at her own philosophy.

Marina, for the first time, cracked a genuine smile at Lori's analysis. "True enough." Then Marina's expression hardened. Whatever was going on clearly was happening behind me. Maybe it was Nick? I hoped not, considering Lori's condition.

I turned and it wasn't. It was a guy. Not an ugly guy either. No one I knew.

I turned back around and gave Marina an inquisitive look. She shrugged.

"Good evening," he said.

"Hi." Lori leaned in and Marina pulled her back. Lori's

top was too low-cut for her to be leaning like that.

"Hello," Marina replied.

I just smiled and nodded. His eyes were on me. It couldn't be.

"Would you like to dance?" he asked.

I glanced at Marina like she was my mother or chaperone or something. Lori had had too much to drink to be a good judge. She threw me a look that told me to be an adult and do what I wanted to do. Poor Marina had Lori to watch. She was right. I needed to make the call.

"Sure," I said too quickly. Not that I didn't get hit on. I was never the first. This time, except of course for Marina and the owner, I was the first. Why did it have to happen when I had a man I was interested in and already semi-intimate with?

As I got on the dance floor, I decided I didn't care. It was a dance, not a one-night stand or anything. He mentioned his name...Bill, I think. I mumbled mine but the music blared over any attempt at conversation.

The beat was fast and it felt good to move. Sitting with drunk Lori was funny but definitely not cathartic. I danced, not really caring how I looked. Bill—or was it Bob?—anyway, he was handsome and kept up with me. Two more fast songs later and there was a slow song.

He pulled me close to dance and I didn't object. It wasn't Lucas. Bill's cologne was different and he was too tall, but it felt nice. Halfway through the song, he slid his hands down my back and cupped my ass. I tensed and tried not to overreact. Lori once told me that I was forever overreacting to things. I wasn't going to do that here.

I kept dancing, waiting for the end of the song so I could return to my friends. Before then, he went from cupping to squeezing, and I shoved him. His hold was too good so I brought my knee up in a swift, sharp motion.

That made him let go. He grimaced and swore at me. I slipped out of his grasp as Marina and Lori appeared. I was surprised Marina didn't have her pepper spray out and at the ready.

"You okay?" Marina asked.

"Fine, let's go." I led the way and helped steady Lori. Marina brought up the rear and I heard her give some specific directions to the bouncer on what she wanted done with that creep.

"Nice shot, by the way." Marina poured Lori into the back seat before she got behind the wheel.

"Thanks." I was rather proud. I joined her in the front seat and stopped. I'd never noticed before because I'd always ended up in the back. "It's a stick."

"So? Didn't your dad make you learn on a stick?" Marina started the car, worth fifty grand if it cost a dime, and eased the car into traffic.

"No. Glad you're here or we'd be taking a cab home and coming back for the car later." I looked back to check on Lori, who, thankfully, had fallen asleep.

"She okay?" Marina asked.

"Sleeping." I nodded. "Sorry tonight sucked."

Marina shrugged. "Nothing special. Lori could've been a lot worse."

"Who were all those people in that back room?" I didn't want to talk about groper guy or Nick and Lori for a change. Anything except that, and we definitely weren't talking about Lucas.

"More friends from high school. I guess it's their regular spot because Louie comps them on almost everything. He thinks he's the king of the high-school crowd. I wanted to tell him we're not in high school anymore. I think his ego needs to still feel that way." Marina had clearly driven Lori's car before. She fiddled with the radio while changing lanes, kicking up the heat, changing gears, and didn't look for a thing.

"They sound sad," I replied.

"They *are* sad. I made a huge splash at my reunion because it said *doctor* before my name. Louie thinks we're the two big success stories from our graduating class. He wanted to hook up then."

"Why didn't you? I mean, he's not ugly or poor." I shrugged.

"I was dating Lucas at the time. Brokers impressed them, too. Better than a guy who runs a perpetual party for a living."

"Think he'll call?"

She laughed. "He'll call. I'll find an excuse to get out of it. Then Lori will want another party night or he'll invite us to some free hard-to-get-into thing at the club and we'll go. I just hope I have a man by then to fend him off. Louie's a nice guy. He's just too..."

"Too...?"

"Like my sisters' husbands. Stuck in the neighborhood and the family. Don't get me wrong. I love my family. I see them all the time. I didn't want to end up a housewife or a baker for my mom or a hair stylist. There's nothing wrong with those jobs. It's just that I had the brains to do what I *wanted*." She gestured as she made intermittent eye contact with the road then me as she rattled, driving with the other hand. Amazingly, I was following her story.

"I know my parents wanted me to be a nurse. I can't stand blood." I shuddered.

"You're a chef. You cut up dead animals and serve them to people every day." Marina looked at me as if I were crazy.

"Not that same thing at all. The meat comes prepackaged. Those animals are supposed to be dead. I don't want a job where I could potentially kill someone if I have a bad day," I explained.

"I always order everything well-done, right?" Marina asked.

"Yeah, why?" I shrugged.

"Just checking." She waved it off. "See, you get it. Louie doesn't get it. He thinks I want to spend every night hanging out with him and the gang at The Rattler. Do you even know what that place is?"

"Like a snake?" I guessed.

"Yeah, it was the name of his band in high school. Sort of cool back then. They aren't anymore. Not for me." She pulled the car into the parking garage and set everything back the way it had been.

We carefully extracted the half-sleeping Lori from the back seat—ass first. Marina insisted on that, and I didn't ask why. As we were about to ease her head from car, so she didn't whack it on the roof, she puked.

That was why. Marina didn't want her shoes ruined.

I grabbed the box of tissues from the front seat and propped Lori up, facing away from me. Marina shut the door and locked the car as I did a quick clean-up of Lori's chin. Guess I might have made it as a nurse after all.

"You're going to leave her car like that?" I stood there stunned. Gross!

"It's her car and her mess. You want to clean it up, be my guest." Marina tossed me the keys and steered Lori to the elevator.

I ran to catch up with them. Lori was going to have a bad morning. I didn't care. I'd had a great night. Seeing Lori drunk. Having a hot guy hit on me, even if he had been all hands. Talking with Marina on the ride home.

I had just enough alcohol in my system to feel good without worrying about a hangover tomorrow. We'd have to do this again! And Lucas no longer bothered me.

Yep! Just the right amount of alcohol and other men.

Chapter Twelve

Marina's Foot Comes Down

So far this week had not been good. It had been a horrid morning at work already. I was hiding in the office for a bit to keep my sanity. Between Nick, Eddie and Lori, all my energy had been sucked out and had left a headache behind. I didn't need this sort of drama.

Sure, I'd broken my drought of sex. Then my best friend had gone nuts and tried to beat me up. The only good thing about it was that Lori clearly still wanted Nick. She couldn't deny it anymore.

One problem down, but today was the day I'd promised to have lunch with Jen and Lucas. I wasn't looking forward to it at all. Even if the lunch was on him and the food was good, I didn't have an appetite.

I didn't want to see him. I didn't care about Lucas. I toyed with the idea of calling it off and claiming a migraine. That wouldn't be fair to Jen. Her hopes were up and her heart was set. It wouldn't kill me but I didn't really want to. Another reason I wasn't compatible with Lucas.

Frankly, I was stunned he'd agreed to it at all. Luckily, the odds of a scene with him were slim. Lucas didn't like scenes or fusses, especially in public. I didn't mind making a scene if that was what was needed.

It was for Jen, I reminded myself again and again. Once Jen saw the total lack of chemistry between Lucas and me, she'd back off and hopefully find a man of her own and get a sex life. Maybe then she'd understand how sex, attraction and love could mix or be totally separate.

The office was slow today. That allowed me to avoid my favorite patient. The puppy obedience class was going on and I knew Seth and Monster were out there.

I *could* go out, flirt casually, and it would end up like every other time. Attracted and frustrated. That pattern had grown tired and old. I didn't have the energy for being nice to two men in one day who weren't interested in me. Lucas, I had to be nice to, or Jen would get upset. Seth, maybe I could avoid him this once.

This time I'd decided to hide in the back, if possible, and fate was finally on my side. I sipped coffee in the office and wished it were after lunch and this was all over. Time was moving unbearably slowly.

A few minutes of doing nothing made me crazy, so I went into the back rooms and took out the litter of kittens to play with. They needed human contact and socialization. The black runt was gaining weight and growing bolder. My little favorite was the family instigator.

I was deeply involved with the kitten cuddling, scratching and wrestling and didn't hear the door open behind me. It wasn't until I felt someone next to me that I turned my head. I tried my best not to react.

It was Seth. I couldn't avoid him, even when I tried. My hope started to grow again. Maybe he was looking for me. Maybe this time it would be different. I squashed that fantasy quickly.

I had to say something. "Hi." I glanced behind him for a staff member. He was alone. "What are you doing back here?" I asked.

"I thought I'd visit the kittens, since they're still here. Class is over and Monster is getting spoiled by the assistants." Seth scooped up the black runt and she started purring even louder.

"She likes you." I had to smile. What could be cuter than a grown man, who seemed so serious and shy, cuddling a helpless ball of fur?

"She's gotten bigger," he observed. "They're not ready to

go yet?"

I shook my head. "No, they're still too tiny. They have to be able to eat solid food. Soon. Another week or so." I began toying with the other kittens. They chased my fingers and pounced on them. Their teeth could barely be felt, but those claws could use a trim.

"Found homes for them yet?" he asked.

"I don't know. I don't think so. The assistants keep track of the applications and stuff. I don't really get involved with that." I didn't even try to flirt. It hadn't gotten me anywhere and I wasn't in the mood. Every time I was ready to give up, Seth appeared to tempt me.

Not that I didn't want him. I wanted him. Dress pants in a slate gray and a maroon sweater made him look very trendy. More *in* than he really was. Odd clothes for a puppy-training visit. Maybe he had a lunch date.

Unfortunately, so did I. Sighing, I checked my watch. I wanted to get lunch over with.

"I'm sorry, am I keeping you from something?" Seth put the kitten down and she meowed in protest.

"No, just checking the time. I have to be somewhere for lunch with a friend and I don't want to be late." I scratched the runt under her chin and she rolled over on her back, wiggling in enjoyment.

I'd be thrilled to be late for lunch just to make Lucas wait. I preferred to get there and be settled first so I could appear calm and detached.

"It's almost eleven now." He ran a hand over the other kittens and smiled slightly at me. "I'll get out of your way. I'm sure you have some work to finish. Have a nice day, Dr. Castini."

"You too, Mr. Lauden," I said. I didn't look at him as he left. I barely smiled a polite, not overeager, smile. Was I losing interest?

No, I still enjoyed him. Felt that tingle when in his company. Maybe I'd just given up hope that he'd catch on. Some men were slow, and if he was that oblivious, he didn't deserve me.

It sounded good, anyway. The kittens and I knew better. This time would be no different.

Seth's runt friend licked my thumb and rubbed her face against it. She had a better chance of going home with Seth than I did.

Less than enthused about the rest of my day, I put the kittens back in their cage with a note to the assistant to trim their claws.

Then I returned to the office and took off my lab coat. Jen, this was for Jen, I told myself. One lunch wouldn't kill me. Lori was on the right track, I hoped. She'd seemed determined to get Nick back.

I wanted to believe her. Unfortunately, she could change her mind in a second for any reason. Lori could talk anyone into or out of anything. And she could do it to herself, too. I had to let that go for now. It was up to her. I was done stalking Nick for her.

I slipped into the bathroom and checked my makeup. Not bad. I touched up my lipstick and powder then dabbed perfume on strategic areas.

Not that I wanted to get Lucas back, but I could make him suffer. A woman never met an ex-boyfriend unless she was at her best.

I grabbed my stuff and headed out. I had a bad habit of being early. I'd rather have the drop on Lucas than the other way around.

I arrived fifteen minutes early and spotted Jen already sitting in a corner booth. I saw Lucas, partially obscured by her, in the booth, too.

My plot to be early was foiled. At least we could get started and get it over with. The first few minutes would be awkward, then it would be all downhill. I wanted it to be over with.

I got a bit closer and saw Lucas' arm go around Jen's shoulder. No, it couldn't be. My eyes were playing tricks. Jen and Lucas were playing a joke. It had to be. It couldn't be true.

I got a little closer again and it *was* true. They were making out like high schoolers. Lucas and a public display of affection?

Even in a low-lit restaurant like this, it wasn't normal for him. He'd changed, all right, yet he wasn't good for Jen. Lucas wasn't the type she should start off with. A terrible match all the way around.

She was too innocent. Lucas was a rough-around-the-edges type. Direct and lacking any savvy. A workaholic who would take her for granted if she wasn't careful. I had to put a stop to this for Jen.

I double-checked for a hidden jealous motive. Nope, I was clean. He was out of my system and this proved it. I cared about my friend, not my ex. Jen was a bit naïve for Lucas. The whole virgin thing wasn't a problem for Lucas to fix. Handling women well was not one of his talents. He lacked subtlety and patience.

The urge to break them up was pounding through me. Adrenaline and increased blood pressure made me feel like a jealous crazy woman. Just like Lori had looked yesterday. Though I wouldn't start a catfight over Lucas. He wasn't worth it to me.

On the other hand, I couldn't let Jen walk into the lion's den. The virgin wasn't up to playing in Lucas' league. I could be diplomatic, I decided. I'd catch them, Jen would be embarrassed, and I'd act like it was nothing. We'd have an awkward lunch and leave. Maybe we could just skip it and forget about it all.

Then, later, I'd explain to her that Lucas wasn't a good choice for her first sexual experience. That was more than she needed to deal with her first time. Shit, I hoped I wasn't too late for that. If I had to, I'd make her feel guilty for going after my ex. That would seal the deal. I didn't care. I'd use whatever I had.

With my plan ready, I took control of my temper as best I could and approached the table. I stood right in front of them and they didn't react at all. I cleared my throat, remaining unnoticed. Jen was practically in his lap to the point where I could barely see the top of his head. This was a new side of Jen.

"Hi, Jen," I said.

They broke apart like I was a nun catching them in the confessional—not that that had ever happened to me. Stupid Sister Mary Regina. I wish I'd been invisible that day! Too much repression in Catholic school for a co-educational environment if you ask me.

Jen was blushing the color of a good merlot but Lucas was... Lucas wasn't here. I opened my mouth and squinted. My contacts hadn't gone blurry. I closed my mouth, looked around for a hidden camera, rubbed my eyes and realized it was a real mess. Bigger than I ever imagined. Did I get the wrong day?

"Who the hell is this?" I asked. Was Lucas coming later? Jen had scored a nice, adorable guy? Good for her, however this wasn't the time or place to get to third base. Why did I have to be there for that lunch?

"Lucas?" Jen asked.

The man looked trapped like the rat that he was and refused to make eye contact. I hated it when men tried to weasel. This guy was up to something.

"I told you earlier. I called," he said. The guy blushed until his ears were red.

"No, that's not him." I put my hands on my hips and felt my mother's tone emerging from my mouth. I stepped closer and directed my voice at him—whoever he was. "Who the fuck *are* you?"

He appeared terrified and guilty. "Tim."

"You were serious? I thought it was a joke," Jen said.

"Tim who? Kidding about what? And what are you doing impersonating Lucas?" I demanded.

Jen was clearly useless. She looked ready to burst into tears, but too stunned to do that just yet. Her gaze darted from him to me, waiting for a punchline for it all to make sense. She was out of luck.

"Tim Richards. I work with Lucas at the brokerage firm." He answered my questions but spoke directly to Jen. "I'm sorry. I did try to tell you. I thought you understood."

"Why are you impersonating Lucas?" I asked rather loudly. Making a scene had never bothered me.

"Ma'am, is there a problem?" a male waiter, no more than twenty, asked.

"No, *ma'am*, there isn't," I snapped. Ma'am, my ass. Who the hell was a ma'am at this table? That guy was lucky I was mad at Tim or he'd get an earful. The waiter left us before I turned on him. I'd definitely inherited my mother's talent for inflicting fear and extracting the truth. Tim needed some fear put into him.

"I didn't mean to pretend to be Lucas. Jen was searching for him and I wanted to keep talking to her," he babbled. He appeared unsure whether to explain to me or to Jen. Neither of us was sympathetic.

"You're really not Lucas?" Jen's lip began to quiver. "You're Tim?"

"I'm so sorry. Everything else is true. I only lied about my name. I swear."

"Excuse me," Jen squeaked. She slid out of the booth and bolted for the door.

Tim looked like he was about to after her, but I stared him down. "Don't you dare," I warned.

"She was so single-minded after him that she barely glanced at me. I'm not a creep. Lucas is married with three kids. It would have been a waste of her time." He was younger than Lucas and lacked the smug ego Lucas wore proudly. Lucas would never apologize or be afraid of me.

"Tim Richards," I said. I needed to make sure I had his full attention.

"Yes?" he asked.

In a perverse way, I was enjoying the intimidation factor. I had the power over Tim right now and I was going to make sure he understood the ground rules. Since Jen was gone, we'd go with my ground rules.

"Stay the hell away from me, stay away from my friend, or I'll call up Lucas and have you fired." I grabbed the mostly full pitcher of frozen margaritas on the table and dumped it all in Tim's lap.

Then I strutted out of that restaurant, glaring at that waiter who'd dared to call me old. I knew this wasn't a place I'd be coming back to, ever, even if the food was supposed to be good. Ma'am, my ass!

This was turning out to be a hideous day. And now, I had to deal with the aftermath. If Lori out of control was bad, Jen was worse. I'd handled Lori countless times before. Jen wasn't normally like this.

I stepped out into the cold Chicago winter and looked up and down the street. I spotted Jen huddled at the corner. She was trying to cross to get to the L platform and blend into the crowd.

She had that deer-caught-in-the-headlights expression. I couldn't blame her, I didn't really understand what Tim had done or why he'd done it, but Jen was my concern now. Tim was history. Depending on how badly Jen reacted, I might get him in even more trouble. A call to Lucas for some real revenge wasn't out of the question. It was certainly warranted and could come later, if necessary.

I ran to get her and she started crying. "I'm sorry." She buried her face in my shoulder and I tried to comfort her as I hailed a cab. Jen was too shy to handle an emotional breakdown in public.

After pushing her into the taxi, I followed. "It's not your fault," I said, after telling the driver where to take us. "Some men are scum."

"Yes, it's my fault. I was a fool. He lied and I bought it. He tells the truth and I don't believe him. What's wrong with me? I fell for him and his story. I was going to tell you today that I wanted to date your ex, except now he isn't—he isn't Lucas." She started crying again.

Big heaving sobs that nothing except time could stop. I

was helpless. Mom would offer food, but alcohol might work better.

"It doesn't matter, Jen. This is about you and Tim." I didn't want to be reminded that I'd started all of this. Then I'd feel bad and it was Tim's fault.

"Then I failed on my end of the plan. I never even found Lucas." Jen's breathing was so fast I knew she'd hyperventilate if she didn't calm down.

"Breathe," I encouraged. What else was there to say? "I never cared about Lucas and Tim told me he was married with three kids. Tim lied to you. You have every right to be furious with him."

"I blew it." She shook her head. "I totally blew the game. I can't do *anything* right."

"I don't want Lucas, Jen. I never did. This was about Lori, remember? I'm relieved I didn't have to see Lucas. This Tim doesn't deserve your tears. He's the asshole here. Don't blame yourself."

She sniffed. "You're not mad?"

"Of course I'm not. And after I dumped the frozen pitcher of drinks in Tim's lap, I felt a lot better." I grinned. "Too bad I had to waste good tequila. It served a worthy purpose almost as enjoyable."

She laughed, and cried. "You didn't?"

"Hell, yes. He deserves worse. Say the word and I'll call Lucas and have him fired." I nodded.

"I don't know. I was the fool. I never got a business card or a phone number other than his cell. I was a complete idiot and I thought I was in love. I just believed that it was the best way to get a hold of him. I was enjoying myself."

"Jen, don't beat yourself up over it. I'm just glad he didn't hurt you." I shuddered to think what a manipulative jerk like that could've done to her if he had had the chance. There was no way of knowing how sick he was. What had possessed him to do such a thing?

"Hurt me? He lied, that hurts enough." She looked to be on the verge of tears again.

"I meant physically. Who knows why he was lying. What he was after. He could've been some perverted *Silence of the Lambs* type." Jen didn't see the big picture of dangers out there in the city.

"No, he wasn't like that." Jen shook her head. "He was nice."

I let my head drop into my palm. "Jen, for Christ's sake, you don't know what he's really like. You just learned his real name. Don't you dare defend him."

My lecture was met with sniffles and blubbering. Yelling at her wouldn't do any good. Lori sure was easier to fight with. Jen needed a more subtle approach.

We arrived at home and I paid for the cab. Jen and I got to her apartment and she was still silent. The zombie look in her eyes wasn't a good sign.

I called off work for the rest of the day and made Jen some tea. "Don't tell me you want him back?" I had to squash that romantic fantasy right away.

Jen was curled up on the couch. She managed to shake her head. "That jerk. We went out three times. He could've told me."

"Welcome to the dating world." I handed her a cup of tea. "It sucks."

She nodded slowly.

I had to say something. The truth wouldn't be as comforting. At least she'd believe it better than hollow consolation. "There are tons of liars, cheaters and complete assholes out there. Lori and I have had our share. Every woman has. You need to develop some instincts to pick them out. That's just practice. There are questions to ask that give you clues if he's hiding a wife or a girlfriend. If he's controlling. There's a lot to look out for."

"Why would he lie about his name?" Jen's tears were drying up.

"Who knows? Don't try to analyze him. Try to learn from this hideous experience with an idiot. That's how you pick out the liars."

"Why bother? Who needs men? I'll die a virgin. At least I'll avoid the zillion horrible men it could've taken me to learn this lesson. They're all creeps, like Lucas." Jen's voice had an edge of bitterness.

"Tim," I corrected. At least I now knew she hadn't slept with this Tim/Lucas imposter. "Don't go that far. My sisters found some decent guys. Lori's Nick never cheated or lied while they were a couple. Those guys are harder to find. You can't give up this fast."

"I deserved this." Jen nodded.

"No, you didn't. You've never done anything mean in your life." I tried to decide if alcohol would help or hurt Jen.

"It's karma. I dated your ex-boyfriend. Or at least a man who I *thought* was your ex-boyfriend. I felt so guilty. I couldn't help myself. He was so sweet and handsome and fun. I really believed he liked me. I was crazy about him. I've never felt that way before."

"And then you found out he was lying," I finished. "Jen, I was through with Lucas a long time ago. I don't want him back. I never did. Don't feel guilty about that part. Especially since it wasn't even really Lucas. Be mad at this Tim guy for lying. I have half a mind to call Lucas and warn him about what Tim did."

"No, don't." Jen seemed concerned.

"Why not? He's impersonating Lucas to pick up women. Lucas has a wife and kids who I'm sure wouldn't appreciate that. I have no idea why, but what if you aren't the only one Tim has done this with?" I suggested. "What if he does this a lot? What if he doesn't even work there? What if he's a scam artist taking advantage of women?"

"I don't think so." Jen sat up and went to the kitchen. She got a bottle of wine and a half-gallon of ice cream. "He had a pass card to the right office and didn't sound smooth or scripted."

"You actually made it up to the office with Tim?" I was surprised.

"Yeah, I got that far and he offered to help me since he

worked there. When I told him I was looking for Lucas, he just acted shocked. He said that I was searching for *him*. It was so genuine." She shrugged and stuffed a spoonful of ice cream in her mouth.

"Okay, so he works there and you knew that much is true." I paced the room and wondered if I should call Lucas.

Tim had said Lucas was married with kids. That made sense and now that I believed Tim worked there, I started to buy that Lucas was married with kids. He certainly wouldn't like the idea that a kid in the office was using his name and higher position to get women. On the other hand, Jen had brought up the name 'Lucas' — not Tim.

"What is it, Marina?" Jen asked.

"I'm not sure if I should bother calling Lucas or not." I wandered to the kitchen and grabbed a wine glass and a spoon. Then I joined Jen on the sofa for the ice cream binge. "I'll let you decide that."

Before my second spoonful, I remembered her saliva phobia. "I'll grab a bowl." I started to get up. Jen shook her head and offered the carton.

"If I can kiss a guy when I don't even know his real name, I can share ice cream." She smiled.

"Now that's *real* progress." I clinked my glass of merlot against hers and took another huge spoonful of rocky road. I was very proud in a big sister kind of way.

Chapter Thirteen

Jen on her High Horse

My apartment looked like a florist shop. At least five dozen roses were scattered around. Tim might be a liar, but he wasn't a cheap liar.

I'd read the first card from Tim, asking me to forgive him and hear him out. After that I just found a spot and stuck the vase of flowers there. I didn't need to start crying again and his notes sounded so sincere.

I'd called in sick to work for the past two days, ever since Lucas had confessed to being Tim. Marina had kept me from going over the edge that first day and quitting or moving home to Wisconsin. The depression had yet to go away, though. I wanted to disappear. I wanted to run away. Gullible me wanted to hear Tim out, yet I'd fallen for too much already.

I'd been a fool. I'd missed all the huge glowing neon warning signs. Lesson learned, but that had been a pretty awful way to do it. I *was* naïve.

The phone rang again. I had the answering machine volume turned down so I didn't have to listen. Tim had given up calling after one day. I'd saved the messages. My friends tried to keep tabs on my mood.

I couldn't bear to listen to his voice.

I'd heard his apology in the restaurant, but that didn't excuse his actions. What possible explanation could he give?

So, my couch and the cast of *Days of Our Lives* had become my friends while Lori and Marina were at work. I'd tried

Jerry Springer on the advice of one of my dumb brothers. He thought I'd feel better about myself seeing those people's *real* problems. All I saw was myself in a bad tube top starring in one of those stories.

Besides, the men on *Days* looked a whole lot better with their shirts off. Jerry's guests, who frequently took off way too much, were mostly gross. And soaps fed my romantic fantasy world. That was probably a bad thing, even though it felt good. Right now, I needed it.

It made me feel safe, anyway. My mom had watched this soap opera when I'd been a little girl and I had gotten to watch it on summer breaks or when I'd been at home sick from school. Bo and Hope looked older, but not the twenty years it had been. Amazing they were the same actors.

And they were still my friends. Their love was pure and true and any identity questions were blamed on the evil Stefano. It was nice to know the good guys from the bad guys so clearly. True love like Bo and Hope's only occurred in Salem, U.S.A. Too bad we didn't know what state that town was in, or I'd move there.

The rest of the day, I avoided my phone, cleaning and any talk shows dealing with relationships. When desperate, I'd replay *Days of Our Lives*.

Tim and I didn't qualify as a relationship, no matter how much it hurt. I understood Lori's fear and frustration, even if only a little bit. Letting someone else hurt you like this was insane. Love was my new definition for insanity.

There was a knock on the door. I turned down the TV volume to make sure it wasn't my shows. Must be six o'clock. "Who is it?" I didn't move from the couch where I lay sprawled in flannel pajama pants and a Curious George T-shirt, cocooned in a fleece blanket.

"It's Marina. Open the door," came the reply. The door shook as she tried the knob. I'd locked my door today on the off chance that Tim had tracked me down. Then again, maybe I wanted him to stop by. I couldn't be caught looking like this.

"Coming." I dragged myself off the couch and undid the locks. I opened the door and immediately turned around and went right back to the sofa.

"How are you doing?" Marina asked. She stepped inside and closed the door, locking it. Marina walked into the kitchen and put some things into the fridge.

I shrugged. "I learned to lock my door finally. Proud of me?"

"Thrilled. Didn't go to work again?" she asked.

I shook my head and grabbed another cookie. My eyes focused on the television.

"Jen, no man is worth this. You can't hide in here forever." Marina made a space on the coffee table, moving chip bags and candy bar wrappers out of the way to sit. "You'll run out of sick and vacation time eventually."

"Don't care." I didn't care down to the tips of my toes. I didn't even care that I was talking with my mouth full. "Haven't heard about my interview, either, and I don't care about that, either. Doesn't matter anymore."

"Lucas called me." Marina took my remote and turned the television off for the first time in two days. She could be so bossy when she wanted.

As long as the TV was on, I wasn't alone with my thoughts. And *Nick at Nite's* sitcoms from my growing-up years were very soothing at two in the morning. *Sleeping is harder than it should be when you're depressed.* It would feel better just to sleep and wake up when it was over.

"Lucas/Lucas or Tim/Lucas?" I asked.

"Lucas/Lucas," she said. "Tim talked to him about the whole mess. Confessed everything."

"Great, now your ex-boyfriend knows what a fool I was." I pulled a blanket up over my head. "Hope the whole office had a huge laugh over me."

"No, not like that. It means Tim isn't doing this regularly or on purpose."

I shrugged. "I didn't even believe him when he told the truth. I thought it was a joke to get out of the lunch with you."

"Lucas actually called to tell me how great Tim is. And how miserable he's been since he upset you."

"Lucas said that he's a good guy?" I asked from under the blanket.

"Yeah, and he doesn't say nice things about people very often. Tim is actually Lucas' employee, so he knows. For whatever it's worth."

"You're on his side now?" I glared at my friend. I needed support, not betrayal.

"No, he was absolutely wrong and he knows it. Lucas was pissed that Tim did this. Apparently, you were so determined to get to Lucas that you weren't willing to give Tim your number or accept a date. Then when he did tell you…"

"I thought it was a joke. Who does that?" I punched a throw pillow hard and stayed under the blanket.

"I know, I know. I'm not defending him. I told Lucas I'd tell you some things about Tim. He's thirty-one, a good employee who has never been married, and has no kids. Lucas said he's a nice and decent guy. Tim screwed up big time, but if Lucas was willing to call on his behalf, he has to have good points, too."

It finally dawned on me that Marina had had contact with her ex. She'd actually talked to Lucas. At least the plan had been completed on my end. I peeked out from under the blanket. "You talked to Lucas?"

Marina nodded. "He's married with three kids, like Tim said. We caught up and we're not interested in each other. Are you happy now?"

I shrugged. "At least you talked to him."

"Are you going to go back to work tomorrow, Jen?" Marina asked.

"I don't know. Might as well call off on Friday, too." I inhaled and tried to wake up. Something smelled good. "What's that?"

"I stopped on the way home. Mom made vegetable

soup and some salad to go with her bread. It's her cure for depression. I realize you and the Frito-Lay Company have a new relationship and Ben and Jerry's is now your primary source of calcium. But a little real food can't hurt. Want a bowl?" she asked.

I nodded and waited as Marina got up and brought back a bowl of soup, a plate of salad and two hunks of bread. She handed me the bowl.

"I can't eat all of that," I protested.

"If you can stuff yourself with junk food for three days, sure you can. Who cares if you blow up to Jabba the Hut size and we have to get a crane to get you off the couch in a year." Marina handed me a spoon.

Fine, she'd made her point. I sat up and rubbed my eyes, focusing on her and making eye contact for the first time. "Sorry I've been a mess." I bit into the bread and felt better.

"Sometimes you have to be a bitch to make your point. Doesn't bother me." Marina shrugged and took the other piece of bread. "You're only hurting yourself by letting Tim get to you like this."

"So what do I do? Hear him out? Forget him?" I asked. The soup smelled so good I dug in. Junk food was not enough to live on.

"I don't know," Marina admitted. "Both would be a step. Which step is right is up to you. Do you want to hear him out? Do you care? If it'll help you get over what he did, do it. If you're better off just forgetting about him, then get back to your routine."

I chewed and thought. "Too soon to tell," I concluded. It was nice that, for once, Marina didn't have the answer. Part of me wanted her to tell me what to do, but I had to be an adult about this.

"Fair enough. You won't find the answer here." Marina picked up the salad and ate, careful not to spill any on the floor. "You might want to start cleaning here first, then get back to work on Monday."

"Wow." I stared at Marina in disbelief.

"What?" she asked.

"If you're telling me I need to clean, I'm really out of control." I started to laugh.

Marina grabbed one of my throw pillows and smacked my shoulder. "You're lucky Lori will be here soon. I can't take much more of the Tim and Lucas drama."

"I don't need either of you to babysit me," I argued. "I can wallow on my own."

"No, just one babysitter. I have to go get my mother's car from Nick's garage. I told Mom I'd go with her. So Lori will be here soon for her shift." Marina went to the fridge and got a can of Diet Coke.

"I'll be fine until Lori gets here," I said. "Don't be late on my account."

Marina studied me, her hand on her hip, tapping her long fingernails. I could tell she was trying to decide if she should trust me or not.

"I have real food, the Soap Opera Channel, and cleaning to do. I'll be fine. And Lori won't let me get away with acting stupid, either."

"You promise you'll be good?" she asked.

"I swear, Mom." I gave her my most angelic face and fluttered my eyelashes.

"Fine, I don't believe you. I'll check in on you tomorrow after work." Marina left and I locked the door behind her. Five minutes later, I was back on the couch, blanket over my head, asleep.

* * * *

The loud pounding on my door pulled me from my weird dreams about Tim. Lori shouted at me from the other side. She sounded pissed.

I rolled off the couch and dragged myself to the door. Lack of movement made my muscles hurt worse than going to the gym. I didn't like the feeling at all.

"What's wrong with you?" I opened the door and Lori

stumbled in.

"I've been knocking for ten minutes." Lori stopped cold. "Marina wasn't exaggerating."

"I know, I know, it's a mess. A disaster area. You still didn't have to pound on the door like I'd swallowed a whole bottle of aspirin. I'm not that bad to be suicidal over a man."

"Glad to hear that." Lori dug into the salad and soup then handed me a large envelope.

"What is it?" I asked.

"How the hell should I know?" Lori shrugged. "It was stuck under your door. Too big for our little mailboxes downstairs, I guess."

I looked at it. There was no return address or postage. I had a funny feeling that it was from Tim. He'd gone from flowers to who knew what?

"Are you psychic or are you going to open it?" Lori settled in an overstuffed chair since I'd clearly taken over the couch.

"You open it." I handed it to her.

"It's not mine," she argued.

"Please," I begged.

"No," she refused.

"It's from Tim. I know it is. I don't want to backslide." It sounded good and rational, I hoped.

"You'll go to work on Monday?" Lori asked. Clearly Marina had briefed her via cell phone before the handoff of babysitting shifts.

"I promise. Cleaning tomorrow and work on Monday." I crossed my heart.

"Fine." Lori ripped open the envelope and scanned the top page of a thick stack stapled together.

"Well?" I asked.

"You said you didn't want to know." Lori set it aside and looked around the room. "You do need to clean in here, Jen. It's not like you at all."

She really wasn't going to tell me. How could she do this?

I stopped the panic. I could handle this, or pretend to. "I know. I'll do it tomorrow."

"Good." Lori nodded and kept eating.

"You don't have to stay late with me. I know you have to go to work tomorrow." Maybe if I got her to go I could peek at the papers. They had to be from Tim or she'd have told me what they really were.

"No, I don't. I took the day off." Lori smiled and kept reading.

"Why? What are you doing?" That wasn't like Lori. An unscheduled day off. Any day off was weird, but normally they were carefully planned.

"I have something I need to do." She shrugged.

"What?" I persisted.

"I thought I might go and talk to Nick." Her eyes stayed focused on the paper.

"Really? That's great." I couldn't hide my smile and hugged her tightly.

"Calm down. We aren't back together yet. And you can't tell Marina." Lori's face went dead serious at that and she jabbed her finger at me.

"Why not?" I pouted.

"She doesn't need to know about this until the results are in." Lori got out of the chair and rummaged through my freezer. Of course, she took the papers with her. She was going to torture me.

"What are you looking for?" I asked.

"Ice cream."

"That won't help your nerves." I helped her anyway and found chocolate ice cream for her.

"You're one to talk. You've got more wrappers and chip bags than a convenience store." She finally settled in the chair again and dug into the carton. "I need a little comfort food."

I started to clean up the garbage. After a few minutes of quiet, I couldn't wait anymore.

"Lori, what was in the envelope?" I demanded.

"A background check complete with a criminal record." She shrugged.

"What? Whose?" I flopped on the couch confused.

"Tim's. There's a note, too. Basically he had a background check run on himself for your review."

"Like that matters. He lied and at the last minute tried to save his ass." I fumed as I tried to take the papers. Lori quickly sat on them.

"Give it. It's going in the trash." I grabbed again. I had to get rid of Tim.

"No, that's not the right attitude," Lori scolded.

"Excuse me? He's a liar, and my attitude is very much justified."

"If Nick feels that way, he won't even hear me out tomorrow. I didn't lie. By believing him, I screwed up our relationship. Do you want to ruin my hopes? Why should I ever go then?" Lori was such a lawyer—too smooth and went for the jugular. I felt like I'd walked right into it.

"I don't know what to do about it. I barely know the guy." I wrapped the blanket around myself again. He felt like a stranger and yet not.

"No, no getting sad again. You're not allowed." Lori caught the tail of my blanket and unraveled me with freakish strength.

"What should I do then?" I asked.

"What should Nick do?" she returned.

"Don't do that. You and Nick had a real relationship. This was a few dates with a guy who told me a big lie." He didn't embellish his job title or what kind of car he drove. That much I knew.

"And you can let it end things or clear the air. Your call." Lori slumped in the chair.

"You're really going to talk to Nick tomorrow?" I pressed.

"I want to. I hope I can bring myself to get out of the car this time. I've tried." Lori stuck the spoon in her mouth again.

"You have to." Why did I have a strong feeling that Nick

and Lori would be okay? Too many romance novels stuffed under my bed? Marina's unshakeable belief in them? I didn't know the reasoning, but I knew it was right.

"I'll talk to him if you read this background check and his note." Lori was negotiating with me.

"Why should I?" I wasn't going to make it that easy on her.

"Because reading his information won't kill you. It won't even embarrass you because he's the one who was wrong, not you. Seeing Nick again could cause me serious humiliation and heartbreak."

"Okay, okay. If I promise to read it, you'll promise to get out of the car and see Nick?"

"Cross my heart." Lori made an exaggerated cross over her left breast and held up her hand.

"Okay, I'll read it."

"And you won't throw it away until at least Monday?" Lori put a condition on it.

"Yes, okay, fine, whatever." I held out my hand and Lori gave me the papers. She kept eating ice cream as I carefully read every word.

"Men suck," I sighed.

"And lick if you're lucky." Lori smiled.

I blushed and tossed a throw pillow at her head. I couldn't look her in the eye. Tim had done both and well.

"Wait a minute. How far did you and Tim get exactly?" Lori asked.

"Lori, I wouldn't. I *thought* he was Marina's ex-boyfriend. I wanted her to be okay with it first." Technically, that was true. I wanted it.

Lori watched me for a few seconds with squinty eyes, letting the silence fill the room. "Nothing?" she asked finally.

There I was, caught. Marina had clearly seen us kissing and no doubt had filled Lori in on everything she knew. "Not sex, but it wasn't nothing."

"Not sex, intercourse sex?" Lori wasn't giving up.

"I'm still a virgin, if you must know."

"I knew it. You had to be intimate with him to be this upset over it. Oral at the very least. Was it good?" she asked.

"I'm trying to read here." I did try, except my brain was now on that night when we'd actually had a real date and I hadn't been able to get enough of him.

"So don't tell me. At least your reaction makes sense now. Better see if he included an HIV test in that background check, just in case."

My face froze. The words on the page blurred as reality hit me. "I wouldn't be that stupid," I lied. "I barely knew him."

"You didn't do him? Okay. Condoms and oral are a real pain." Lori shrugged.

I had. "Check to be sure." I tossed Lori the pages and she looked at me with a raised eyebrow.

She knew I'd lied. Why hadn't I thought of that? I knew better. I hadn't been thinking at all at the time. My first really good sexual experience and it could kill me. How could I have been so stupid?

"He is thorough. And negative." Lori folded back to that page and showed it to me.

"Thank God," I exhaled.

"Now you're sure you can't be pregnant, right?" Lori went back to eating ice cream. If she wasn't careful, she'd finish off that entire half gallon on her own.

"How could I be? I swallowed." I felt like my mom was giving me the third degree. Lori was so matter-of-fact about it.

"It's not always just about where the cum landed. How do I put this? Did the sperm stick ever venture near pussy central?" Lori kept a straight face as she sounded like a character from *Sesame Street*.

I burst out laughing at her. She sounded like a cartoon, not a sex lecture. I laughed and she laughed. My eyes began to tear and my sides hurt by the time I got control. I felt better if nothing else.

"No," I managed. "Nowhere near."

"Good, because it's been a few days and I don't want to find out you're knocked up and have to go through that stuff, too." Lori sat back and looked down at her ice cream. "I ate this much?"

"Yeah." I nodded. "Might as well finish it now. I don't need any more junk."

"Why did you let me eat so much?"

"I didn't know I was your food monitor." I rolled my eyes and started reading Tim's background check with a more skeptical eye. Maybe he'd left the bad stuff out. Or maybe this was all a fake.

"I'm stress eating." Lori put the spoon in the sink and tossed the rest of the ice cream in the trash. "It's all Nick's fault."

"You're in the right place for it." I waved at my sea of wrappers and bags. "This is what men do to us."

"Exactly. I did the same thing after Nick and I broke up. Only more alcohol than sugar." Lori was clearly on a sugar high as she paced my living room.

"Then you'd better go and see him tomorrow so you can burn off all those calories." I grinned.

Lori shot me a dirty look with a smile behind it. "Nick did have the touch. I could never get enough of him. Even if he won't talk, we could always just hook up. I bet I could still seduce him first and he'd ask questions later."

"Doubtful. I think there is too much emotion there for that. Fight first."

"Fine, fight first. Screw later. You're probably right. Just as long as we get there." Lori sat back down and seemed lost in thought.

I kept flipping through Tim's report. How could I be sure? I mean, one hundred percent sure this was true? "Lori, would you do me a favor?"

"What?" Lori asked absently.

"Can you get another background check run on Tim? I want to make sure he's not lying. This could be a fake."

I dropped it on the coffee table with the other garbage. "What if he just filled it out himself?"

"No problem." She picked it up. "Give me a day or two. Think he might be worth another look?"

I wasn't sure, but didn't want to confess that weakness. That strong temptation to be near him again, whatever his name was.

"I need to know he doesn't have any diseases and that really is his clean criminal record."

"Medical stuff can be hard to get, but I'll try." Lori tucked the report next to her. "All the reports won't restore the trust. For that, you need to talk to him."

I glanced at the clock. It was nearly two in the morning. "If you're going to talk to Nick tomorrow, you'd better go get some sleep or he might not want you."

Lori looked at her watch and did a double take. "Okay. You go to bed, too."

"I will, I promise." I tugged my blanket around me on the couch.

"No." Lori grabbed the blanket and pulled it and me off the couch with a thud. "You're going to sleep in your bed like a normal person."

"Okay, okay." I stepped out of the blanket and went to the door to lock up after Lori left.

"Straight to bed," Lori lectured as she walked into the hallway.

"You know, you and Marina will make great moms someday. You both nag and guilt like pros." My sarcasm was not lost on her.

"If you didn't need it, we wouldn't do it. You're the one who blew a guy and you didn't even know his real name," Lori returned.

I stuck my tongue out at her and closed the door. She was right. I'd lost my mind.

Chapter Fourteen

Lori and the Mechanic

I'd barely slept all night after leaving Jen. The thought of seeing Nick had kept me up and when I finally had slept, the dreams had been about him. They hadn't been good. Bad karma, as Jen would say. In every nightmare, he'd turned his back and wouldn't talk to me. That was my worst fear. I needed to talk to him. At ten in the morning, I gave up sleeping and forced myself out of bed.

A quick and very hot shower freshened up and cleared my head, then I carefully shaved every inch of my legs and touched up the bikini area. I didn't have any real hopes for today. What a lie!

Better to be safe than sorry, I decided. I'd been going over and over my possible outfit options all night and had yet to decide completely.

Getting dressed took forever. Jeans and his old sweatshirt was a tempting outfit. He'd see through it. He'd like it, no doubt, and he'd tease me for it. I wanted to do as much of the talking as I could.

I dressed like normal, except with a few alterations. The skirt was simple and black. It was also one of my shortest skirts, with a slit even Marina wouldn't approve of.

I refused any thought of pantyhose. They'd get in the way of things if they went well.

Topping off the outfit was his favorite blouse, a sexy red that would get me noticed by every man in Chicago. Even the gay guys would approve of my fashion sense.

Of course the topper was the shoes. Nick was well over

six feet tall so I could wear stilettos and not even look him in the eye. Red stiletto heels would be unforgettable and so would the contortion of my feet.

I'd touched up my nail polish last night. Even Jen had noticed the 'I'm Not Really a Waitress' shade. I did my makeup carefully and layered on the red lipstick. Didn't know why, but red lips had a strange effect on men. And I was determined it wouldn't rub off until I rubbed it off on Nick in as many places as I could.

The base lipstick was one of those that wouldn't come off under water, kissing or chemical peel. Next was a less matte, long lasting one. Then I let those set, patted with face powder, another coat of each and topped that with shiny red lip-gloss. It was perfect. I hoped it would have the desired effect.

If he didn't shut up long enough to hear me out, I'd have no chance with Nick, ever. He could still show me the door, but I'd jump-start his hormones for sure. Maybe that would buy me some extra time.

I covered the outfit with my ankle-length black wool trench coat. The element of surprise was another advantage I wanted on my side. I even wrapped a long scarf around my neck to hide any hint of cleavage. It was the first time I was glad Chicago had such rough winters. Who knew what type of attention I'd attract walking through Nick's garage without the long coat?

Driving in stilettos wasn't easy, especially in slushy Chicago weather, so I took my time on the way to the garage. It was that, or I kept growing more and more nervous the closer I got to Nick's place of employment. I had to be subtle and try not to get him into trouble.

Parking the car, I took a deep breath and counted to ten. Moments later, I stepped into Nick's garage. I noticed the sign said 'Nick's Southside Garage'. Marina had never mentioned that. I must have missed it during my drive-bys. All I'd ever been looking for was Nick.

As I made my way through the rows of cars and men,

I got plenty of whistles and winks, and that was with the coat buttoned! Finally, I spotted Eddie, Marina's sex toy. I'd almost missed him with his clothes on. Maybe he could help me not chicken out.

"Morning, Lori." Eddie nodded.

"Hi, is Nick around?" I tried not to fidget with my hair or anything else. My nerves were getting the best of me. I knew I wanted Nick back. It wouldn't be easy. It might not even be possible.

"Nick, sure. The boss is in the office. Right back that way on your right." Eddie smiled and went back to his brake job.

"The boss?" I confirmed.

"Yeah, Nick bought the place about a year or so ago. Old man Jerry retired and sold it to him." Eddie shrugged. "Good luck."

"Thanks." I nodded and walked slowly in the right direction. He'd bought it? Nick really owned a business? I could see him in the office through the door's window. He was on the phone pacing and looking seriously sweet. Sexy as ever and so adorable.

I couldn't stand there forever. Waiting wouldn't help. Every second made me more and more nervous. I knocked on the door and opened it. Nick turned to see me and his expression went from normal to poker face.

"I'll call you back," Nick said to whoever was on the other line. He hung up slowly and put the file in his hand down on the desk.

"Hi." What a great opening. Had I practiced that? My brain was blank. How could I be completely at a loss? This was worse than any jury or judge.

"What brings you here, car trouble?" He sat and folded his hands behind his head.

The façade was intended to look casual. Thankfully, I could see through him. He was nervous, too. I wanted to touch him so bad my fingers ached.

"No, the car's fine. I'm the one having some serious

trouble." I took off the coat and tossed it at a metal and vinyl chair.

"You sick?" he asked. His gaze roamed slowly up and down.

"Mentally." I nodded. "I screwed up years ago and I've been a mess since."

"Did Marina tell you that?" he asked.

"No, she came to make sure you wouldn't throw me out. Marina doesn't tell me what to do. She's my friend and I needed help. I was afraid I couldn't get this far." A tiny little lie, but I wasn't about to tell him about Marina's plan until I had him back. I took a step closer and toyed with his nameplate. "Will you hear me out?"

"I haven't kicked you out yet." He shrugged as he watched my fingers like I was a shoplifter. It was the nails, I realized.

"Okay, I made a mistake. I've been paying for it ever since. I want to fix it."

"And you think red lipstick, nail polish and slutty heels will do it?" he asked.

"No. I missed this. I missed dressing sexy and feeling sexy. I missed you. I miss how I felt when I was with you. I liked myself better." I forced my voice not to shake and my eyes never left his.

He just stared back. His eyes were cold and unreadable. Maybe the outfit had been too much? I'd overdone it and ruined everything.

"What about your parents?" he challenged.

"I don't care. They can't stop us. I won't let them. I want to take you to their Eve of Christmas Eve party. I want you back in my life." There, I'd said it. I'd swallowed my pride, put my ego and heart on the line. Now it was all up to him.

Why did this feel like a bad TV movie all of a sudden? Unfortunately, the anticipation was real and I couldn't expect a happy ending.

"Why me? Why not find some other inappropriate guy who they'll hate?" Nick got up from his chair and came closer to me.

"I don't want anyone else. This isn't about my parents. I don't care if they love you or hate you." I took a deep breath and tried to stay calm. I'd never thought about how hard it would be to say the right words.

I'd been so focused on getting there that what to say had never sunk in. Everything I'd practiced before felt stupid and there weren't enough words to express what I felt. Marina had frequently told me I had a degree in arguing. Why wasn't it helping now?

Nick was so mad he was calm, which was the worst level. I held my ground as best I could. I had to take it, let him get his anger out. Yet, he remained silent.

"I don't care what they say to me or think of me. I'm sick of living my life to avoid upsetting people. I'm thirty fucking years old. I finally know what I want and I want you."

"Why?" he demanded through a clenched jaw.

Nick, my Nick, was just a few inches from me now. I could barely think straight.

"Hate me if you want, I deserve it." I shrugged. "I'd have hated myself forever if I didn't come here and try to get you back. I'm not great at this emotional stuff. I'm trying."

"That's not an answer. I'm not a birthday present or consolation prize because you haven't talked any blue blood, inbred moron into marrying you." He turned his back on me. That was it. That couldn't be it. He had it all wrong. I had to do something.

"No!" I grabbed his arm. "This isn't about my birthday. That was just the wake-up call I needed to see that my life wasn't mine, not really."

"What the hell does that mean?" he snapped.

"I was myself with my friends and at work. I kept that separate from my family. I led a different life for them. I can't do that anymore. I can't be happy like that."

"Marina was good enough to meet the parents." He tossed a pen at his computer.

"Not really. You should hear the things they say about her behind her back. She's my friend. You should know

190

they'll be ten times as hard on you. They'll probably hide it less, too.

You don't have to worry."

"Why?" He folded his arms, trying to put me off more. "What's the difference?"

"Because I love you and nothing they'll say can ever change that." I looked him the eye, then looked at my shoes before the tears started. They slipped down my face anyway.

The silence made me want to give up and leave. I wasn't running away. Not this time. I rubbed my neck nervously. A tension knot was forming fast. "Say something," I whispered. I loved hearing his voice, though he could ruin my hopes with one word.

He didn't. Nick just walked closer. He reached behind me and I knew he was going to open the door and throw me out. I didn't hear the door. Instead, I would've sworn I heard the blinds close.

I turned to see how mad he was and reached for him before he opened the door. My blouse gaped and his hand reached for my neck. His medic-alert necklace had come out from under the blouse and caught his eye.

"That's mine," he said.

I nodded. "I saved everything. I needed to have something of yours on me today."

"Not your usual jewelry." He swallowed.

"I have unique taste, not really expensive." I shrugged.

He crushed his mouth against mine in a sneak attack. Nick pulled me to him hard and he tongued his way into my mouth. I was so stunned I couldn't react fast enough. I could taste my own tears on his lips and my brain finally registered it wasn't a dream.

Years, my brain screamed, as I kissed him back. I'd been waiting for this for years. I'd wasted three years without Nick. That was never going to happen again.

Never again!

I clutched him like he was my purse on the L. Nick was

the only place I truly felt safe and I'd forgotten how good it had felt. He lifted his head but didn't let me go. His body felt so good.

"You're sure?" he asked.

I nodded in a daze. "Move in with me?" It was all I could think of. The words flew out of my mouth before my brain even processed them. That was too much, too fast. He'd never agree. I'd pushed my luck. The heart was talking and I didn't want to take it back.

"Not in your dad's building," he replied. He was smiling at me. I loved that smile.

What? Was that a yes? "Okay, we'll find a new place together."

He nodded. Nick was finally smiling at me. "How much of your red lipstick do I have on me?"

I laughed, trying to stop crying as I wiped off the lipstick I'd smeared on him with every kiss. He wasn't going to torture me with guilt or humiliate me. He wasn't going to make me pay or beg.

"All better," I said.

"Good. Let's go." He grabbed my coat and his, pulling me by the hand out the door.

"Where are we going?" I asked.

"My little brother is at my place for holiday break, so I guess we're going to your place. I'm getting you alone one way or another." Nick didn't stop walking for a second, even when applause rang out from his employees.

I just smiled and kept up with him. Suddenly, everything fell into place.

When Nick got something in his head, it was impossible to get it out. He took my keys, drove my car, then parked it in my own building without a word.

Normally, I hated it when other people drove my car. I'd loaned it to Marina once, but that had been a special occasion. She drove it when I was too drunk, too, of course. Nick had been the only other person to drive it, ever. Somehow, it felt sexy to have him driving my car. I couldn't explain why if I tried. I liked it.

Instead of annoying, it felt like a dream to have him behind the wheel. To have him back with me. I didn't care where we went. His place, my place or a hotel. As long as he was there, too.

I kept touching him to make sure I hadn't lost my mind. This was really happening. My fingers knew his body by memory. The texture of his hair, the muscles in his arms, and the roughness in his hands were familiar and exciting. The memories flooded back happy now, no longer painful. It was just the beginning.

The fact that we were headed to my building was a great relief. I rested my head on his shoulder and inhaled. Same cologne mixed with the smell of grease and sweat. He must still work on cars, even though he was the boss. I could see the grease on his hands.

"Falling asleep on me?" he asked.

"Not yet." I grinned. "You smell good."

"You always were weird. I like that, Lori." He turned off the engine and kissed my forehead, nose and mouth. Then, rather reluctantly, we exited the car.

We boarded the elevator alone, thankfully. My hands were under his warm winter coat and up his back in no time. Nick sank his fingers into my hair as I kissed his neck.

It was a fast elevator or I'd have pushed for more contact. One day, we'd try sex in that elevator. I didn't want experimentation now. I just wanted to be alone with him. I longed for that familiarity.

"You never were patient," he joked.

The elevator stopped and I pulled him toward my door.

"Don't I get to meet your friends?" he asked. "You can't hide me anymore."

I glanced down at my watch. "It's only four o'clock. They'll both still be at work. Later, if you're not too exhausted." I grinned and pushed him into my apartment. I wanted to be alone with him first. Then I'd show him off. I knew he was worth it.

The door closed behind us and Nick stripped my coat off me before anything else.

"You like it, don't you?" I turned around so he got the full effect.

He didn't say anything as he removed his own jacket and closed in on me. Before I could say anything, his hands were on me. He went down my neck, back, hips and thighs. I shivered under his touch.

"Your legs are cold," he whispered.

"No pantyhose." I shrugged.

Nick knelt and used his rough hands and warm mouth to heat my legs slowly all the way up. Did he have any idea what he was doing to me? He was so close. I'd bet he could smell how wet I was.

"Are you trying to drive me crazy?" I moaned.

Nick didn't say a word. He bunched my skirt up around my waist to get a look at the red thong I had on. "Who's driving who crazy?" he asked.

I grinned and suddenly found myself over his shoulder like he was a Neanderthal. "What are you doing?" I squirmed and tried to brace myself.

He didn't answer me as he marched into the bedroom and dropped me on the bed. He tugged away my blouse, and the see-through black bra I had on underneath seemed to meet with his approval. Nick groped my breasts through the bra like he'd never seen them before. It had been so long that neither of us could wait. Finesse would come later.

It was my turn. I pulled off his T-shirt and unzipped his jeans, pushing them down to his knees. He tried to kick off his boots while standing up. I threw him off balance and brought him onto the bed. I made quick work of his shoes, socks and jeans.

I eased my hands up in his legs to his underwear. He had a great ass and nice legs for the boxer-briefs he had on. That red color on my nails looked good against the gray cotton as I traced and teased his swollen package.

"Come here," he growled.

I glanced at him, innocently. I ran my fingers up his chest and he grabbed me so I landed flush against him. A glorious feeling.

Nick kissed me while unhooking my bra. I responded by grinding my hips into his. I pushed his underwear down. I kissed down his chest, over his flat stomach, until I nipped his narrow hip.

"Now you." He nodded.

I glanced down and realized he wanted the thong gone. "You don't think it's sexy?"

"You'd be sexy in granny underwear. Now get out of them and those insane shoes before you stab me or fall and hurt yourself." He reached and pulled the thong down but didn't get far before the material snapped back.

I finished the job, even getting rid of the shoes that made me feel like Jessica Rabbit and killed my feet. He thought I'd be sexy in anything. I fell back onto him, teasing his cock with my mouth and that familiar taste of him reminded me just how long it had been.

"No games," he warned. Nick pulled me up and pinned me with a quick flip. The deep kiss and sudden warmth zapped all thoughts away. "You're really sure you want me back?" he asked with a grin.

I dug my fingernails into his shoulders and arched my back, trying to push him beyond teasing. "Damn, Nick. Please," I demanded.

"See, I did make you beg." Nick pressed his cock against my pussy, rubbing along the inner folds until I was biting as his neck while my hips matched his.

Nick's mouth caught mine and I opened my eyes. I couldn't look away. He watched my eyes as he sunk into me slowly. I'd never felt so wonderful and so vulnerable in my life. And it was so familiar, like we'd never been apart. This feeling should last forever.

"Nick," I whispered. He kissed me and our bodies took over. It didn't take long for both of us to hit intense orgasms.

"Next time you won't get off so easily." He nibbled my

shoulder as he stayed on top of me.

"As long as there are a lot of next times, I don't care." I stretched and he responded by rolling over. The most I could manage was to snuggle against him. He'd sucked out all of my energy. "I'm starving."

He laughed. "Same old Lori. Eats like a horse and still too skinny." Nick ran his hands over me, taking inventory. "We'll have to stuff you with food."

"I ate almost an entire half gallon of ice cream last night."

"That's a start." He reached over on the nightstand and grabbed the phone. "What do you want?"

"Chinese." I smiled and at some point must have drifted off to sleep. He knew what I liked.

* * * *

Half an hour later, the doorbell was ringing. I found Nick had fallen asleep, too. I remembered the food and jumped out of bed.

Nick groaned, still mostly asleep, while I tugged on Nick's T-shirt and a pair of pajama shorts from the hamper. I needed money and dug through Nick's jeans for his wallet. I fished out a couple of twenties.

I made it to the door, got the bag loaded down with food and gave a big tip. Seconds later, I had the cartons on the table and Nick and I were refueling.

He was still naked and he looked good that way. Most men didn't look great naked. He did. I had no intention of letting him get dressed all weekend unless, of course, I let him meet Marina and Jen.

I'd finished off my second egg roll and had grabbed some beers from the fridge when he pulled me into his lap. I didn't resist for a second. Still, I had to toy with him.

"Can't wait until we're done eating?" I teased.

"I was getting cold." He took the beers from me and set them on the table before he slipped his hands under my shirt. Nick cupped my breasts and held me to him. Instantly,

I wanted him again.

Nick began kissing my neck and gently pinching my nipples. He knew what I liked. It was an amazing sensation to be with a man who knew just what I wanted. I got comfortable on his lap and sipped my beer. I hadn't had one in years, but it tasted good. Just like Nick.

There were voices in the hall. "Marina and Jen must be home. If you're good, I might let you meet them later." I nibbled him and wiggled in his lap.

Nick kissed me. His reaction to my efforts was obvious. The voices outside seemed to get louder, distracting me. I focused on kissing him and getting him harder and harder.

Before I could suggest Nick and I take dinner into the bedroom, my front door opened.

"Oh, my God," Jen said from the doorway.

Shit! I'd left it unlocked after I'd gotten the food. I tried to get up out of automatic reaction. Nick held me to him. He had nothing to be ashamed of, he was just more modest than some would give him credit for.

I looked over, and Jen was blushing bright red and Marina was smiling at me. Clearly, they hadn't expected this.

"Sorry, Lori." Marina gave me a knowing wink. "We're going to see a movie and wanted to invite you along. I see you have other plans. Hi, Nick. You should lock your door if it's naked time. We'll go." Marina pulled on Jen's coat as Jen stared.

"Hi, Nick." Jen let herself be tugged away by Marina, but her eyes were on my man.

Marina closed the door behind them and I barely heard my two best friends break down into laughter over my own. I scampered to lock the door, put the chain on and bolted it. "Sorry about that."

As if reading my mind, Nick was already half at attention for another round in bed. He picked up the cartons and headed for the bedroom.

I pulled off the shirt and the shorts, grabbed the beers and followed him. This naked thing wasn't so bad. I just had to remember to lock the door.

I climbed back into bed and kissed his cheek softly.

"What was that for?" he asked.

"I love you."

"I love you, too." Nick dumped a packet of soy sauce into the fried rice. He hated soy sauce but knew I loved it.

We were an odd couple. Screw odd. We were happy.

Chapter Fifteen

Jen's Decision

I'd gone all out for our third week wrap-up. The problem of Tim had by no stretch of the imagination been solved. I wasn't going to let that ruin Lori's happy news.

Marina and I knew, of course. She and Nick were back together in a big way. No thanks to her telling us. We'd walked in on the very happy couple in afterglow. Still, we hadn't heard the details of how it had all worked out and curiosity was killing me. *A happy ending for someone, please.*

The coffee table was set for a celebratory dinner. We never seemed to eat at the actual table anyway. I'd made chicken Marsala and had the wine breathing when Marina knocked and entered carrying a large bag.

"What is that?" I asked.

"I told Mom about Lori and Nick and she went cheesecake crazy." Marina set it on the island like it weighed a ton then pulled it from the large brown bag. The circular tray was twenty inches across at least.

"We're not throwing a party. How much cheesecake does she think we can eat?" I joined her at the island and sized up the tray versus my refrigerator.

"Lori'll be taking home whatever is left. Mom and Nick agree she needs fattening up. Consider it a conspiracy." Marina took the lid off the massive cheesecake. "There is a quarter of every type of cheesecake they make, from chocolate to strawberry and everything imaginable."

"Wow. They look amazing. I may just have to sample them all. Your mom is too good to us." I poured two glasses of wine and handed Marina one. "Maybe Lori'll be too excited for her share."

"Still depressed about Tim?" she asked.

I knew she knew it was true. She had asked to be nice and supportive. What were friends for?

I shrugged. "I don't even know what to think. He's stopped calling me. I thought I'd be relieved. I'm half hoping he'll give up."

Marina took a seat on the couch and nodded. I hated when she nodded like that. There was nothing I could read into that nod, but it made me think. It felt like my mother's eyebrow raise—I tried to figure it out.

"At least your plan came through for Lori and Nick. I'm really happy for them." I sat down, too. "I'm so relieved it worked out for her."

"That was the whole point. I don't have any regrets. I talked to Lucas. I know that he wasn't the right thing for me. And the Seth crush will fade now that I'm tired of trying to flirt or get attention without results. Bring on thirty." Marina drank.

I wasn't totally convinced she meant what she'd said about Seth.

"I guess. I mean, I don't regret Brian. It wasn't meant to be, obviously. Now I know why. Tim was an unexpected sidetrack. I don't know why it's still bugging me." I rubbed my temples, trying to get him out of my head. "Why can't men make it easy?"

"No law says you can't give Tim another try," Marina reminded. "It's not an all-or-nothing prospect. You can just give him a chance, a date, whatever. Tim isn't part of the plan, so you can't succeed or fail. If he's bugging you this much, Jen, just try it."

"You threatened to have him fired and yelled at him." I pointed out.

"We were both pissed at him that day. Now, get the whole story. You can't punish him really good unless you're around him to inflict it."

"True. I'm not sure how I feel. Do I want to go to that much trouble just to be mean?" I wanted a different subject. "Any progress with Seth?"

Marina's face went blank and she lifted a shoulder. "Not really. He's just a customer. It's a crush on my end and it'll go away."

"Hasn't yet," I added.

Marina sighed. "It will. It has to, eventually."

"Hi, hi!" Lori burst into the room with a champagne bottle in each hand.

"Hi!" I replied. I did my best to sound upbeat and happy, like Lori.

"Glad you could join us," Marina teased.

"Hey, I wouldn't miss this for anything. Well, almost anything. I won." Lori opened one of the champagne bottles with a practiced hand.

"Won? I didn't realize it was a competition." Marina frowned.

"I didn't mean it like that. I was competing with myself. I did it. And it worked! I won him back. I did it." Lori toasted herself, downed a flute of champagne, and refilled her glass.

"Are you sure you should let him out of your sight tonight?" I asked. "He might rethink it when you're hung over and puking on him tomorrow."

"He's out with the boys from the garage." Lori waved. "We love being together, and we're not completely co-dependent. I refuse to be one of those women who abandons their friends as soon as they get a man. I owe my happiness to you guys. And I'm not going to get *that* drunk. I was promised a great dinner to absorb it all. I've landed my man so I can let my figure go."

"Glad to hear it. I'm sure we'll be seeing plenty of Nick. Though hopefully with clothes on." Marina winked at me, and I blushed.

Seeing Nick like that had made me laugh all the way to the movies. Luckily we'd gone to a comedy, because that was burned on my brain. We hadn't gotten a view of anything, really, but it had still made an impression.

"Actually, we're going to move in together," Lori said proudly.

"Good, then we'll be seeing lots and lots of him." I nodded.

"Nick won't live here," Lori corrected bluntly. "My dad owns the building and he won't take any charity from my dad. Don't worry. I'll still see you guys. We're going to find a new place that's all ours."

Marina smiled. "Wow."

"Wow, what?" Lori put her hands on her hips. "Thought I wouldn't do it?"

"Wow, you did a complete one-hundred and eighty degree turn. And you seem so calm about it. What about Mommy and Daddy's holiday affair?" Marina mocked in a snobby accent. "Shall Nick's presence be amiably tolerated by the filthy rich set?"

"We're going. You're both invited with guests, by the way. Nick could use some friendly faces. Mom and Dad won't make too much of a scene there, and if they accept it, they'll let me know."

"And if they don't?" I asked.

Lori shrugged and shook her head. "Fuck 'em. I don't need them. I make enough money, so if they want me in their lives, they'll accept Nick, too. If they don't accept him, then too bad. I've never been this happy or free. If they don't like it, tough."

"Good for you! Does Nick have any brothers? You might be able to share the wealth." Marina raised an eyebrow, finished off her wine and started in on her share of the champagne. "We could use some good cute men around here who don't lie about their name."

"Nick only has one sister and no brothers." Lori waved off the question like she'd snagged the last Kennedy. "He's all mine."

"Things with Seth not going well?" I felt she was holding something back. Odd for Marina to bring him up, then stay quiet, so I mentioned it again.

Marina shrugged. "Nothing good. I'm good at being alone. It'll go away."

"One out of three isn't bad." I shrugged.

Marina's original goal had been accomplished. I could tell she wasn't overly happy. Seth was such a mystery man there wasn't anything to say.

"Oh, that reminds me. I'll be right back." Lori left the apartment and returned a minute later with papers. "Your background check."

Marina looked confused. "What background check are you talking about?"

"Tim ran a background check on himself and sent it to Jen," Lori explained. "She wanted to be sure that he has the truth on there so I had one done, too. It's all there in black and white."

"It's all true." I read it again. I didn't really believe it, or I hadn't, until now. I was sure Tim would've filled his background check with lies and cover-ups to get me to see him. "You're sure about this?"

Lori nodded. "I had it done independently. They even followed him for a day to be sure."

I nodded. I needed to think about this. I set the papers aside and served dinner. Taking the garlic rolls out of the oven, I almost burned my finger thinking about Tim. My heart demanded one thing and, oddly enough, my brain wasn't fighting it anymore.

We sat down to dinner and everyone seemed to enjoy it. Lori recounted her fight with Nick and their night together with a grin so fixed to her face that, if we hadn't known better, we might have suspected Botox. I half-listened and did my best not to be jealous.

I knew it hadn't been easy for Lori to take the plunge and swallow her pride. Should I? Would it work for me?

I hadn't done anything wrong. I hadn't lied or deceived anyone. Letting Tim into my life again could spell more embarrassment later if it went wrong. Why should I be the one to make the first move? I could just wait until he called again and listen. *If* he called again.

Marina was right. I wasn't that great a judge of character when it came to men. At least I knew Tim wasn't gay. I'd felt that much.

"Jen?" Marina clanged her fork on the side of her glass, ringing me out of my funk.

"Sorry, what?" I shook it off.

"What's wrong?" Lori asked.

"Nothing, I'm fine." I looked down and realized I had barely touched my dinner. Marina and Lori were already done. I cleared off the table and brought the monster tray of cheesecake to the coffee table. I carefully cut three pieces, not too big or too small.

Neither Lori nor Marina made a move for the cheesecake. They were both looking at me.

"What?" I asked.

"You're not happy." Lori folded her arms.

"I'm thrilled for you," I argued.

"You're happy for me, and not really happy with yourself, or the Tim thing." Lori shook her head. "Why don't you just talk to him?"

"That's my vote," Mariana added.

"I don't want to be a doormat." I took a piece of cheesecake.

"Hearing him out isn't being a doormat. Clearly, you two have chemistry. Talking to him doesn't mean you're moving in with him or marrying him. You can just see." Marina grabbed her own piece.

"Maybe I just need time." I didn't want to make the move. I wanted to be a wimp.

"Don't wait," Lori said intently.

"You don't want to take the same chance Lori did with Nick," Marina agreed. "Lori got lucky that Nick hadn't moved on. If you want him or even think you might, don't wait until it's too late."

"She's right. You know he's not an ax murderer or anything. And you clearly like him and can't get over him." Lori put the background check she'd run back in my lap, then she took two pieces of cheesecake. Happiness made her eat as much as depression did. Good thing nothing would put an ounce on Lori.

I stared at the pages and believed it. I had the truth and yet it didn't matter. I hadn't been true to the spirit of Marina's plan. No regrets meant more than just the ex-boyfriends.

I might not be fighting Tim anymore, but a part of me still distrusted him. I needed to know the whole story so I could decide if I was doing the right thing or not. At the moment, I was mad at him and getting nowhere fast.

"Hearing him out would mean that I'd know for sure that I don't have any regrets," I said. I hoped it would be true and I could put him behind me.

"Exactly." Marina nodded.

"Thanks." I got up and grabbed my purse and coat. They could lock up for me when they were done. "Gotta go. See you guys later."

* * * *

I'd left my apartment in a rush, with my friends still there eating dessert. I knew exactly where I was going. Tim might not be home. I had to try. And I had to do it now before I changed my mind.

I'd memorized his address and even walked by it on my lunch hour one day. I knew it was weird, but this time I was going in. I had to get this out of my system. This man was like the stomach flu. I hadn't heard about the new job yet either but I could make a move with Tim to be happy on one front.

It wasn't far, so I walked. Sprinted was more like it. Thankfully, I was dressed for comfort in gym shoes and jeans. Not my best look, but good for running like a crazy woman in bad weather. December in Chicago, slipping on ice and slush while not getting hit by falling ice. He was worth it. I got to the door and pressed his apartment intercom button. Please be home!

"Yes?" Tim replied.

"It's me. Can I come up?" I did my best not to sound too excited or desperate.

The door buzzed. He didn't say anything else. I was too excited to wait, anyway. I opened the door and ran up to the fifth floor, apartment C.

Tim was in the doorway. He looked confused and closed off. Not his regular friendly self. This wasn't normal for either of us. Nothing had been easy since that day he'd told the truth. Maybe we could redefine normal. Or just redefine our relationship on the truth.

"Can I come in?" I asked.

He nodded, let me in first and followed. "Can I get you something to drink?" he offered. He left the door open like I was afraid to be alone with him and would bolt.

At least he wasn't being smug, as though he'd done nothing wrong. That was how my brothers always acted when they screwed up, like they were the innocent and injured party. I wasn't going to let Tim try that on me.

"No, I want the truth." I sat on a plaid sofa. His apartment was sparse and comfortable. Pretty much what I'd envisioned for a bachelor.

"I don't understand." He sat next to me, smelling so good I had to build up my self-control. First, I had to look him in the eye to believe he was honest. Then I could enjoy him again, maybe.

"I saw the background check and Marina told me what you told Lucas. And she told me what Lucas told her. I'm sick of second-hand information. I want the truth from you." I nodded. "Why did you lie to me and keep lying? And you agreed to see Marina. You knew she'd know you were lying. You still didn't try to tell me until the last minute."

"I wanted to keep seeing you. So, I just said or did whatever came into my head to keep you with me. I've never met a woman I actually had instant chemistry with." He sounded so sincere and looked so cute. I wanted to believe him. I needed answers, not to give in to the feelings.

"After a while…" I shrugged. "Why not tell the truth sooner?"

"I didn't want you to hate me. My name didn't matter. I didn't lie about anything else. I know I waited too long." He leaned closer.

"I just don't know if I can trust you after all that. We were intimate and you still didn't tell me the truth." I turned away from him. That was the most humiliating part of it.

"So women are the only ones allowed to get caught up in things?" Tim's hands were on my shoulders and he felt so good.

My restraint was slipping. "Did Lucas really give you hell when he found out?"

Tim chuckled and looked at his shoes. He had this cute pouting expression, as though he was a little boy. "He nearly decked me. I was in his office all afternoon giving him the details. I had to explain everything and it wasn't easy. Men don't generally talk about this stuff and Lucas really doesn't. If his wife had found out, or anyone in the office, he'd have fired me in a split second. I had to bug him for a day solid to call Marina and convince her I wasn't a complete ass. The way you weren't responding, I thought maybe he'd refused to call her at all."

"He called. You're still not her favorite person." I slipped out of my coat.

"I'd like to make it up to you and her, if you'll let me." He rubbed his neck nervously. "Did you get the flowers and the messages?"

I nodded and shrugged. "It was nice, but I just needed some time."

"Understandable. I'm an open book. I was an idiot but can't go back and change it now. The only other thing to confess is that I don't make as much as Lucas. He's my superior. So there, you know absolutely everything now."

I nodded. "So what do you think about twenty-nine-year-old virgins?" I asked.

Tim's eyes bugged out of his head. "I never gave it much thought. Why?"

"I just wondered if you thought that it was a pathetic state and wouldn't want a woman without that kind of experience and skills." I tried not to blush but we were being honest. He might as well know all.

He inched in. "You?"

I shrugged and looked away. Blushing like a fool, I was sure.

"It'll be a first for both of us, then." Tim pulled me into his arms and I felt instantly better. His words took a few seconds to sink in past the feel of his strong arms and warm neck.

"You're not!" I didn't believe it for a second. "I won't believe that."

"No, no," he backpedaled. He was blushing deep red. "I'm not a virgin. I didn't mean that. I've never slept with a virgin before."

"Oh." I took a deep breath in relief. "Good, because if neither of us weren't experienced it could really be a mess trying."

"You had a little experience with me that night," he reminded me.

I blushed. "If I accidentally call you Lucas, you'd better not be offended."

I don't know when I'd decided to take him back. We weren't going to be crazy like Lori and Nick. I wasn't about to ask him to move in with me or anything. This was more like starting over. Fresh and with a clean slate. I'd regret it if I didn't try.

"I guess we can date. See if I like the real Tim." I smiled and scooted a bit closer.

"You did see the real Tim. You just called me by a different name. I'll start quoting Shakespeare if you want. I minored in literature. I can do the entire 'Rose by any other name' speech by heart." He closed the distance between us and kissed me. "We'll go as slow or as fast as you need, Jen.

And I promise I won't lie about anything else. Even if it's just to keep you."

"Then I guess I can give it a shot."

There was a long way to go before I trusted him, but it was a start.

Chapter Sixteen

Marina's Reality Check

I'd ended up taking home two pieces of cheesecake after the celebratory dinner. It made for a most unhealthy breakfast. I had an afternoon and evening schedule at the animal hospital today so the morning was mine.

Jen had called last night, telling Lori and I not to worry. Clearly, she and Tim had found some common ground to build upon. Two out of three wasn't bad.

Not that Jen was with her best sex ever. Things had changed over the course of our little game. They were both happy and in love. I watched boring morning shows and marveled that our plan had actually worked. Lori had a solid future, I hoped, with Nick. Jen was at least out there and experiencing things. Namely a man.

Up until that morning, I'd been so happy Lori had taken back her man and grown a real backbone that it hadn't hit me. Lori was happy and would be moving out.

An unintended and unwelcome side effect. *That* didn't make me happy.

Not that I blamed Nick. He was smart to draw lines early. The Eve of Christmas Eve party would be the first test. It was the tip of the iceberg. I could see Lori's mom now, clenching her jaw, the too-tight skin straining. Lori's dad would be bewildered that his princess would do such a thing. I couldn't wait.

Jen was a total surprise. Leave it to her to accidentally fall for a guy and have it turn out better than expected. Clueless luck. Damn, I envied her. I overthought everything.

I overanalyzed, as Lori would say. Lori, who didn't overanalyze so much as overreact. Drama queen.

Right now, she was at work, happily arguing something or writing something full of big lawyerly words. She had Nick. I'd heard a lot of it through my wall over the past few days. She had him and he had her in too many variations to think about. The walls between our apartments weren't that thin — the neighbors were just that loud.

Maybe their moving out wouldn't be so bad. I poured myself more coffee and wondered if Jen was home. Instinct told me no, and if she were, I'd have to hear her first-time story. Not in the mood I was in.

I should be happy, and I was, for them. It had all worked out. Except nothing had changed for me. Not that I had planned any differently. This wasn't supposed to totally change our lives. I had wanted it for Lori, even if it had been a fifty-fifty shot at best that she'd do it. She had. And then Jen.

So where was my luck? No luck for me. Here it was, the week of Christmas. All these parties and dinners to go to and no one to go with.

If every sister I had weren't married, it might not be so bad. The only single and unattached cousins I had were at least five years younger than me.

And loving Mom had brought it up. I was dreading the holidays now. I didn't want to go to Lori's family's Eve of Christmas Eve party alone. I knew I was being selfish and self-centered. The odd one out was not my favorite role to play at these things. Single I could deal with, but the only single one over the holidays was just pathetic.

The phone rang and I looked at it for the first two rings. I grabbed the handset and noticed that it was Jen's restaurant on the caller ID. Might as well get this over with, I decided. It would be now or later and, over the phone, I could fake happy better. Not that I wasn't happy for her, but in that moment I wasn't feeling it.

"Hi," I answered in my most upbeat voice.

"Marina, glad I found you. I tried work."

"Late day," I filled in.

"Anyway, I just wanted to thank you."

That was the last thing I expected from her. "For what?"

"For doing this whole thing. I would have never have met Tim if it weren't for your little game."

True enough. "That's just dumb luck." Now I felt guilty for feeling cheated. "Did you and Tim have a lot of fun last night?"

"Yes, and I'm now proud to say I'm no longer of the untested variety. He tried to wait. I wore him down." She sounded so proud of herself. Like it was hard to get a guy out of his pants.

"Was it good?" I hoped she'd hold off the details until she wasn't at work. Jen was clearly bursting.

"Amazing. I don't know what I was waiting for. I'll tell you more later. Thanks again. I was ready to run home to Wisconsin after I screwed up Tim and Lucas. And don't worry, Tim and I are taking it slow. I just wanted to get over that hump."

"Nice choice of words," I teased.

Jen laughed. "Yeah, well, I'm no longer G-rated. You should be proud. Bye."

"Bye." I hung up the phone and stretched out in my recliner. At least that was over. Jen could meet thirty not as some repressed virgin, but as a sexually active woman with a real boyfriend.

No telling if she and Tim would last, I reminded myself. The phone rang again. My peaceful morning was slipping by me. It was Lori's office. "Hey, Lori." I was determined to be upbeat this time. This was the monster I'd wanted to create.

"Hey, Marina. Hear from Jen?" she asked.

"Just now. Happy doesn't do her justice." I felt better sharing the blame.

"She told me the story this morning. Apparently, he caught her before she fell over his gym bag. Talk about fate.

We could have had a friend in a hospital bed instead of smoking up the sheets in Tim's bed."

"Sounds like a sappy movie." I rolled my eyes. Who did that stuff really happen to, except Jen?

"Then he took her to lunch and escorted her to the brokerage offices. It wasn't until they got there that she threw out Lucas's name and he claimed it was him to keep her talking to him," Lori rattled.

"She went to lunch with him? She held a conversation with him and never knew his name?" I couldn't believe it. "I'm glad you ran that background check, because our friend is just a tad clueless."

"We knew that, but she came out on top," Lori replied. "So I guess Tim is coming to the
Eve of Christmas Eve party with Jen. Should I put you down for a guest or not?"

"What do you think?" I tried not to snap at her. I swear, I tried.

"Wrong side of the bed?" she asked. Her tone let me know I was being bitchy.

"Holidays alone, you remember what that was like, right?" I felt bad. "Christmas sort of sneaked up on me this year. I have the presents bought and everything. We were so busy with my little game that I forgot to mentally prepare myself for facing mistletoe and mobs of family all alone. I don't mind being single, but it's all the couple events around the holidays that bothers me."

"You'll be fine. You're best when you're on your own and making smart-ass remarks. Everyone loves it. I'll put you down for a date just in case you get brave and ask out Sethy boy."

"Don't bother," I argued.

"No, too late. I emailed my mother's housekeeper and you're down for two."

"Now I'll have to explain why I don't have a date."

"No, you won't. Trust me, my parents will be so busy dealing with Nick and that trauma they won't notice you're there. Except of course to demand why you let this happen." She laughed.

"I'll take the blame." I shrugged. Why not? At least it would make my evening more interesting. And it was sort of true. I *had* started it.

"Oh no, this one is all mine. The idea for looking up exes was yours. You didn't force me to do it. I didn't think Nick would even talk to me, so the heat is on him and me. Don't worry, if Mom and Dad throw us out, we'll be at your parents' for Christmas."

"Good, she'd love to have you." And I'd love the diversion. All the focus would be on them and I'd get some credit for my matchmaking skills.

The old aunts said there was a gift in the family for it. They'd been praying and working on me for at least five years and nothing had worked. Maybe I had the touch for others but was cursed not to find a match for myself.

"We'll stop by at least. I'd rather torture my parents if they're willing to sit through it."

"I think they will. They won't admit defeat that easily. You'll have to go a few rounds before they give up. Nick ready?" I asked.

"Tux shopping tonight. What about you? Do you have a dress?"

"Sure, I have that green velvety number I got on clearance last year after the New Year's dresses were marked down. It's fitted, yet not revealing. Did you warn Jen to get Tim a tux, too?"

"Done," Lori chirped. She was so happy I could hear it over the phone. Thank God I had to work tonight so I didn't have to see it firsthand.

"Good. If he walked in wearing a suit your mother would faint."

"Maybe I should make Nick just wear a suit and watch Mom have a fit?" Lori mused.

"No, don't make him look clueless to bait them. I bet he'd look good in a tux. Pull that hair back into a short ponytail and give him a clean, close shave and he'd blend well." I didn't want Lori to set up a huge blow-out at the party. Her parents would start enough trouble.

"The tux and the hair are no problem. He likes that stubble look, though." Lori made contemplative noises on the other side of the line. "We'll see. I *would* like to see him like that. He'd look so much younger without that scruffy layer of a beard."

"Not like it'll take him long to grow it back, either. A week, at most." I really didn't care about Nick's appearance. He wasn't a slob or a jerk, so why set him up? Obviously, he wasn't my date, and Lori liked to push the envelope. Her parents would be pissed enough. "Don't give the parental units more ammunition."

"You're right. You're right. I don't care what my parents think but I think Nick will put his best foot forward so they see his good points. I have to go back to work. See you later." She hung up before I could even respond.

"Bye." I pressed the off button and glanced at the clock. I'd made no use of my morning. I needed to go shopping. It was too late now.

The best I could do was get out of the chair and make my way to the kitchen. After picking up a notepad and pen, I opened cabinets and the fridge, making a list of what I needed. I'd stop after work and get it all. The stores would be less crowded then. I hated the holiday crush so I normally scheduled my trips around them.

As I finished my list, the phone rang again. *Who the hell could it be now?* "Hello?" I answered.

"Marina?" It was a man's voice, not a family member. I didn't recognize it at all.

"Yes, who's this?" I dropped the notepad and pen on the counter and leaned against it in my fuzzy robe and kitty slippers. I had yet to shower and dress, so this better not drag on.

"This is Louie from The Rattler. I told you I'd give you a call. Is this a bad time?"

Louie? Damn, had I really given him my number? Probably to get rid of him. Not that he was a bad guy. I didn't need this now.

"Hi, Louie." I had to be nice. He was harmless and I knew him from high school. That probably was why he held little appeal. I'd known him at his gawky and geeky stages. And he'd seen me at mine.

"I was wondering if you'd like to grab a drink or dinner one night."

Great. I got a guy I didn't want asking me out, and the guy I did want, wouldn't say a word. What to do? What to do? I knew he'd take the heat off Nick. He wasn't the tux type. At least I wouldn't be alone.

My common sense vetoed that thought. First, you didn't accept a first date during the holidays. Too much pressure. Secondly, if I took him to any holiday function, that would give him minimum of boyfriend status which he hadn't earned. Bottom line, I didn't want Louie.

"You know, Louie, it's the holidays. I have a lot of parties and family stuff for the next few weeks. How about you give me a call after New Year's and we'll try to do lunch?" I hoped he'd get the hint.

"Sure, I know it's a busy time, I just didn't want you to think I was blowing you off. Talk to you later." He hung up and I exhaled.

"You waited a week." I rolled my eyes at the phone and hung up. I didn't want him, anyway. Not my type at all. Of course, my type wasn't working out so well. Was that my problem? Maybe, but the thought of dating Louie made me sick. That wasn't the answer.

I finished my list and got in the shower. I dressed for comfort and only bothered with minimum makeup to keep my face from drying out in the windy Chicago air. I tossed the shopping list in my purse and made sure I had everything.

I needed to stock up on wine again. This little game of mine had caused a large thirst. I made sure I had my license, too. Not that I really got carded anymore, but occasionally I'd find a new employee who carded everyone and their grandmother.

With no energy to move, I forced myself to go out into the hall and locked the door behind me.

"Hi," a man said behind me.

I turned. Nick. I couldn't catch a break today. "Hi, Nick. On my way to work. I've got afternoon and evening."

He nodded. "I'm going in late today."

"Perks of being the boss." I smiled. "Glad you and Lori worked things out."

Nick grinned. "Thanks for pushing her. She told me about the little game."

I shrugged. "You know how she gets with her birthdays. I had to do something or she might have panicked and married the first halfway normal snob her mother threw at her. Luckily, her mom usually picks guys that seem nice, however twenty minutes with them and the loser comes out."

"I'm guessing she's fixed you up a couple of times?" Nick asked.

"I put a stop to it real quick. Her mom lives in a different world. Don't worry, you'll get to visit. It's an adventure." I walked to the elevator and he went back into the apartment.

The one day I didn't feel like conversing with people and they were coming out of the woodwork. I couldn't wait to get to my job and avoid the emotional relationship and deep conversational crap for a while.

* * * *

It would be a slow day. Few people brought their pets in for routine stuff around the holidays. Though there would be the inevitable cat that had eaten tinsel or had chewed on the lights, which could be more dangerous. I wandered in and chatted with the techs. There were a lot of boarded animals for the travelers so staffing levels were high, but there wasn't much activity.

I dropped my junk in the office and noticed Dr. Percy was working. He owned the animal hospital and he was about a hundred years old, plus he liked to come in now and then. His wife was our office manager.

However, he never came in over the holidays. His wife was home cooking already.

She'd called to invite me if I could pop in. Sometimes I felt like their adopted kid.

"Hey, old man," I said affectionately. "You get lost or forgot to fly south for the winter?"

He grunted and kept reading. "Had to check on something. You here all afternoon?"

"Yeah. Need something?" I asked.

"Later." He waved.

I shrugged and headed to the front. No patients, so I ducked in the back. My litter of kittens was now officially ready for adoption. We'd held off announcing it because too many people gave them as pets for the holidays and ended up returning them.

So, they were all still there. I took them out and played with them a bit. Gave them a free check up on their reflexes as they darted after toys and each other. All healthy, playful and socializing well.

The doorbell rang. I stayed with the kittens. If they needed a doc, they'd get me. Probably just another animal to be boarded.

"Marina?" Dr. Percy poked his head in. "Can I talk to you for a minute?"

"Sure." I piled the little balls of fur back into their cage and went to the office.

I sat and he closed the door in his puttering old-man fashion. He dropped into his chair with a sigh. "I need to retire."

Not a surprise. We'd known that for years. The question was, what would happen with the place when they did? "Big plans?" I asked.

"Maybe moving somewhere warmer. The frigid winters here are just getting to my wife's arthritis too badly now." He nodded. "We don't just want to put this place up for sale."

"I understand." Was he firing us all? Closing up shop to sell the property and move? Not the old man. Not days before Christmas.

"We want you to buy it." He looked at me as though I should've known or suspected.

"I'm sorry, you want me to what?" I must've heard him wrong. Not possible.

"Buy the place. Then we'll know it'll be run well. It's a great location. Business is good and customers are loyal." He handed me a folder. "Financial statements for the past ten years. It's profitable."

"I'm sure it is. I can't possibly afford to buy this place. The location would make it worth... I can't even imagine." I shrugged. I was flattered, but this was far more than I'd planned for today.

"That's what loans are for. You think I didn't have one?" He handed me another folder. "Women seem to get them more easily for small businesses. You won't have a problem either way. Here are some forms and programs my wife found."

I didn't take the folder right away. I was frozen in my chair. No April Fools. No joke.

He waved the folder at me. "I'm not getting any younger. Take them."

I added that folder to my lap but didn't open either one. "Are you sure?" I asked.

"Of course I'm sure. I've watched you here. You're good, everyone likes you, listens to you, and you don't take crap. No reason not to settle in and start paying off that loan while you're young. Unless you don't intend to stay in Chicago?" He looked concerned.

"I never planned to move." I shook my head. That wasn't the problem. "It's just such a big thing. You never mentioned it before."

"If I had, it would've meant picking a time or giving you an idea. I wasn't sure when I'd be ready to let go. Most of our friends have moved away and we want to be near them and somewhere we don't have to worry about ice and snow. Now is a good time for me. You take your time. Think about it. I don't want an answer now. I want you to read all that stuff and let me know after New Year's. You're off starting tomorrow, right?" he asked.

I nodded. I'd take December twenty-third through the day after New Year's off so I could make all the parties and family stuff without missing anyone.

"Well, then you'll have time to ponder it away from here. It's not just a job. It's a business decision, so make sure you're ready. I know you are, and I'm not going to be around to tell you so." He wagged an arthritic finger at me. "You have to want it."

"Okay." I didn't know what else to say. He was offering me his life's work. "I really appreciate this confidence in me."

"Don't you think you're up to it? You are. And the boss gets to make their own schedule." He grinned.

"One of the perks." I nodded.

A knock on the door ended the conversation. "I need a doc out here for an exit exam."

I nodded to the old man and set the pile of papers next to my bag before I headed out.

"Who's leaving?"

"We sold your runt." She handed me a file.

"I thought we weren't letting any of them be adopted until after Christmas?" I'd gotten attached to that little runt. Occupational hazard. It didn't happen too often to me.

"It's not for a present and he's a regular customer." The tech shrugged. "I didn't think you'd mind."

I glanced down at the paper and smiled. "You're kidding?" I looked at the tech in disbelief.

"He asked for you." He pointed to exam room two.

I knocked briefly and opened the door. Monster greeted me instantly with a wagging tail and cold nose in my hand. "Hi, Monster."

Seth tried to catch his leash. I got to it first. His hand hit mine and I did my best to ignore it. I handed Seth the leash and he secured Monster to the table so he wouldn't go wild. "Glad you were working. They said you're off for a week or so after today?"

"Yeah, I'm taking the holidays off. Too many family gatherings and holiday parties to deal with. So you decided to take home our runt?" I stroked the little kitten on the table, who looked lost without her siblings.

"She and Monster seem to get along okay. Besides, he needs someone to play with while I'm at work or he'll wreck the place." Seth shrugged.

"Keep an eye on them for a while. They get along now. There could be territorial issues and she's still pretty small to defend herself. The claws would do some damage, though." I did the routine checks on her. I knew she was healthy, but it was policy. I spotted a cat-size carrier on the counter next to me. The man planned ahead! "Do you have a name for her?" I made notes in the file in my usual scribble. I tried not to look at his body in jeans and a T-shirt. He'd taken off his wool coat. The heat was a little high in the room, and I couldn't help but be distracted by his form.

"No, I'm not very creative," he admitted. "Any ideas? You must see every name in the book."

"Well, an all-black cat who ends up on the doorstep of an animal hospital. My sick sense of humor would call her Lucky. I'm sure you'll do better."

"No, I like it." He picked up the two-pound furball and looked her in the eye. "What do you think, Lucky?"

She licked his nose. Seth laughed. "I think you have a winner."

I wrote in the name and checked when her shots were due. "You have a couple of months before her next round of shots. We'll send you a reminder card in the mail. She can't be fixed for a few more weeks, until she gains enough weight. That's highly encouraged. Any other questions?" I asked.

"De-clawing?" He dislodged her claws from his shirt.

"I wouldn't. Especially not with a dog in the house. She has to have a way to defend herself and he'll bite a lot harder than she will. Just keep them trimmed. Nail clippers are good. No matter what people say, de-clawing a cat hurts them." I got a pair of clippers out of the sanitizing solution and took Lucky from him.

"You pull back the paw pad and make sure she stops wiggling. Then just get the tips. Don't go too low. When she's bigger, it'll be easier to see. And a scratching post is a must. Train her to use it and you'll be fine." I did a couple then handed the clippers to Seth. With great intensity and determination in his face, he trimmed the rest carefully.

My mind wandered while he was working. Not to my business proposition, which was more than I could take in at the moment. Back to Lori and Jen. The deal had been no regrets. They didn't have any. Lori had tried and won. Jen had tried, failed, then found someone else and had gotten rid of her virgin status for more fun. And what had I done? Nothing different.

I reviewed. Not one thing different. Talking to Lucas? I'd talk to any of the idiot exes if they called. Pushing Lori into mischief? No problem, I did it all the time. For her own good, of course. What had I done? I'd got asked out by a club-owning, aging college kid. Not for me.

It was now or never, I decided. If he said no, I just wouldn't look after his animals anymore. There were plenty of other good vets in the office.

"Seth?" I started and stopped when he looked up.

"What?" he asked.

"About all those holiday parties I have to go to. You're probably really busy now, too, right?" This was smooth. I'd laugh at myself if I weren't so nervous.

"Actually, no. I don't have a lot of family. My brother

and his wife aren't far so I'll take Monster and Lucky over there Christmas Day. Other than the company party, I'm not overbooked. Why?"

"I was just wondering…" *Spit it out, Marina. You can do it. It won't kill you.* "If you'd like to go out sometime? With me."

My eyes darted to the cat. As though the words hadn't just left my mouth.

"Is that allowed?" he asked.

"Allowed?" I repeated. "What do you mean?"

"I just thought you might have a rule against it, office or personal policy. I mean, you must get owners hitting on you all the time." He shrugged.

"No, no policy and definitely not hitting on me all the time. Not a lot of single men, I guess." It sounded good, anyway, even if it wasn't an answer from him. How did men do this? I so much preferred being a girl, but for now, I had to follow it through. "Is that a yes?"

"Absolutely. I'd have asked you out sooner, but I didn't think it would be appropriate." He stuffed his hands in his pockets and grinned.

I knew I was blushing like Jen would. "Great. When is good for you?"

"What about those parties? Aren't you booked?" he asked.

"Depends if you want to see how the other half lives?" I teased.

"What do you mean?"

"My friend's parents are loaded and they have this formal fancy party the Eve of Christmas Eve every year. It's lobster, caviar and the best champagne. My friend put me down for a guest, even though I'm not seeing anyone. If you want to join me, I promise the food and alcohol will be good."

"It's not a family thing?" he asked.

"No," I assured him. "Not for a second date. You'll meet my friends. That's enough."

"Second date?" he asked.

"Yeah, if you're free for dinner, we could break the ice

tonight." I wasn't going to waste two days waiting to see him. Breaking the rules was working. He was a 'by the rules' sort of guy, and that was fine with me.

"All I had planned for tonight was settling in Lucky, so I thought I'd order in. Do you like Chinese?"

I nodded. Dinner at his place. Even better.

"Then it's four for Chinese. Why don't you come by about six o'clock?"

"Sounds great. I've got your address." I nodded to the file. "See you then."

He put Lucky in the little carrier and grabbed Monster's leash. I helped him manage the doors and kept smiling. I couldn't have stopped if I'd tried.

"What are you smiling for?" the old man asked. What he was doing at the front desk, I had no idea.

"I have a dinner date."

"You're on until nine," the tech reminded me.

"Actually, Dr. Percy is going to cover for me." I looked at him and winked. "One of the perks, right?"

He nodded at me. "Right."

Being the boss wouldn't be such a bad thing after all.

Chapter Seventeen

Lori's Family Face Off

Today was the day. The Eve of Christmas Eve. My parents' annual holiday party — so pretentious my family named the event and that day was strictly for their party with their circle of friends — was tonight. I'd warned Nick it was black tie over a week ago and he'd insisted I not get involved. He wanted to handle his wardrobe.

I checked my watch. He'd be here any minute. I couldn't wait. Why hadn't he agreed to just move in with me now? I knew it was stupid to move his stuff just to move it again, but I hated being without him.

A quick turn in the full-length mirror reassured me. I'd gone with a silvery blue gown that showed off my eyes and didn't wash me out too much.

Time for a last-minute check. Earrings, necklace and a tasteful bracelet — check. Hair done by my favorite stylist — check. Shoes that matched the dress and were elegant yet dance-ably comfortable — check. Makeup done — check. Perfume! I knew I'd forgotten something.

At the vanity, I had five scents to choose from. I could go with the one my mother had bought me for my birthday, try to flatter her indirectly. No, I had to go with Nick's favorite. If only he knew it ran one hundred dollars an ounce. He had expensive taste and he didn't even know it — in perfume and women.

I dabbed the perfume strategically on my body in anticipation of the after-party activities. I'd just added another layer of glossy lipstick when the doorbell rang.

Taking a deep breath, I walked out of the bedroom and opened the front door.

I stared at Nick, stunned. For the first time ever, he wasn't in work overalls or jeans and a T-shirt. He was in a tux. A very nice-looking tux that did great things for his already good build. I wasn't about to check the collar. I knew it wasn't a rental and it hadn't been cheap.

"Hi, Nick." I knew I sounded like an idiot. It didn't matter. I could be a fool for him. He did look good.

If only I had the time to take it off him, have my way with him and get him back in this perfect state in time for the party. I wasn't going to be late, not for this holiday event.

There was time for fun stuff later.

"Ready, gorgeous?" Nick asked.

I checked my appearance one last time in the hallway mirror and nodded. "Are you sure you're ready?"

"No sweat." He took my hand and grabbed my coat for me. I hadn't realized how much I'd missed him until he was back doing those little things again.

We took my car, with him driving through the icy and slushy Chicago streets. I grinned at him like a silly schoolgirl. There was a flutter of fear in the pit of my stomach. I was happy, but about to make my family very frantic. I wanted it to be over with.

Nick parked the car and we went up. I smiled and put on my game face for dealing with Mom. Nick's hand was on my back and it reassured me.

I opened the familiar door with tense fingers and a knot in my stomach. I refused to hesitate. The room was already filling in, thankfully. We handed over our coats and picked up flutes of champagne.

"Okay?" Nick asked.

I nodded a little too quickly and took a slow breath. As long as Nick was there, I'd be fine.

"Are Marina and Jen coming, too?" He filled the silence.

"Yes, thank God." I looked around for them. "Jen's bringing Tim."

"And you think I'd fly solo." Marina appeared behind us with a man in tow.

"Hi." I hugged her and instantly felt better.

"Nick." Marina nodded at him. "Nick, Lori, this is Seth Lauden. Seth, my friend Lori Craig and her boyfriend, Nick Jared."

The men exchanged handshakes while I nodded in approval of Seth to Marina. I'd heard a lot about him and pictured a geek. A little stuffy-looking, maybe, but handsome and social. This would be a topic of conversation later. The more friendly faces, the better.

"Sorry we're late." Jen rushed up to the group, dragging Tim by the hand.

"You're not late." Marina tapped her neck and looked at Jen. I checked out the spot. Yep, Jen had a hickey. They really were like kids.

Marina and I exchanged a smile, then she introduced Seth to Tim and Jen and then Tim to Nick. I loved how she made it look simple. I'd been lectured by my mother on etiquette and protocol all my life as though I was going to be the next First Lady. When the moments came, I always forgot.

"We should meet the parents," Nick whispered in my ear. "Let's get it over with."

I nodded. "We'll be right back. We're going to say hello to my parents."

"We'll join you." Jen nodded and started to follow, pulling Tim by the arm. I could tell she was eager to show off her new boyfriend.

"Later," Marina added and shook her head at Jen. Finally, Jen took the hint and stopped.

I inhaled deeply and held on to Nick's hand. I spotted my mother and we made our way. Relief washed over me when I saw Dad standing next to her. He was less likely to go after me and Mom wouldn't be too unbearable with Dad there. But his reaction was unpredictable.

"Lori, I'm glad you're here." Mother pecked my cheek and Dad did the same.

"Mom, Dad, I'd like you meet Nick Jared. Nick, these are my parents."

The men shook hands, but my mother made no attempt to extend her hand. "Nick?" she repeated.

"My boyfriend," I added.

Her eyes glazed. "I'm sorry, I don't believe I know your family, Mr. Jared. Where are you from?"

"Southside," Nick replied proudly.

She clenched her jaw and nodded stiffly. "And what do you do?" she squeaked.

"I own a car repair shop. I'll be opening another soon." Nick's voice didn't waver. I was so glad he was doing the talking.

"I'm glad you could join us," Dad piped up. His small talk wasn't so good.

"Are the two of you...serious?" Mother asked. She held her chin as though she were trying to hold it up and yet act casual.

I could tell she was carefully watching her words. Maybe she feared I'd brought more of them, and that her party would be overrun with blue-collar men.

"We're moving in together. We found a new place." I smiled. It was over and I hadn't vaporized under her gaze. What was it about parents? They could always make me feel like I was five. Not this time.

"Why would you do that, princess?" Dad asked. "What's wrong with your apartment?"

"Nothing's wrong with it. I'm just not taking any more handouts or deals or whatever you call them. I appreciate it, but I don't need them. *We* don't need them." I stepped closer to Nick.

"I see." Mother glanced around to be rescued from a scene and spotted Marina, Jen and their men getting drinks. "Marina, dear. Have you met Nick?"

Marina tossed me a supportive nod. "Yes, Mrs. Craig. Nick and I have met. His shop did some excellent work on my mother's car."

"I see." Mother's vocabulary had shrunk quickly. "Won't you play something for us?"

"Play?" Jen looked totally confused.

"Marina is an accomplished piano player. We paid for Lori to take lessons — of course, she never had the patience to practice." Mother got her dig in at me even if it didn't have anything to do with Nick.

"You should've done what my parents did. Hire a nun with a big ruler and Lori would've learned real fast." Marina had the last word and everyone laughed, even my mother. In her polite and sophisticated way, of course. She'd never give a real laugh, but she wouldn't be rude to Marina either.

At least not when she was trying to get Marina on her side against Nick. Mother had plenty of tricks up her sleeves. Marina wouldn't fall for any of them.

"Please play," I encouraged.

"I want to see this," Seth agreed.

"I'll play," Marina relented. "First, I want to make a toast."

My face drained. *Too much, Marina. Too far. Please don't. I know you're proud of yourself, but save it for later, when they're drunk.*

Everyone in our little circle had glasses of champagne and Marina got the center of attention. "To Lori and Nick. We should all be so lucky."

The circle was quiet at first, looking at my parents for their reactions on the *proper* thing to do. They appeared frozen. They didn't drink.

No one drank. I started to panic, then Seth jumped in. "To Nick and Lori." Seth lifted his glass and drank, which triggered Jen and Tim that it was okay. It also guilted my parents into behaving well.

Freakily, Seth seemed in tune with Marina's plans. Either she'd found a man who understood her or she'd trained him really well in a very short time.

"What'll you play?" Mother asked Marina. Glossing over any reference to me and Nick, naturally, she had to have it her way with the conversation.

"I'll make it a surprise." Marina handed her glass of champagne to Seth, approached the grand piano and winked at me.

I followed her. "What were you thinking? That was too much," I said.

"They'll get over it." She sat with a shrug.

"The sheet music is in the bench you just sat on," I pointed out.

"I don't need sheet music. I know what I'm going to play. Go dance with Nick." She poised her fingers over the keys and waited.

"I'm not dancing to Christmas carols." I laughed. "Just play."

"I never said I was going to play a Christmas carol. Go." Her posture made it clear she wouldn't start until I went back to Nick, so I did. She could be so stubborn when she wanted to be.

I noticed my parents had moved to talk to a group of their friends as I got back to Nick, Jen, Tim and Seth. Then I heard the familiar first notes and turned back in the direction of the piano.

Marina just grinned and pretended to stay focused on her playing. She could play that with her eyes closed and we both knew it.

"She's good." Nick hugged me.

"Marina's played harder pieces than that." Jen looked confused. "Not very Christmassy."

"Nick meant the song choice, not her performance." I glanced up at him and wanted the world to disappear so we could be alone.

"What is the song?" Jen asked.

"The theme from *Arthur*," I supplied. "It was our first date at a retro movie theatre and our song." I sighed and rested my head on Nick's shoulder. My parents had no clue that song had any special meaning. They'd just think Marina was a little strange and they already knew that.

"Excuse us. I think we're going to dance now." Nick tugged me away from the group and we started to slow dance. Nothing had ever felt so good.

* * * *

After eating way too much at the traditional lobster-and-pheasant feast, I wandered away from Nick and found the girls. Marina and Jen were returning from the powder room and covering the evidence of Jen and Tim's necking.

"I'm proud of you." I gave Marina a nod.

"For remembering yours and Nick's song? Nothing impressive about that. You wore out the soundtrack twice. It's burned on a section of my brain. I've tried to kill it with vodka, but it never works." She grabbed another drink from a passing waiter's tray.

"No, I mean you asked out Seth," I clarified. "That's huge for you."

"He's cute." Jen nodded.

"It's only the second date. He said he would've asked me out. He thought we had some policy against dating customers." Marina poked Jen in the shoulder. "Just so you know, you can't have this one."

"No, thanks. I'm still breaking in the one I have." Jen sipped her drink and grinned at

Tim. "Relationships are a lot of work."

"That's the truth." I looked over to see Nick, Tim and Seth in an animated conversation. Nick appeared comfortable. He was actually enjoying himself. I'd never expected that. He was with the boyfriends of my friends, while my family showed little interest in him.

"I'm sure Tim and Nick are warning Seth what he's in for," I teased.

"Tim wouldn't," Jen defended. "If he does, I'll dump ice on him tonight."

"Careful, he might like it." I laughed.

Jen blushed. She was clearly comfortable doing it, but

she'd have to get used to talking about it. I wanted some details.

I looked over at Nick and exhaled. The men appeared to be getting along fine. I could only hope it was a good sign for the future.

"My turn to make a toast," I said. "To Marina, whose bossy attitude and crazy idea brought us here tonight with these cute guys."

Jen and I toasted as Marina rolled her eyes and drank, too. "Just don't blame me when you guys have your first big fight," Marina warned.

Over Marina's shoulder, I spotted my mother and cringed. She was heading for me and I knew I was about to be cornered for *the* talk.

"Excuse me, girls," Mom said. "Lori, I'd like to have a word with you."

I nodded and slipped away with sympathetic looks from Marina and Jen. "Yes, Mom?" I smiled. She was not going to ruin this.

"How could you do this to me?" Mother sounded offended and angry.

"I didn't do anything to you, Mother," I insisted.

"You brought that man to my party. An uneducated mechanic." She talked as though he was a homeless rapist who stepped on puppies for fun. I wanted to point out her time at finishing school hardly qualified as an education. She was qualified to plan parties and give courses in snobbery and nothing else. Those words didn't come out of my mouth. I wasn't going to drop to her level.

"He isn't uneducated. Not that it matters. I love him. You don't have to like him, but I'm not hiding him." I folded my arms.

"Is this how I raised you? To fall in love with a man who changes oil for a living?" She shook her head. "You should be ashamed of yourself for subjecting my party guests to such a person. At least Marina's and Jen's young men are respectable, professional men."

I toyed with the idea of pointing out that Nick owned the shop. Not worth it, really. Mom had already set her mind on this. "The only person I'm ashamed of is you, Mother. Nick has behaved perfectly tonight. He's been nothing but polite to you and all of your guests, plus very attentive to me. And he's even dressed the part with an expensive tux to fit your snobby party. All you've done is belittle him and look down your nose at him. At least Daddy's dropped it for now."

"Your father isn't happy about this, either. Nick's hardly appropriate. It's not as though you don't meet decent young men. Your Aunt Gilda told me how she introduced you to a proper man at the last party and you ran off. Rudely, I might add." Mother wasn't going to give up, just change tactics whenever she was backed into a corner.

"Did Aunt Gilda also tell you Freddie tried to molest me on her terrace? I had to defend myself, Mother. Ask Daddy if you don't believe me. And if Nick found out about it, Freddie would be over that terrace in pieces." I grinned at the thought of Nick defending me.

"Just as I thought, a man prone to violence and stuck in a manual labor job." She rolled her eyes. "Not what I dreamed of for my only daughter."

"At least he keeps me safe from the creeps you and Aunt Gilda throw at me. I won't be scolded or criticized and I won't hear a word against him. If you don't want Nick here, we'll leave," I offered. I wanted it clear I wouldn't stay without him.

"No," she said quickly. Her eyes bugged out in horror. *Her* daughter walking out on *her* party? Never! "Fine, I'll be nice to Nick. As nice as I can be. We can discuss this in more detail later. It's better in private, anyway. Try to keep him away from me, please."

"No, Mother, we won't discuss this later. No more conversations. Nick is in my life and it's not negotiable." I turned and walked away.

Marina and Jen were lurking at a respectable distance and

I needed their friendly faces. I took a deep breath. "That was fun," I lied.

They smiled sympathetically.

"You survived." Marina handed me a drink.

"Thanks." I downed it and felt a bit better. I could do this and survive it. The earth had not opened up and swallowed me. As a little girl, I'd always avoided my mother's wrath like if she had to raise her voice it would be the end of the world. I'd faced her and the solar system hadn't exploded.

The men approached and any beginnings of conversation were put on pause. Girl talk was not for their ears. Not that I wanted to discuss my mother's behavior at the moment. I wanted details about Seth and if Marina thought he was worth it. Later would have to do.

"So, did you really dump a pitcher of frozen drinks in Tim's lap?" Seth asked Marina.

"He deserved it." She shrugged unapologetically. "He impersonated an ex-boyfriend of mine to get Jen to keep seeing him."

"If I apologize, will you promise not to hurt me anymore?" Tim teased.

Marina shrugged with a smile. "It's not for me to punish you anymore. That's Jen's prerogative now. You're her problem."

Seth looked more confused than before. Not that we could blame him. Our little game had had some strange results. Luckily, none of them had been tragic.

"It's true. Be afraid," Jen warned. Then she tugged Tim out to dance.

"Good luck." Nick slapped Seth on the back in male-bonding fashion.

"Be very afraid." I smiled.

"She's not that scary." Seth shrugged it off. "I do want to hear this ex-boyfriend impersonation story. I know you guys are close, but exactly what sort of group am I getting mixed up with?"

"Maybe I'll tell you one of these days. If you last long

enough." Marina seemed un-fazed. "At least you can't say you weren't warned." She pulled him out on the dance floor.

"We're fairly harmless." Nick held me close and we started to dance, too.

I kissed his neck softly. "I'm so glad I turned thirty," I whispered in his ear.

"No, you're glad I clean up so well." Nick squeezed me tighter.

"Actually, I really prefer you naked. Jeans and T-shirt are better if you must wear clothes. However, you do clean up very well." I adjusted his tie like a fussy girlfriend. "You always did surprise me."

What I really wanted to do was open his collar. He had the sexiest neck. That would have to wait for later. For the moment, I was completely content.

"Did I survive round one?" he asked.

"So far, so good. There will be major retaliation and reaction from the parental units. This was the shock meeting in public where they can't make a scene. At least, not too big." I felt the need to warn him just in case he thought the worst was over.

Better yet, I had to offer him an out. "Are you sure you want to take this on? It'll be a long time before they settle down or leave us alone completely. My parents don't take losing well."

"They can lose you or accept me. Either way, do I seem scared? This time I'm not going away. Even if you tried to get rid of me." Nick looked me right in the eye. "I love you, Lori."

"I love you, too," I confirmed. I broke my mother's cardinal rule. Public displays of affection were inappropriate, unladylike and vulgar. Tough shit. I kissed my mechanic boyfriend in the middle of my mother's snobby holiday party and didn't care who saw.

Chapter Eighteen

Marina's New Normal Life

The weeks after Christmas were insane for me. Dr. Percy had taken my agreement to buy the animal hospital to heart. He'd had papers drawn up and sent over before my vacation had been done.

I'd already applied for the loan and things seemed to fly through faster than I'd expected. Call it old-world paranoia, but I'd never been big on debt. My student loans were minimal—thank you, scholarships—and no car loan because no car. The apartment was leased and the rent was reasonable. Not paying stuff late had worked out to give me an excellent credit rating.

That and the rosary vigil by my mom and her sisters had made the large bank bless me. I was magically in debt up to my eyeballs like the rest of the world.

The closing took place at the bank and I dressed for it. Being a vet, I rarely got to wear what could be called a suit or anything really professional. So, I went all out. The black pants flared, the subtle silver blouse was fitted, and the trendy cut jacket was long.

I felt like a professional. I'd even received an application to join a businesswomen's organization in Chicago. This was real.

I arrived ten minutes early and was offered coffee, tea and water by three different receptionists in the loan department. I'd always avoided deals with my money. After seeing my sister and brother-in-law struggle to get a mortgage approved, I had been content to lease the apartment from Lori's dad at a friend-of-the-family rate.

Maybe now I'd look into buying a car or maybe even an apartment in the city one of these years. Owning a business made paying rent look like a waste. I wouldn't end up with anything or get any money when I moved out. First, I had to get used to the business. Maybe then buy a condo.

Dr. Percy arrived with his wife, both smiling ear to ear. Damn, I'd just realized I'd have to replace her. Mrs. Percy did all of the scheduling and a good deal of the paperwork. My first management decision — I'd need an office manager.

Shelley was Mrs. Percy's right hand. Maybe she would get a promotion. That would go over well. She was dependable, well-liked and always there. Good first move.

Of course, I'd have to hire another vet eventually. Percy had cut back his hours to almost nothing about a year ago. That was less critical as long as I kept myself on my regular schedule for now.

Before I could exchange more than a hello with the Percys, we were ushered into a room with the bank representative. My brain couldn't absorb all of the legal blather.

I'd had Nick's lawyer look over the papers before I'd even read them so I could ask questions of someone knowledgeable. He'd helped Nick when he'd bought the garage, so that was a relief. I'd convinced myself there was a clause in there taking my first-born if I missed a payment. The lawyer promised there wasn't and I hadn't found anything odd.

For about twenty minutes, we signed things. I'd never written my name so many times in my life. It felt like the ultimate Catholic school punishment. My hand cramped and my signature was barely recognizable by the end of it. Luckily, I had a manicure scheduled for tomorrow so the damage could be undone.

Then it was over. I was handed the keys and I felt it was real for the first time. We were shown to the lobby and told our copies would be mailed in a week or so. It was all a blur really.

"Bye, dear." Mrs. Percy hugged me.

"Bye? Are you guys leaving already?" I asked.

"We're heading down to Arizona to stay with some friends for the worst of the winter. Don't worry, we'll be back for the spring to sell our house. No point in putting it on the market with the deep snows ready to start." Mrs. Percy smiled hard. They were eager for this change.

"Sounds perfect." I smiled.

"If you have any questions, we're not leaving until this weekend. Not that you don't already know how it all works. You can call me anytime. I'm keeping the cell phone." Dr. Percy patted his pocket and hugged me. "I won't be one of those puttering, retired old men who can't handle technology. I may even get a computer, so you'd better email me."

"I will. Thanks." I watched as they walked out of the lobby and into the brisk wind to get in their brand new Cadillac.

For a moment, I just stood there. Free and without responsibilities no longer described me. I'd just signed away my life and it feel oddly good. I stepped out of the bank as someone who owned something. I had more than a degree and some furniture.

I started looking for a cab. I had to get back to the apartments. Today was moving day for Lori and I'd been enlisted to help with last-minute stuff.

Honestly, I couldn't wrap my brain around the urgency. Her dad owned the building. The building manager hadn't, as far as I knew, leased the new apartment to anyone or threatened to have her stuff tossed if she stayed an extra day. That was Lori. Miss Independent now, with Nick, of course.

"Where do you think you're going?" a voice called in my direction. I knew that voice.

I turned and saw Seth leaning against a shiny new black Lexus.

"What are you doing here?" I walked over.

"All signed and officially a grownup?" he asked.

I nodded. "I thought you had to work today?"

"I lied to throw you off my little surprise." He shrugged. "Get in."

"This is your car?" We'd always taken the L or a cab from my place. We'd only been dating a few weeks. Maybe the car was new or just a lease.

"I never said I was poor. Get in." He held the door open, waving me in.

I hopped in and examined the inside. Lori's car was nicer, but this was good, too. I'd never had a boyfriend with money. He rounded the car and dodged traffic to get in the driver's side.

"You're not an illegal sort of pharmacist, are you?" I asked.

He laughed. "No, totally legal. My grandfather was a stock-market dabbler before it was the thing to do. He didn't blow it and did a little trust fund stuff. I turned that into some serious cash with pharmaceutical and med tech stocks. I invest in what I know."

"So what does your brother do for a living?" I snuggled into the heated seats. A girl could get used to this. Way to go, Grandpa! And Seth played with stocks, too. Maybe that was my fate with men, stock traders. At least Seth was a lot more fun than Lucas.

"He's a cop."

I laughed. "A cop? A Chicago cop?"

Seth nodded and looked at me as if I'd lost it as he pulled out. "Why is that funny?"

"I don't know. He's rich with a trust fund and deals with the worst this city has to offer. I have to work. I never understood people who don't have to work and still do."

"Come on, your parents hated what they did?"

"My dad only wanted to put in his years and get his pension. My mom went to work after Dad retired to get away from him. Her bakery is like her second kitchen. Work is work."

"What about Lori?" Seth shrugged.

"Lori's parents didn't do the trust-fund thing, they spoiled their kids and kept the cash in their name. Control is everything there." I took off my gloves and ran a hand over the leather. "This is nice."

"Thanks." He didn't seem to care that I loved his car. "I thought Lori liked being a lawyer."

"She loves it." I nodded, toying with mirrors and compartments.

"If Lori had all the money in the world, you think she'd stop?"

I shrugged. "Probably not. She might be more selective with the cases she took or start her own firm, though. It's the freedom, I guess."

"What about you? Would you really stop working?" he asked.

I thought about it for a minute. "I might. At least for a while. Maybe I'd do it a couple days a week just to keep myself in the swing. I think it would be different if you didn't *have* to work. That's the real problem with work. The *have to* part. If you're rich and wanted to take a vacation at the drop of a hat, you do. You see, us working stiffs don't have the luxury."

"Actually, you're a boss now. You don't count as a working stiff anymore." He grinned. "Ever notice I don't have the tensest schedule in the world?"

"Actually, yes. Some of the girls were commenting on how you didn't seem to have a consistent day job or shift or whatever. I should've known you weren't normal. Pharmacists need to fill meds at all hours of the night. My cousin is a pharmacy tech at a chain drug store and loves the midnight shift." I studied him. No, still cute. He might be rich, but he hadn't turned into a frog yet. "You're really a rich guy and not normal at all. I like that."

"For that I should take you back home and cancel my surprise," he threatened.

"Why? Where are going?" Home was where I'd expected us to be headed.

"You'll see." He nodded.

I started paying attention to his driving instead of his car and had no idea where we were going. He pulled up to a building and had the valet, who addressed him by name, take the car.

"What are we doing?" I asked.

"Aren't you ready for lunch? It's nearly one." He guided me through some etched-glass double doors. I found myself in an elegant restaurant.

"I'm not dressed for this," I whispered.

"Don't worry, neither am I. We don't have to be." Seth nodded to a guy in a tux and we were shown to a quiet table with a gorgeous view.

"Reservations?" I asked.

"My sister-in-law owns this place. It's nice and keeps her out of trouble when the kids are in school. She's not here today or I'd introduce you." The staff members greeted him by name as they passed.

I nodded and glanced over the menu. Seth was well off. No, not possible. My brain was still processing this. I knew pharmacists pulled in a good income, but a trust fund? I couldn't even attempt to process the prices I was seeing on the menu. Was that dinner or my loan payment for the month? No lie, he was a *rich* guy.

"It's all great. The pasta sauces are amazing," he recommended.

I nodded then remembered I didn't have all day to play. Lori, damn. "Do you think we can be back at my apartment by three?" I asked.

"Sure. Trying to get rid of me? I knew you'd hate me for my money."

I looked over the menu and laughed. The fake pout was priceless. Thank God, he was teasing. "It's not the money, though, you could've told me before. We went to Lori's parents' party in a cab. I'm surprised your family doesn't know her family."

"All rich people don't know each other and their type of

rich seems different from my family. Besides, if I'd told you, how would I know if you liked me or my bank account? You'd be surprised what's out there. Some women are after any straight single guy with a little money."

"Fair enough. Any more secrets? I don't want to find out you have five kids or insane ex-wives or something." If he thought I was going to be sweet and perfect because he was loaded, I'd better squash that right now. This relationship wasn't even a month old yet.

"No, no kids or ex-wives. I'm only thirty. I haven't had time for that much trouble. What's happening at three o'clock?" he asked.

"At three?" Oh, right. I wanted to be back by then. "Sorry, I promised Lori I'd help her wrap some of the very expensive breakables in her apartment. She and Nick are moving to a new apartment today."

"I'll help," he offered.

Yeah, okay, the millionaire helping us pack. "You don't have to. Lori hired movers so most of it went earlier today, I hope. It's just some figurines and crystal she wants handled personally. We're going to wrap and Nick has a truck to take over these boxes. It won't take long."

"Good, then you can cook me dinner."

I froze. Me? Cooking was not my best skill. "I'm not really great in the kitchen."

"Jen said your mom owns a bakery." He looked surprised. "You can't cook?"

"I'm not great. Mom does have a bakery. I take care of animals. If you want to risk it, I'll try. Don't blame me if you need your stomach pumped."

"We can call delivery." He nodded. The waiter arrived and we ordered lunch. Today was going to be all about the food, I could see.

"Considering you just invited yourself over, you're paying." I pretended to examine the Wedgwood china and smiled. Expensive little bread dishes. His financial situation was still sinking in.

"Considering the fact that you just put yourself in businesswoman debt, I'm definitely paying." He winked. "You did a big thing today."

A wave of seriousness hit me. "Promise me there are no more surprises."

"What's wrong?" He lowered his voice and sounded a bit nervous.

"Nothing's wrong. The animal hospital is a great move for me. You having money isn't a bad thing. My mother always warned me not to date a man who had less money or education than I did."

"Education, we're about even and money isn't a problem." He shook his head.

"I just can't take any more shocks or surprises today. Okay?" I sipped the water already on the table. "Let's get the weird stuff out of the way."

"I promise, no more shocking revelations. Unless you think my being an identical twin is shocking." His face read honesty, no hint of a joke.

That was unexpected. I thought about it. "Not shocking. Still, I think it's good information to have. What if I ran into you in the city, only it wasn't you? What if it was your twin brother and he was making out with another woman? Then it would be a problem. Remember what I did to Tim? And I wasn't even dating him at the time."

"The warning comes back to haunt me." He laughed. "*You* never actually dated Tim. Right?"

"Right, he was supposed to be Lucas, whom I did date a few years ago. Lucas has since gotten married, so he's no threat. Don't worry, it's complicated. Just trust that my friends know me well. If they get to know you better, they might give you a few more warnings." I had to keep him on his toes. "Of course, that would take some of the fun out of me."

"I prefer to be surprised. You know about my brother now. What about your family?"

"Four sisters, all married. They all live on the south side.

In the suburbs mostly." I shrugged, not knowing what else to share. "You know my mom owns a bakery with her two sisters. I have six first cousins from those two aunts alone. My dad was a union guy and has been retired in front of the television since before I started college. Which made my mom open the bakery."

"Sounds like a fun family."

"If you're still around for Easter, we'll see how you feel about meeting the mob in a concentrated dose." That would be a true adventure. My turn for questions. "Is your twin the cop, or do you have more than one brother?"

Seth nodded. "Just the one brother. I preferred a line of work where I'm not a target."

"I think I prefer dating a pharmacist to a cop. From a safety standpoint, anyway."

He just grinned at me. Lunch arrived and we could barely stop talking. I'm not sure what it was about. The topics varied and flowed.

The fact that he'd never mentioned his money or that it didn't seem to impress him only impressed me more. He talked about his family, his nephews and the pets with animation and affection. And he actually listened to me when I talked. Not like most men I'd been out with.

It wasn't the money that impressed me, either, I realized. I'd even forgotten about it once the shock wore off. He was one of the good ones. As my mother would say, don't let this one get away!

Mom didn't have to worry. I liked him a lot.

* * * *

Shortly before three, we arrived back at the apartments. Jen and Lori were already wrapping and Nick and Tim were moving boxes. Sweating and grunting like they were studs. I wished I had time to get my camera and get this moment on digitally transferable media.

"Impatient to be rid of your friends?" My cute way of

announcing our presence.

"About time you got here." Lori didn't even look up. "I'm behind schedule."

"Was there any doubt?" I grinned at Seth. "Where do you need us?"

"Come in, I don't want to dwell. I want everything moved and done tonight. Then I can have you all over for dinner." Lori was dressed in ratty jeans and a worn old T-shirt I suspected belonged to Nick.

She was so serious about the move, I tried not to laugh as she pulled me in and put me to work on her Waterford crystal. Nick was apparently in charge of the manly endeavors.

"You're going to cook?" Jen sat up from her wrapping and stared.

"Lori, cook?" I shook my head. No way I'd buy that she'd gone that Martha Stewart on us.

"You're criticizing her?" Seth teased me. "You warned me you're not a good cook."

"I'm not a great cook. Not like Jen or my mom. However, I can manage a dinner without supervision if I'm in the mood. I've never heard of Lori using her stove. The microwave, sure.

Popcorn, Pop Tarts, she's good at heating things. To actually cook?" I shook my head.

"Come on, I'm not *that* bad!" Lori stomped.

"We can always order pizza if it's that scary." Jen shrugged.

"Or you could help her and we'll eat it and live," I suggested.

Jen nodded as Lori shook her head.

"I'll do it myself," Lori insisted.

"Nick's trying it first," I added.

"I can help you cook," Nick offered to Lori.

Lori picked up the nearest heavy object and wound up to pitch it at Nick's head. Not sure if she was kidding or having a true hissy fit, I grabbed her arm first.

"Not the Tiffany vase, please, Lori." I pried it from her fingers as Nick tackled her into a pile of bubble wrap. They laughed and wrestled and kissed while the bubbles popped beneath them.

"Get the hose," I joked to Jen.

"Just for that, Nick'll be cooking dinner for everyone," Lori declared.

Same old Lori. It felt good to know being with Nick hadn't changed her, except to make her happier. I'd never seen her this happy.

"Thank God," I mouthed at Seth.

"Are we fighting or packing here?" Lori clearly wanted a subject change.

Hands got busy. The conversation grew dull.

"Jen, did you ever hear about that job?" I asked.

"No," she groused. "I left a message at the restaurant the day before the Margarita incident. They never called me back. I've given up."

I grinned. 'The Margarita Incident' was how we now referred to the day Tim had come clean about his identity and I'd dumped that pitcher of frozen drinks in his lap. The timeline didn't add up right.

"Wait a minute." I paused in wrapping a piece of crystal. "You left that message the day *before*?"

"So, that was two weeks and a day from my interview. I didn't want to be pushy." Jen shrugged. "They said I'd know in two weeks."

"Right, weren't you screening your calls the days *after* The Margarita Incident? If I remember correctly, you were deleting messages without listening to them. Who knows what else you deleted."

Jen's eyes bugged out. "I need a phone!"

Seth produced his cell phone and Jen lunged for it and dialed. She slipped into Lori's now-vacant bedroom for added privacy.

I shrugged at Lori, who returned it. We both knew how badly Jen had wanted that job. A gay-owned French restaurant. It was bound to be a success.

"I got it!" Jen ran out screaming. She hugged everyone, including Nick and Seth who both looked a little bewildered. Jen clung to Tim, jumping up and down and kissing him. "I'm hired!"

"What did they say?" Lori asked.

"They were worried I'd gotten another job, but were waiting until the holidays were really over to call again. They thought I might have gone back to Wisconsin for Christmas or on some extended vacation. They were going to call me tomorrow." Jen caught her breath.

"Let's finish up here and go celebrate," I suggested.

* * * *

Seven hours later, the boxes had been loaded, we'd gone to dinner and stuffed ourselves in honor of Jen's new job and the men were gone.

Lori had decided she wanted to spend one last night hanging out with us before moving. So the three of us were sprawled around Jen's apartment in pajamas, eating junk. The guys weren't too happy about it. They'd learn that the world didn't revolve around them.

"I can't remember the last time I had a slumber party." I sat curled up in one of Jen's overstuffed chairs in my favorite sweats.

"I'm going to miss you guys. Too bad my new building is full or I could take you with me and things wouldn't have to change." Lori looked around the room like she was moving to Outer Mongolia for the rest of her life.

"You're only moving a couple blocks up the street," I reminded her. "And I'm not moving all of my stuff to be near Nick."

"It won't be the same, but you don't need us barging in at inappropriate times," Jen agreed.

"We're good at that. You can always give up Nick and stay," I suggested. Couldn't resist playing devil's advocate

247

with a love-smitten lawyer. Some things wouldn't change and I was glad for that.

We'd still be friends. I'd still harass Lori and she'd harass me. Jen would, no doubt, continue to look for advice as she ventured farther into Chicago and possible couplehood.

"I love you guys, but not that much." Lori grinned. "Remember what I was like without Nick?"

"Good point." I nodded. "So, I never did hear the verdict on Seth. Does he pass?"

"Absolutely. He's cute and rich." Lori sipped her hot chocolate.

"Rich doesn't matter. I didn't even know until he pulled up in a Lexus, which isn't that impressive a car." I shook my head.

"I know," Lori relented. "It's better than a beat-up Chevette. He could be poor and unemployed."

"Marina's poor enough now. I can't believe you really took out that huge loan for the business." Jen popped a marshmallow in her mouth.

"I have a business in return. I'll actually own something. I'm an adult." I shuddered at the thought. I was a boss. Good thing it was done or I might have changed my mind once it completely sank in.

Lori laughed. "You shouldn't turn thirty until you're at least an adult. You just made it."

"I don't own anything. Maybe I'm not an adult." Jen poked at the marshmallows now floating in her hot chocolate like a left-out kid.

"You're not a virgin anymore. That's good enough." Lori nodded.

"True, being a thirty-year-old virgin would be serious cause for alarm. And you've got a new job, too. Maybe you can buy a car. That's owning something," I suggested. The idea of Jen driving in Chicago traffic scared me. She'd have to learn eventually.

"This new job is farther than my old one, but Tim already has a car," Jen mused.

"Moving the boyfriend in already?" Lori asked.

That had my attention. "Jen?"

"No, no. We're not moving in. He doesn't live that far. That's all."

I leaned in Lori's direction. "I give it six months and they'll be living together."

"A hundred bucks says they're engaged by then." Lori and I shook on it.

Jen blushed deep red. "What about you and Nick? No ring yet?"

"No, I told him we had to live together for at least six months before we can even talk about that, to make sure he wasn't going to throw me back. I'm not rushing anything. I've got him. That's all that matters."

"That's smart. You don't want to actually kill your mother." I smiled.

"Are you agreeing with me or trying to talk me into dragging Nick to the courthouse tomorrow?" Lori glared at me. "Because I'll do it."

"Whatever. Just make sure I'm invited. I'm content that you'll stick with Nick now so whenever you want to make it legal is fine with me." I stretched with satisfaction.

"As long as you're content." Lori rolled her eyes.

"You did start all of this, Lori," Jen said. "You're the one who freaked about turning thirty."

"So? I was the first one to do it. I didn't make Marina come up with that crazy idea, but it worked out for the best." Lori crossed her arms.

"Actually, you did make me come up with the idea," I corrected.

Jen giggled and I gave her a knowing smile.

"What?" Lori seemed paranoid.

I shrugged. "I figured if anything, you regretted not keeping Nick. The game gave us all a chance to check for regrets. I thought *you* might actually get your guy back. And you did."

"She's the only one who got the guy she looked up." Jen

nodded.

"True. You didn't do too badly with Tim," I teased.

Jen grinned so hard my face ached as I stared at her. If Tim hadn't been as goofy at dinner, I might have been nervous. He was whipped, too.

"I'm not sure if I'm mad at you or not." Lori leaned back on the couch and stared at me.

"Would you be happier without Nick?" I challenged with smug satisfaction.

"Of course not." Lori's mouth remained open for a moment. She never completed her thought and simply shook her head.

"Then you're not really mad. Think of me, I spoke to Lucas for Jen. And I fought with Nick for you, too. Poor Jen had to track down Lucas and hear that Brian was kissing boys in California."

"I don't mind. I got Tim out of the deal." Jen blushed. "I'd probably still be a virgin if you hadn't started all of this, Marina."

"And you did okay with Seth," Lori reminded. "Though I guess you didn't make him part of the game. You've been mentioning him off and on for months."

Time to come clean, I decided. "To tell the truth, if I hadn't seen how taking those risks worked for you two, I probably wouldn't have asked Seth out in the first place. I was a chicken."

"You? Scared?" Jen looked shocked.

"She acts tough, but she's putty in Seth's rich hands," Lori teased.

"I wouldn't go that far. It's very early. No talk of moving in or anything even remotely serious. Just dating. That is how normal people do it. I'll have my hands full running the animal hospital at first anyway. One thing at a time, please." I liked Seth. Hell, I was crazy about him, but I didn't want to overdo it and end up ruining the relationship and the business all at once.

"If you want some advice from someone older. Don't get

so obsessed with your career that you pass up the right man." Lori sounded like one of my sisters.

"You mean like you did with Nick and taking the job at the big law firm?" I wasn't about to let her get away with that crap.

"I know. I don't want you to make my mistakes." Lori nodded.

"Now you're proud to be older than us?" Jen asked.

"That's not what I meant." Lori rolled her eyes.

"I thought you gave up Nick because of the family thing?" Jen seemed puzzled.

"It was parts of both, okay? I was stupid. Details, details. Just recognize you've got a good guy and don't let him go just because he gets on your nerves a little. They're bound to screw up occasionally."

"Okay, Mom." I rolled my shoulders at the long day. "Speaking of Mom, she's thrilled you and Nick are together. You'd better bring him by the bakery to see her or I'll never hear the end of it. Which means you'll never hear the end of it."

"I will. Maybe I'll take him tomorrow to get some good pastries before we unpack our lives." Lori glanced a few blocks away at her new apartment.

"Poor Nick, home alone in your new apartment." Jen yawned and tugged a throw around her.

"Don't make me feel guilty. I'll smooth it over with him tomorrow. We've got a lot of stuff to do. Plenty of bubble wrap to pop." She grinned mischievously and snuggled into a ball on the sofa.

"Now I'll never sleep." What an image!

We sat around watching late night movies and not talking. It wasn't a sad affair, but no one wanted to say anything remotely like a goodbye. It wasn't, after all. Just a change of apartments and not that far.

The two lightweights fell asleep at only three o'clock and with nothing more than a glass or two of champagne in their systems from the toast to Jen's new job.

I wasn't quite ready to go to sleep. That would mean it was really over. Things would be different, in a good way. Better, though they'd never be the same again. As hard as I'd tried to change things for the better, I'd miss the way it had been.

I got up to grab a blanket from the closet and noticed Jen had left the door unlocked. I walked over, dimmed the lights then flipped the deadbolt lock and put the chain on the door. Not bad for a month and a half. I still hadn't trained Jen to lock the damn door.

Maybe before we all turned forty.

More books from
Totally Bound Publishing

Part of the Celebritease collection

*Chasing dreams can be tough, even when you run as fast
as your bespoke stilettos will take you…*

Book one in the In Other Words series

Can she overcome her consuming desire for him? Can he make her comfortable with the other C-word… commitment?

667 WAYS TO F*CK UP MY *Life*

Lucy Woodhull

Sometimes, there's nowhere to go but f*ck up

Sometimes, there's nowhere to go but f*ck up...

A CREATIVE GUIDE
TO GETTING A

Life

MJ EASON

Carrie Sinclair thought she knew exactly what she wanted from life.
Until she came face-to-face with the bluest eyes in Texas.

Carrie Sinclair thought she knew exactly what she wanted from life until she came face-to-face with the bluest eyes in Texas.

About the Author

Cheryl Dragon

A lover of unusual things, Cheryl Dragon enjoys writing unique stories with steamy romance. Her two favorite settings are Las Vegas and New Orleans…where anything can happen! Cheryl lives in the Chicagoland area.

Cheryl Dragon loves to hear from readers. You can find contact information, website details and an author profile page at https://www.totallybound.com/

Home of Erotic Romance